Published by Three Worlds Productions LLC
P.O. Box 8774
Red Bank, NJ 07701

This is a work of fiction. Names, characters, places a. ⸺ɯents are used fictionally or are the product of the author's imagination. Any resemblances to real places or people are purely coincidental or fictionalized.

700040962788

Acknowledgements

It would require a second volume to list all the people who have helped make Dark Dealings possible. But you know who you are and how much I appreciate you. However, a few special mentions are required.

First and foremost --- my life-long gratitude to the angels of Faded Denim Productions for the cover art, formatting and encouragement. This book would not have happened without you.

To Jennifer Gracen, Copy Editor *par excellence*, friend and head writer's cheerleader. Find her at:
http://jennifergracen.wordpress.com/contact-info/

To Marlo Montanaro whose photographic skills can make even me look good. See his work and contact him at
http://www.marlopix.com/

To Barbara Rogan
Teacher, Mentor, Friend.

Who, through her wonderful instruction in The Next Level
Workshop, deserves credit for the best parts of this novel and
anything else I ever write.

Dark Dealings

By

Karen Victoria Smith

Samhain

Her hopes for a nice, normal weekend away from the office died on a dark bend of Massachusetts' Route 7. Micaela flicked on the high beams, wary of the deer that often darted into the unlit road. She downshifted the Porsche Cayman and guided it around a sharp curve. The crisp air that flowed through the open window smelled of late October snow in the Berkshires. As much fun as it might be to floor it, she wasn't in any great hurry to get to her grandmother's farm. A mile later, a shadow at the edge of the road made her slow to a crawl. On the shoulder, a man dressed in bloody shreds of clothes sat hunched over his knees. He looked up and stared into her eyes. His mouth formed words she couldn't hear.

Reece.

Micaela pulled over and grabbed a halogen flashlight from the glove box. She jumped from the car and dashed back to the place she'd seen her friend to find no one there. A dark stain gleamed in the ray of her flashlight. She touched her fingers to it and then lifted them to her nose. Motor oil. Micaela paced up and down, scanning the brush and road for clues.

"Reece, where are you? If this is some sick Halloween joke, come out now!" she shouted into the darkness. No sign of him or anyone on the road or in the woods beside the two lane highway, no footprints and, thankfully, no blood.

Reece wasn't the type to pull this kind of stunt. His brother Adam, maybe. But Adam would have already stumbled into the road, doubled over in laughter. She walked slowly back to her car, ears straining for any noise she might have missed. Back behind the wheel of the Porsche, Micaela stared into the night sky. Until five minutes ago, she'd looked forward to time away, even if it meant being in Bridewell for Samhain.

She looked around one more time. No sign of Reece. Her stomach was a basketball-sized knot. If this wasn't a trick... *Damn.* She slammed her hand against the steering wheel. It was just a delusion, she thought, spawned by exhaustion. She must have been micro-sleeping behind the wheel. Too many late nights hunched over the prospectus of a recent deal. The alternative was unacceptable. It meant the visions had returned. Why now, why had his spirit, ghost... No, she refused the idea that he had passed over. Then again, Samhain was the time of year when people and spirits moved between this world and the Otherworld. *Shit.*

She wanted to call Reece from her cell phone, but she'd never programmed any of the Bridewell numbers into her contacts. Dread gnawed at Micaela's mind for the remainder of the drive to her old hometown.

Over an hour later, she turned off Cerwiden Street and onto the narrow country lane that led to the Rourke-O'Brien Farm. Flashing red lights slashed through the darkness between the gnarled apple trees of the Rourke orchard. She swerved left as she rounded the last turn to avoid the police cruiser stationed near the foot of the drive. The wooden gate, meant to keep sheep in, was pushed open. A patrolman in an orange vest flagged her down. Her dread turned to fear.

"Miss, you'll have to park on the road." The strobe from the light bar illuminated his name tag.

"Sean, Sean Murphy... it's me... Micaela O'Brien. Is my grandmother all right?"

"Jeez, Micaela, I didn't recognize you. Nice car. Is it new? I haven't seen you since… "

"Sean! Is she all right?" He had always been easily distracted, especially by high powered toys.

"Una's okay. I think. Some kind of accident in the hills behind the farm."

"Is Reece at the house?" Please say yes, she whispered to herself.

Sean shrugged. "Don't know." He waved her through the gate.

Gravel sprayed behind the car as it sped up the driveway. Micaela left the car in the first open space amid the Jeeps and vans. EMTs sipped from Styrofoam coffee cups beside an ambulance.

In three steps, her four-inch heels were kicked off. She finished the sprint across the brittle late season grass in stocking clad feet. A jack o' lantern leered from the wood porch while a scarecrow twisted in the wind. She slammed open the screen door and crossed the dark parlor toward the light of the kitchen. The aroma of coffee and baking soda bread filled the kitchen, familiar scents, so different from the sight that greeted her. The crisp linens, flowers and canned fruits and vegetables that usually adorned the counters and shelves were crammed into a cupboard. A kettle screeched on the stove. Dirty dishes overflowed the sink. On the oversized black farm stove, bangers sizzled while the oil danced in the cast iron skillet.

Una Rourke leaned over a massive blue pottery bowl beating the daylights out of the potatoes. Her grandmother was fine, but things must be bad; Una always turned worry into action usually involving food. Micaela wrapped her arms around Una from behind and planted a kiss on her cheek.

"Ah, Micaela, you're here. Good. Would you get the large platter from the pantry, then slice the soda bread and set it out. The butter is in the fridge." Una brushed a lock of her still black curls from her face.

3

"What happened? Sean said there was an accident?" Micaela opened the wood and glass-paned cabinet door and pulled out the pewter bread platter. The knot in her stomach tightened.

"A group of the boys from the enclave were up on the mountain. Reece got separated from them just after dusk. There are teams of searchers looking for him now." Una spooned the ivory mounds of potato onto a large ceramic platter. "Can you turn down the flame on the bangers, dear."

"Reece? He's hunted these hills since middle school. He doesn't get lost." He was the son of Chief Deerfield of the Pokanoket enclave, a splinter group of the main tribe near the Cape. He had grown up just outside of Bridewell and knew this part of the Berkshires better than anyone. If he was missing, Grandma had cause to worry. Micaela's heart sank.

Five men filed in through the back door. In the mudroom, they pulled off suede coats and leather boots. Hunting rifles were balanced against the whitewashed bead board wall. Reece's younger brother, Adam Red Hawk Deerfield, led the group that included four of Reece's cousins from the enclave. It was a different entrance from those of their childhood, when the Druids, led by Una, and Pokanoket had played together because the old blood Yankees would have no part of either group. As always, Una's door was open to all, whenever they needed her.

Behind them, Peggy, Reece's bride of six months, leaned against the doorframe. She was pale with the shadow of tomorrow's dark rings under her eyes. They hadn't spoken since Micaela's parents had died, but the anxiety that poured from Peggy made Micaela cross the room to hug her. Peggy lurched away, her hands locked at her side and her eyes wide. But Reece must love her and she him, or they wouldn't have crossed the line between Pokanoket and Yankee to marry. So for Reece's sake, Micaela reached out.

Peggy's emotions flooded into Micaela: dread about Reece, concern for the child she carried, regret she hadn't told Reece, and,

4

after all these years, Peggy's terror of Micaela's visions. Micaela gasped and stumbled back. Peggy stared wide-eyed at her.

For ten years, Micaela had tried everything, from psychotherapy to alternative medicine, in the hope of burying the visions and sensations. Except for the occasional nightmare, she believed she had succeeded. She couldn't… wouldn't go back down that road. A gift, they called it. *Bullshit*.

"It'll be okay, Peg. They'll find him." Micaela grabbed the edge of the slate kitchen counter as the room wavered. One of those headaches was around the corner. "You need to take care of yourself, Peggy. You're no good to anyone sick."

Peggy searched Micaela's face. "Are you just saying that or is this something you know?"

Micaela caught Una watching, cautious, waiting for Micaela's response.

"The only thing I know for sure is that they are doing everything possible to find Reece." She steered Peggy to a chair. "Can I get you coffee? Some herbal tea?"

"I guess the tea makes more sense. Thanks."

Henry, Reece's cousin, laughed. "Hell of a time to give up coffee. Peg's always got a latte in her hand. Her kindergarten students can already spell caffeine."

Una's and Adam's eyes darted from Peggy to Micaela. It wasn't Micaela's place to tell them about the baby.

Adam perched on the counter next to the stove as Micaela poured Peggy's tea. Six years younger than Reece, he had been the little brother who tagged along on adventures in the woods. Now, he sat there, the image of Reece with the same coal black hair, chocolate brown eyes over arched cheekbones and broad chest.

Adam whispered, "I don't pretend to understand everything that happened to you or why you and Peggy haven't spoken. But we need any help you can give us; whatever it is. Reece needs you."

"There are dozens of searchers out there. Someone will find him." She refilled the kettle and set it back to boil. The aroma of

5

Peggy's tea drifted up. Lavender, oat, catnip and lemon balm, Micaela blended the herbs just as Una and her mother had taught her. She poured a second cup for herself, although she doubted it would help.

Peggy looked up, tears glittered in her eyes. She'd heard their conversation. "It's been hours, Micki. Please."

Reece's family, members of his tribe, her childhood friends sat at Una's table, half eaten meals in front of them. Their hunger had been replaced by a greater need. Behind Peggy, Una radiated comfort and warmth. Six pairs of eyes poured their pleas into her soul, colliding with her nightmares.

Micaela set Peggy's tea on the table and took her own cup out to the back porch. She wrapped her hands around it and inhaled the fragrant steam. The evening dew had hardened into frost. A late October fog crept down the hills and across the lawn. Tendrils of mist sought the house. On the hillside, a beacon from a searcher's flashlight shimmered in the darkness diffused by the vapors. It would be a bitter night on the mountain.

She had stuffed all the metaphysical shit in a box and shoved it into the darkest recesses of her mental closet. The jump into Peggy's mind had been a lit match in the closet and Micaela didn't want to look. Of course, it would be Peggy who opened that door in Micaela's mind. The look of horror on Peggy's seventh grade face when Micaela came home after her parents died was diamond-etched in her memory. She could still hear Peggy and her other so-called friends whisper at the lunch table words like "freak," "crazy," "just like that girl in the Stephen King movie". She placed her empty cup beside Una's garden basket on the white cast iron table.

The screen door creaked. She knew it was Una before she spoke.

"Micaela?" A word. A whisper. A thousand questions.

"What am I supposed to do?" She stood at the edge of the porch and shivered.

Una joined her on the top step and draped an Aran Isle cardigan over Micaela's shoulders.

"Peggy still thinks I'm a monster. But she needs me to be one now." Micaela slipped her arms in the sleeves and started pacing. Her hands clenched and unclenched. "Reece, his family, the whole tribe… they were my friends when everyone else treated me like a side show attraction."

"Reece could be dying up there." Una's steady gaze fixed on Micaela's face.

"You don't think I know that. It's what they think I do, right? Know things." She stared out at the dark hillside and fought back tears of frustration. "What if I don't know, what if I can't find him?" What if the vision on the roadside meant she was too late?

"And if you don't try?" Una smoothed Micaela's auburn waves the way she had when Micaela was a teenager waking from one of her nightmares.

"I'm not sure I know how." Micaela slumped against the porch rail.

"You'll figure it out." Una kissed her forehead. "You know I'll be here if you need me."

Mrs. Ryan rounded the corner of the house; her ceremonial robe embroidered with Ogham and triskeles billowed around her. She had been part of the family and the community for as long as Micaela could remember.

"You haven't changed, Aunt Evelyn." Micaela hugged her old dance teacher. Evelyn Ryan wasn't Micaela's blood aunt, but that had never mattered.

"Any word on Reece?" Mrs. Ryan asked.

Micaela shook her head.

"You'll find him," Mrs. Ryan said, "Then we will celebrate his rescue and your promotion. Your parents would be very proud of you and the community is too." By community, she meant the Druid Grove, of course, not Bridewell's Yankee elite, who barely acknowledged the Irish or the Pokanoket.

7

"My stuff can wait," Micaela said. Why she had driven to Bridewell in the first place no longer seemed so important. But tonight was also one of the most important festivals in the Druid Community. As Priestess of the Bridewell Grove, Una Rourke had to be there.

Micaela turned to her grandmother. "It's Samhain; shouldn't you two be on your way?"

"I must go." Una had stopped asking her to attend years ago. "Can you handle things here?"

Micaela rubbed her temples; the tell-tale throbbing had begun. "Of course I can. It's what I do." She stared up at the mountains. The full moon floated above the peaks. Reece was out there somewhere.

2

Una and Mrs. Ryan disappeared down the path, leaves swirled around their feet. Micaela pulled the sweater around herself in an attempt to chase away a chill that came from inside. She had never tried to call the knowing, in fact just the opposite. She had worked hard to block the images. Now, when she needed them, would they come? If they did, could she put them away later?

Samhain and a full moon. If she could believe the stories, tonight was her best shot to make the visions happen, not just let them happen. It had started with the brief vision of Reece. Hugging Peggy opened the door a crack, so contact was important. She couldn't touch Peggy again. The poor thing was swamped by emotions and hormones. Maybe Adam; he'd been on the mountain with Reece. Would he cooperate or shut down? Well, he'd asked for her help. As she crossed the threshold into the kitchen, she thought: that'll teach him.

Adam stood over the sink washing dishes and strategizing with the other searchers. She crooked her finger at him to follow her outside.

"What's up, Micaela?" He eased the screen door closed behind him.

"I'm not sure how to start this conversation without sounding like a lunatic. I've worked years to avoid what I'm about to say and do."

"Spit it out. Our families have known each other for generations, you can trust us. You can trust me."

Micaela stared out into the oaks. "Things were said about me when I was a teenager…. I was different, I saw things."

"I was little, but I kind of remember. Is that what Peg was talking about?"

"I thought it was gone. That I'd outgrown it. That I could be like everyone else."

"But something happened in there." Adam made it sound more like a statement than a question.

"I've opened Pandora's Box. But if I can help find Reece, I can't close it now."

Adam leaned on the porch railing. She watched the emotions play across his face. His eyes lost focus and he seemed to go somewhere inside.

"Micaela, I understand, more than you know, what we're asking of you. We've looked for Reece for hours. Time's running out." His eyes were haunted. His voice was barely a whisper. "It was my idea to go out tonight. I said it would be easy to hunt by the light of the full moon. Reece didn't think we should ignore the Elders."

"I can't guarantee anything, Adam."

"But you'll try, that's all that matters." He pushed off the porch rail and faced her. "Tell me what you need."

"I'm not entirely sure. For starters, I think we should sit, in case someone passes out." She moved to the bottom step. After the dizziness brought on by her brief contact with Peggy's mind, she didn't want too far to go if she went down.

"Now what?" Adam sat beside her.

"Take my hands." They faced each other. His large hands swallowed hers in their grip.

At first nothing happened. Micaela struggled for a way into the vision. What happened in the kitchen had been so sudden and violent. She had been overwhelmed by the emotions. That was it --- Peggy's strong feelings acted as a trigger. It must have been Reece's own emotions that brought the vision on the highway. Micaela would have to ask Adam to relive the event and the sensations. She wished she could protect him from them, but she didn't know how.

"Adam, I need you to think about the last time you saw Reece, about what happened up on the mountain." And I need to stop resisting, she thought, for now.

He chewed his lower lip, his dark eyebrows knit together. Micaela exhaled and focused on releasing the stress in her shoulder. She opened herself to the magic. Images slammed into her. She could see through Adam's eyes. She *was* Adam.

Reece and the other four men headed into the woods. The temperature dropped as the sun set. She reached beyond their muted voices. The forest air filled with the hoot of an owl, the skitter of small feet, the final screech of a small rodent, and the snap of branches as larger things moved.

Adam signaled to Reece that Henry had spotted a six point buck. She felt Adam's confusion turn to concern when Reece wasn't bringing up the rear as usual. Adam retraced his steps. At first he scanned the path, then whispered Reece's name, no reason to spook the buck. But another noise and a different scent drove the buck deeper into the woods. Silence was no longer necessary.

The men called out to Reece, but there was no answer. They retraced their steps but couldn't pick up Reece's trail. Micaela needed to get past what Adam saw and to Reece's vision. She would not leave another child fatherless. How could she find Reece without touching him? Then, in Adam's memory, a gift from the gods, Adam found Reece's rifle at the edge of the path and picked it up. The same rifle he'd used since he was a teenager. The stock of the gun was infused with Reece's sweat, his skin cells, and his energy. Micaela followed the energy into Reece's mind. Chaotic images flooded her. The part of her that was separate and logical hoped Adam couldn't see what she saw.

The hand clamped over her mouth was barely human and covered with hair or fur that scratched her face. No, not hers…

11

Reece's mouth. She struggled to keep her mind apart from Reece's. She sensed danger if she was sucked in too far. Reece fought back against the beast until it dropped him to the ground. A blow to his head left Reece dazed. The creature dragged him into the forest, threw him over its shoulder, or maybe its back, Micaela wasn't sure, it didn't feel like it walked upright. The image was lost. Reece had blacked out.

Every nerve in her body strained to regain the thread of contact. If she didn't, Reece was lost. *I don't know how to do this, I'm not strong enough*, she cried out to the darkness in her mind.

Voices chanting seeped into her from beyond the blackness. Barely audible at first, they grew louder. She heard the crackling of a fire. Una whispered through her mind, "We are here. We will help you until you can make the journey alone."

A new image appeared. Adam was gone, the others were gone. She stood alone outside Joshua's Cave. They had played as children in this cave tucked into the side of a ravine. As she walked in, a low moan reached her ears. She knew she hadn't left the porch, yet she felt the mat of pine needles under her bare feet. Where had she lost her shoes? She reached out to touch the damp moss covered rock, her hand passed through it.

Another moan. She couldn't see more than a few inches ahead. In the darkness she'd never find Reece or know if the beast was still here. She held her hand out again in what she knew was a futile grope in the dark. This time a small glowing orb formed in her palm. She curled her fingers around the edges of the softball-sized object. It was bright but cool to the touch. It allowed her to see several yards out. In the light, she saw Reece naked and propped against the rough cave wall; his head lolled to one side. His torn and bloody clothes were scattered around the cave. She could smell the air; it reeked of blood and beneath it the musky scent of sex. A new vision of what had already occurred materialized before her. A vision within a vision. Whatever it was stalked into the cave with the unconscious Reece. The beast was definitely female, but more wolf than human. Unable to stop what she saw, Micaela screamed in frustration.

The beast stripped away Reece's clothes, inflicting the first set of wounds. Reece jolted from unconsciousness and he tried to scramble away. The wolf creature overpowered him and began to use its hand-paw to arouse him enough to force him into her. It made a sound that was a cross between a hum and a growl. It sounded like a chant. Reece's eyes glazed over and he stopped struggling. Had the beast somehow gained control of his mind? The beast mounted him and ground itself into him until he climaxed. Micaela watched helplessly. Tears streamed down her cheeks.

Reece regained awareness. His face twisted in horror and rage as he swung at the she-wolf. She lunged at him again, this time clamping her jaw into his shoulder. He brought his knees to his chest and kicked up with his two feet to gain leverage. She lost her grip and staggered back. She howled, a furious sound, and slashed at him, tearing into his chest and flinging him against the cave wall. Without a further glance at him, the creature turned and left the cave. The air shimmered and Micaela was back in her original vision of Reece dying in the cave.

Reece's eyes fluttered open. "Micaela?"

"You can see me?" If he could, there was hope. She smiled at him.

"I never thought you'd be the last face I saw." Reece's skin was pale, almost translucent.

"You are not dying." She hoped she sounded optimistic. Two of his ribs jutted out from under the torn chest muscle.

"Could have fooled me." He coughed out a laugh. Blood sprayed from his lips as he struggled for air.

"Hang on, please."

"Don't tell Peggy what the she-wolf did to me. Peg doesn't understand the power your totem animal can have over you. How it can make you do things." Reece squeezed his eyes shut.

"I won't. I know how hard these things are to explain." She tried to reach out and take his hand, but like the wall her hand passed through his.

His voice was a broken whisper. "I know you two aren't close anymore, but promise me you will tell Peg that she's the only one I ever loved."

"Tell her yourself. No child should grow up without a parent."

"Child? Peggy's pregnant?" A red-tinged tear trickled down Reece's cheek.

"Yes. Hang on, I'm going for help."

"I'll try to be here when you get back." His head slumped forward.

3

Micaela stared into chocolate brown eyes. Not Reece, Adam. She shook out the cobwebs of the vision. Her fingers were cramped and curled. She had let go of Adam's hands and wrapped her own hands first around the invisible rifle and then around the orb. Her palms were warm.

"Micaela, are you okay? You were gone a while." He massaged her palms and knuckles.

"How long?"

"Ten minutes, maybe more," he said.

Ten precious minutes. Panic squeezed her chest. "Joshua's Cave. He's in Joshua's Cave. He's hurt bad."

"That's over a mile from the trail."

From the shadow of the trees, Chief Deerfield, Adam and Reece's grandfather, emerged and spoke to Adam. "Listen to her, Red Hawk. You know what she saw."

Micaela let out a soft gasp. "Adam, how much did you see?"

"We'll talk later, Micaela." Adam called to the men. "We know where he is. Grab the two-ways and the rifles."

They raced in the direction of Joshua's Cave. No questions.

Her head throbbed and her stomach churned. Years before, after the doctors had eliminated a possible brain tumor, they told her

15

the auras, the headaches, the nausea were the result of migraines, but she knew better. Micaela crawled off the step, threw up into Una's azaleas, and then passed out. When she opened her eyes, Chief Deerfield and Peggy stood over her. Tears ran down Peggy's face.

"They radioed. They found him, Micaela, just where you said. They're bringing him down now."

Chief Deerfield helped Micaela stand up. Her head still pounded and her legs were rubber. He handed her a piece of willow bark. "You remember what to do with this, White Crow."

When they were seven, Reece had begged his grandfather to make Micaela a member of the tribe and give her a Pokanoket name. Her parents and Una had been at the ceremony.

"Is Reece all right?" She chewed on the bark. The pain started to recede.

"He will be. We will take him to the enclave and help him through this time."

Micaela's first inclination was to insist Reece be airlifted to New York; she had a friend who would arrange a police escort. Micaela would call in favors from anyone necessary to ensure Reece's survival. But she had grown up with the Nation and knew better, they had their own resources.

She watched as the enclave's EMS vehicle pulled closer. Paramedics in scrubs climbed out accompanied by the aged shaman of the Pokanoket. "If you need anything, Chief Deerfield, Peggy, please tell me."

Peggy's eyes were locked on the path to the mountain. She didn't answer. But knowing now how much Reece loved Peggy and how she returned that love, Micaela didn't mind.

Chief Deerfield took her hand and walked with her and Peggy to the edge of the forest to wait. "I know what this has cost you, White Crow. We thank you for what you have done for Reece and Peggy… and for Adam."

"I didn't want Adam to blame himself, I know how that works."

16

"Adam has a destiny and you have helped him on his path."

Could she get off this path? For now, she would wait in the darkness with the others for Reece to come home.

The search team crashed back through the underbrush with a makeshift stretcher holding Reece. Paramedics met them; one grabbed Reece's arm and, barely breaking stride, started an IV line. They eased Reece onto a gurney and slid an oxygen mask slid over his nose and mouth. The shaman stepped up with Adam as Peggy stood on the other side of Reece and brushed his hair back from his face. When she took her hands away they were smeared with his blood. The shaman began a chant. Micaela stood silent as Adam mirrored the shaman's motions and words. When they had finished, Peggy bent over and lifted Reece's oxygen mask so he could speak. She whispered back and laid a kiss on his cheek, then called Micaela over to his side. Reece's face was gray; his brown eyes had a scary milky film.

"Hey Reece, long time, no see." Micaela felt the tears pool in the corners of her eyes.

"You were there." He attempted a smile.

"You'll be all right. It will be just like before."

"I'm going to be a Dad. I owe you, if you hadn't told me...."
His eyelids sagged and then shut.

Micaela eyes rose to meet Adam's. "Is he okay?"

"We gave him something so he could sleep and heal."

"Any idea what attacked him?"

Anger flared in Adam's eyes. "Yes, the warriors will deal with it." He took Micaela's hands; a tear trailed down his cheek. "Thanks for telling him about the baby. It probably saved his life."

"When I came out of the vision, you knew, too."

Adam looked to the old shaman before he answered. "I told you I understand more than you realize."

Peggy and Adam climbed in the back of the ambulance while a stone-faced warrior escorted the shaman to a waiting Jeep. Micaela watched the motorcade pull away, and then went inside.

She woke the next morning on the sofa; a quilt covered everything except her cold bare feet. Her grandmother must have taken her stockings off. Micaela swung her feet to the floor, ready to head upstairs for a shower. Her headache was gone, but her body ached with exhaustion. She rested her elbows on her knees and weighed the merits of standing. Brown, dried pine needles protruded from between her toes. Maybe someone had used the quilt for a picnic. She carried it out on the porch and shook it over the railing. No needles. She pressed it to her face. The quilt smelled of detergent and fabric softener.

Una fussed over her the rest of the weekend. She cooked Micaela's favorite breakfast of Secret Recipe pancakes. They went to Lafferty's on Saturday night for Shepherd's Pie. Una insisted on a private booth and Lafferty made sure they weren't disturbed. Micaela noticed the furtive glances and whispers but no one came near; a blessed change from years ago. Afterwards, they drank tea with a side of Paddy's Irish by the hearth.

Adam called Sunday morning to tell them that Reece was hanging in. It would be a long road but they were optimistic. After lunch, Micaela sat on the front porch draped in a crocheted throw while Una sat beside her sipping tea. It had rained through the night and into the late morning. Tears of water dripped from the leaves that remained on half-stripped branches. Soon the ground would be covered in frost and then snow. And so began Samhain, the Druid winter when life retreated beneath the earth and darkness ruled.

"I should get on the road. I promised Parker we would meet for a late dinner."

"You tell your young man I expect to see him for Thanksgiving dinner. I don't want to hear either of you are too busy." Una shifted in her Adirondack chair to face Micaela.

"He won't be able to make it. He's leaving in the morning for a new office complex project in Vancouver. It's a great opportunity. He should make partner when he's done."

"How long will he be gone?" The furrows between Una's brows deepened.

"It's supposed to take several years. He'll be back every couple of months." The next part was going to be hard; she knew how much Una liked Parker. "We've agreed to take a step back in our relationship. Just friends and all."

"The wheel turns." Una nodded. "Are you all right with this arrangement, dear?"

"Parker is great guy, he's smart, sweet. We're good together. I suppose it should be enough." Micaela twirled a multi-hued yarn tassel on the throw between her fingers. "Not everyone can have what Mom and Da had. Can they?"

"Your mother asked me the same question not long before she met your father. Will you be here for Thanksgiving?"

"I'll do my best, but I was just assigned to a new financing deal, my first international assignment. I don't know what my schedule will be yet."

"You tell Brian Moran that Una Rourke wants her granddaughter here. He won't argue."

"It's not entirely up to him. One of our major clients asked for me specifically and I don't think they celebrate Thanksgiving in Ireland."

"Ireland. Who would the client be?"

"Knowth Corporation. Judy will have a briefing file waiting for me tomorrow morning. I understand they're headquartered north of Dublin."

"Knowth Corporation. Interesting."

"You've heard of them?"Micaela asked.

19

"They've been around for a long time. Would it be Byrne Connor, you're dealing with?"

"Actually, my day-to-day contact will be a Liam Farrell. We are supposed to speak by video conference on Tuesday morning."

"Of course." Una nodded. "The Farrells have always worked for Knowth."

Micaela knew her grandmother kept tabs on things back home. She didn't realize it included major players in the financial community, especially ones who were as reclusive as Byrne Connor. "Is there anything else you can tell me, Una?"

"Nothing right now. Give my regards to Liam and Byrne."

4

Imbolc

"You'll be wanting to step carefully, Miss O'Brien. The snow's started." Seamus, a chauffeur for Moran & Boru since her father's days, held the limousine door open with one hand. He offered his other to her. Flakes melted into the shoulders of his black jacket, not daring to mar the crisp perfection of his uniform. Company lore said he had once been assigned to the Queen's Guard at Buckingham, until someone noticed he was Catholic and, worse yet, especially in the seventies, Irish.

"My fault for listening to a weather forecast that predicted no snow." Micaela tugged her satin shawl around her and questioned her decision to sacrifice warmth for fashion.

"Could have told ye a storm was coming. My Missus' bones started aching last night. But 'tis good news the weather is so treacherous."

"Really now? And why would that be?" She knew the answer, but Seamus enjoyed the telling.

"Means the Cailleach is asleep. She'll be out of firewood soon and the cold will end."

"Not a moment too soon," she said.

"What time shall I return, Miss O'Brien?"

"You go on home, see to Mary. I can take a cab when I'm done."

Seamus peered at the sky. "Are ye sure? These February storms can be tricky."

"It won't be a late night. I'll be home before the worst of it. Mr. Moran and his wife will be here. I'll get a ride from them, if I need."

"If anything changes, you call me." He tipped his cap and headed for the driver's seat.

Scarlet banners proclaiming the Exhibition of Russian Imperial Art of the Late Middle Ages cascaded down the front of the building. The sponsor, Baron Ivan Vasilievich, was a principal in Les Anciens du Groupe Financier. Micaela had been asked by Knowth and others to facilitate the negotiations that would form AGF, as it was referred to by the participants.

A blast of wind caught her ankle length skirt and hastened her steps. She joined the stream of people entering the great brass doors of the Metropolitan Museum. Micaela took the time in line to scroll through her emails on her smartphone until something in the tone of the whispers around her drew her eyes upward. Men dressed as Cossacks stood at military ease on either side of the Grand Staircase, their hands clasped behind their backs. They wore authentic blue leather-belted tunics and loose woolen pantaloons tucked into knee-high boots. Each rigid face carried the signature bushy mustaches. The coldness in their eyes was enough to deter anyone who might think to disrupt the event or snap a photo with their phone.

At the foot of the staircase, a stone-faced man in a tuxedo stood like a human watchtower. A Cossack in a silk suit with a trimmed mustache and goatee, he scrutinized the invitation of a white-haired woman in a full length sable. She passed inspection and was announced, "Madame Maxine Reynolds, United States Ambassador to the United Nations."

The Cossacks stared ahead as she proceeded up the stairs.

The woman ahead of Micaela turned to the man beside her. "Those swords can't be real. NYPD would never allow it."

"I wouldn't want to find out." He smoothed his thinning hair back. Micaela caught a glimpse of his profile. He was a prominent New York real estate developer. She had seen pictures of his petit brunette wife on the Society pages. The blonde on his arm was not his wife.

Micaela handed over her invitation. The stone-faced man skimmed it and placed it in the pile with the rest.

"Are you accompanied by a guest tonight, Ms. O'Brien?"

"No."

"Just as well," he said.

For who, she wondered.

He bowed and smiled at her as if she were royalty. "Mademoiselle Micaela O'Brien, of Moran & Boru."

The Cossacks snapped to attention. The metal of long curved sabers sang as they were unsheathed. The guards pressed the blades flat across their chests in a salute. From behind, she heard the whispered "oohs" and the murmurs of "who is she?" She felt the muscles in her back knot. Eyes straight ahead, she lifted the hem of the forest green gown and ascended the wide marble stairs. She'd learned to ignore stares and unwanted attention a long time ago.

She was halfway up the stairs when a tingle like an electric current danced on her skin. She glanced around for the source; the entire squadron's eyes trained on her. Each guard dipped his head as she passed. This was odd, even by her standards. If she could, she would have turned around and called Seamus. Unfortunately, duty called.

A young girl in crisp white shirt and black pants with her blonde hair pulled back tight against her skull in a ponytail presented her with a program and champagne. Micaela moved through the L-shaped Robert Wood Johnson Galleries and made polite conversation with the mayor and council president, then the senator from Connecticut. A string quartet played music from Tchaikovsky's

Romeo and Juliet, a soft counterpoint to the murmur of voices and the clink of plates and glasses. Breaking away, she set her drink down and took a moment to scan the room.

Liam Farrell stood in front of a wall-sized display case of pikes and axes. She needed no one to point him out; they talked almost daily on her computer. Tonight, he wore the traditional *lein-croich*, or Irish kilt, under his tuxedo jacket. *Nice legs*. He had told her he was six-two, but with his broad shoulders and muscular build he seemed even taller. His chestnut hair hung in a braid down to the middle of his back. The glistening steel blades behind him appeared ready to remove body parts in the hands of a capable warrior. He looked every bit the Lord of the Manor. Deep in conversation with two other men, he scowled as he grasped the upper arm of one of the men. The debate ended when Micaela arrived.

Micaela nodded a greeting to Liam. She turned to the other men and extended her hand. "Micaela O'Brien, Moran & Boru."

"François Leveque, of Société de La Tène. I hoped to meet you. I have heard so much about you." Undeniably handsome, he was also over six feet tall, with curly brown, shoulder length hair. Worn loose the curls framed his face and drew one's gaze to blue eyes the color of sapphires.

"All good, I hope?" She extended her hand. They had spoken on the phone several times. But his baritone had not hinted at the face before her with its classic Gallic nose and chin that framed sensuous lips.

"Absolument. My employer, Henri Montbelliard, sends his apologies that he will be unable to attend our first meeting."

As François took her hand, an image of murky blue water flashed in her mind. He was nervous. More than nervous he seemed afraid. His pupils dilated in surprise as though he felt her mind brush his. Then, he slid his hand away and like a door slamming, the impressions from him disappeared.

Micaela continued on. "My understanding is that none of the principals will be in town for the meeting, except of course for Baron Vasilievich. Where is our host?"

"I saw him head into the second room of the exhibit with some of his guests." François indicated the archway that led to a side gallery.

She could feel the second man's scrutiny. "And you are?"

"Ethan Lowell, First Colony Shipping." His cultured Boston accent screamed Beacon Hill, even though he wore his dirty blond hair longer than might be acceptable in Society circles. It was tied back and bound by a crimson satin ribbon that matched his cummerbund and bow tie.

"So what brings you to New York, Mr. Lowell?"

"I had other business to discuss with Monsieur Leveque and Mr. Farrell, unrelated to your current transaction."

Liam had told her that Lowell had passed on the project. "When you have a moment, I would be interested in your decision not to participate in AGF."

"No reflection on present company. This was not a project that fit in our strategic plan." He arched his eyebrow at Liam. "Despite Mr. Farrell's eloquent attempts at persuasion."

"Perhaps we can talk further about what would fit with your long range plan." *Never miss an opportunity for future business.*

Liam chuckled. "I thought this was a social event and not work. You do know how to take an evening off, don't you, Ms. O'Brien?"

She turned as if finally noticing his presence. On their almost daily calls he preferred to call her 'Caela. His use of Ms. O'Brien sounded so formal.

"Well now, Liam Farrell in the flesh. From what Mr. Lowell says, you haven't exactly been discussing Ireland's prospects in the World Cup." She heard a soft laugh and a 'touché' from François. From the corner of her eye she saw Lowell cover his mouth to muffle a cough.

"Well, the flesh is under here somewhere. And my preference runs not to football, or soccer as the Americans call it, but to Leinster Rugby. Now there's a sport to get your heart to racin'."

"You do clean up well, Mr. Farrell." She bit back a grin. Normally he showed up on her monitor looking like an unmade bed.

"Well darlin', you've only seen me on a seventeen inch screen." Liam played up his Irish accent. "What do you think of the real thing?"

"Please do not flatter him, Mademoiselle. He's quite impossible tonight." François' smile highlighted a soft cleft in his chin. "If you will permit, I shall steal you away from such tedium. Will you walk with me? Perhaps I could share the Impressionists in the next gallery with you."

Liam opened his mouth to speak, but a tall, attractive woman with a mass of ebony curls joined the group. She was poured into a burgundy silk gown that accentuated her pale skin and ample curves. Her hair pulled tight against her scalp, tumbled with deliberate carelessness from the jeweled circlet which held it all in place. François shifted so that he was between Micaela and the woman.

"Shall we go? Messieurs Farrell and Lowell are quite capable of handling Ms. Vilkas." His eyes darted to the woman. His tone was serious, urgent.

François plucked a glass of champagne from a passing tray and handed it to Micaela. They strolled through the galleries in silence until he stopped in front of Monet's *Rouen Cathedral: The Portal in the Sun*. The gallery was empty but for the two of them.

He stood beneath the spotlights and stared at the painting. "I always enjoy Monet's works, especially the play of light and shade. This is part of a series. In it, he wasn't really interested in the façade but in the time of day and angle of sight."

Up close, she could see lines of strain around his eyes. "We didn't come in here to discuss the Monet, Monsieur Leveque."

26

"François, please. I was told you were direct." He glanced down at the hand she had grasped earlier when she had felt the fear in his aura. "They failed to mention how perceptive."

"What can I do for you, François?"

"Ah, Ms. O'Brien, I was told you had strayed in this direction." The deep Slavic accent washed over her. Baron Vasilievich, sole owner of Eudoxia, approached from the Russian exhibit. Strands of his ashen hair curled at the nape of his neck. His flawless face was a living version of Michelangelo's David. On a delicate gold chain around his neck, he wore the Russian Imperial double-headed eagle.

François turned toward her; his blue eyes glowed like the center of a flame. His voice was barely a whisper. "We cannot speak now. Breakfast tomorrow. Seven o'clock. The Cadwalader Hotel."

"I'm in Philly. What about Friday?"

"Friday, then. My suite. Be safe until then, Micaela." François bowed deeply to the approaching man. "Monsieur Le Baron, pardonnez-moi, the temptation to share my countryman's art with such a woman was too great."

"Ah, we have that in common, François. Perhaps Eudoxia shall find other common ground with Société de La Tène." The Baron's smile didn't quite reach his eyes. The body language between the two men was stiff, formal.

"Anything is possible, Baron Vasilievich." François kissed the back of Micaela's hand. "I thank you for the honor of your company, Mademoiselle."

"The pleasure was mine, Monsieur Leveque." Micaela studied his face trying to read him. Nothing. This was good. Maybe what had happened was only a small crack in the walls around her so-called gifts. She could fix that.

"Ms. O'Brien, would you honor me by allowing me to share my family's treasures with you?" He extended his left arm to her.

27

"I can imagine no better way to see the exhibit, Baron." She slipped her arm through his. No alarm bells went off, in fact, she felt very relaxed. He will be easy to work with, she thought.

"If I may call you Micaela then you must call me Ivan, please."

"I shall try… Ivan."

5

The stunning ebony-haired woman in the skintight gown and jeweled tiara ambushed Micaela and the Baron as they re-entered his exhibit. François had said her name was Ekaterina Vilkas.

"Baron, our guests were wondering what happened to you. I told them it must have been urgent as you are not easily distracted."

His voice chilled like the February winds. "Ekaterina, I am never distracted. See to our guests."

Ekaterina ducked her head and retreated with her eyes downcast. She never turned her back to him.

He turned to Micaela. "My apologies for the intrusion. Please, let us continue."

"Baron, if you need to attend to your other guests, don't let me detain you." He might be easy to work with, but not for. But then, most chief executives of his level were taskmasters, pushing others as hard as they pushed themselves.

"I have promised you a tour of my collection and I am a man of my word." He smiled at her; his pale blue eyes sparkled like icicles at sunset.

He led her from case to case. Each contained jewelry, hairbrushes, gold plate and religious icons, each one more beautiful than the other. He regaled her with intimate details of the pieces and his family. Against the long wall, the largest case contained a richly illustrated bible that rivaled the Book of Kells. He bowed his head for a moment. He then moved on to a series of portraits on the wall behind the case.

"Vasily the First. He is called a Grand Prince of Russia, but we think of him as the first true tsar of Russia. He was a powerful and strong ruler intent on uniting Russia. And this is his Grand Princess and wife, Sophia."

"They look like remarkable people." Her eyes travelled from the portraits to the Baron and back again. "After all these centuries, I still see a strong family resemblance, especially with Sophia."

"Do you think so? Some have said I am more like Vasily."

A picture of another young woman with auburn hair in a green brocade gown hung beside Sophia. "Who is she?"

The Baron turned his gaze to Micaela. His eyes were warm and intense.

"Elena Petrova, Grand Princess of Ryazan, the wife of their eldest son and heir, my namesake, Ivan."

Micaela studied Elena's portrait. "She's beautiful but there is such sadness in her face. Do you think she and Ivan were happy?"

"Absolutely. Despite it being a marriage arranged to consolidate powers, they fell truly and deeply in love." His hand drifted toward the face on the canvas. "Today, you would call her his soul mate. Beautiful, intelligent and strong enough to rule in her own right."

"They must have been an impressive pair. They reigned after Vasily and Sophia?"

A soft sigh escaped his full lips. "Unfortunately, no. Not long after their marriage, he was sent to the Khan's court on a diplomatic mission and never returned."

"How terrible. Did she remarry?"

"Because she carried Ivan's child, she was forced into a loveless marriage with Ivan's younger brother to preserve the diplomatic alliance between Ryazan and Muscovy, as well as her life and that of the child."

"I don't see an image of your namesake. Does one exist?" she asked.

"Regrettably, it had been damaged beyond restoration."

30

Micaela accepted a blini from a server who stood nearby. The tray trembled in his hands. The Baron waved him off. She watched the young man's aura glow the green of relief as he skittered away.

The Baron smiled. "I should apologize. I spend far too much time with the dusty memories of family history. How could I be so rude as to ignore the beautiful woman beside me for one who has been dead for nearly six hundred years?"

"It's hard to separate ourselves from family history sometimes. It seems to find a way into the present whether we like it or not." She looked at Elena's portrait; Micaela knew what it was to lose people you love.

"We understand each other." The Baron lifted her knuckles and kissed them lightly. A brush of the lips. His eyes had changed to the color of the winter sky at home in Massachusetts, clear and crisp, an invitation to a warm fire. Heat rushed up her arm and down to other parts of her body. She felt the blush rise in her face.

His laugh was low and very masculine. "I am pleased my clumsy attempt at gallantry is so well received."

"Clumsy is not a word I would use to describe you, Baron." Micaela took a slow deep breath and re-centered herself. As she extracted her hand from his, Micaela flashed on black pools with spatters of crimson. She needed to dial it down and get the metaphysical crap under control, or six months of yoga, meditation and sheer stubbornness would be out the window in one evening.

She retrieved her champagne glass and looked around the room to see if anyone else had noticed their exchange. Lowell was talking with François, who looked her way, but glanced away when she met his gaze. Across the room, Ekaterina talked to Liam. She leaned closer to him, her arm reached under his jacket. She whispered in his ear, her eyes locked on Micaela, a challenge in them. Liam stepped back and gently removed the woman's arm from his waist.

The Baron rested his hand on Micaela's elbow and steered her in the opposite direction. "Let me show you the heart of my collection, Mischa."

They turned the corner of the gallery into a side room. The focal point of this display was a dais with two thrones under a burgundy velvet canopy. Two Cossacks, bigger and scarier than the ones on the Grand Staircase, stood on either side of the dais. When the Baron entered, they drew their sabers in the same salute that had greeted Micaela. Long daggers with elaborately carved hilts rested on their opposite hips and short studded whips dangled from their belts.

With one eye on the Cossacks, she moved closer to the platform. The thrones were a splendid combination of exotic woods carved with bears, griffins, and other mythic figures. Tigers of white, yellow and rose gold reclined across the top of the backs of the thrones. She drew nearer. The eyes of the beasts were blue-white diamonds, the same color as the Baron's eyes.

"This is remarkable, Baron. I thought all of this had been destroyed when the Communists took over?"

"We were able to secure our heritage in remote locations over the centuries." He was inches from her and his voice was a whisper. "It is the first time they have been seen by the public in nearly three hundred years. I am particularly glad you are here for it."

She was drawn to the thrones. They both pulsed with energy. The smaller one called to her, wanting her to sit in it. She froze less than three feet away. A low, angry growl of a sound came from behind her. The hold of the chair on her broke and she stepped back. Her hands trembled and her heart pounded in her ears. She struggled to sound calm.

"Baron, I have taken you away from your obligations for too long. Perhaps we should return to the main exhibit."

He stared at her, his eyes narrowed. "Are you well?"

"I'm afraid it is my turn to apologize. It's been a very long week and I was thinking about the meeting on Friday." She forced a smile. "I am told I need to learn to relax."

His face brightened. "Perhaps I can help you. I have a box for the opening of the Kirov at City Center tomorrow evening. Will you be my guest?"

The ballet seemed harmless enough. The box would probably be filled with business associates of the Baron.

"I would like that," she said.

"Wonderful, I shall send my car for you at seven o'clock."

"I'll be in Philadelphia, but I should be back at my apartment well before then."

"I have arranged a small reception after the performance in the Center's banquet facility. I hope you will stay for it," he said.

"It sounds lovely." She turned back to the main room in time to spot François as he walked away from the throne room. Had he heard her conversation with Ivan or that strange animal growl she'd heard? She needed to speak to him again, preferably tonight.

Brian Moran, her senior partner, approached the Baron and Micaela.

"Baron Vasilievich, I don't believe you have met my boss, Brian Moran," she said.

Brian laughed. "Don't let her fool you, Baron. I cannot possibly be her boss. No one tells Micaela what to do." He extended his hand to the Baron. "It's a pleasure to meet you. Your collection is impressive."

Micaela shifted toward the rest of the room. "If you gentlemen will pardon me, I see several clients I must speak with before the evening ends."

She tried to make her way across the gallery but was waylaid by the CEO of a start-up search-engine company, and then the CFO of an Australian mining group, in town to launch the shares of the company on the New York Stock Exchange. As she turned to look for François, she came face to face with Liam Farrell.

33

"Liam, are you enjoying the exhibit?"

"It's interesting, but I've grown accustomed to the Baron's displays and saber rattling."

"He seems quite immersed in his family history." Micaela glanced around in time to see François leave with Ethan Lowell. She spotted the Baron with Ambassador Reynolds. He looked over at Micaela and smiled. His smile faded as his gaze moved to Liam.

Liam followed her gaze to the Baron. "More likely buried in it."

"I know half of Europe tries, but few are able to legitimately claim descent from royalty the way he can."

"Now that's not true, all good Irishmen know they are descended from kings." Liam cocked an eyebrow. "Might this Lord of Eire buy Milady a drink?"

"Thanks, but I have a busy day tomorrow and should be going." And if she hurried she might catch François. "Maybe after the meeting on Friday."

Micaela extended her hand to Liam. After four months of near daily conversations, it felt too formal, but even a peck on the cheek could cause whispers among colleagues.

She reached the door in time to see Ethan Lowell and François pull away in a limo. Almost an inch of snow had fallen since she'd arrived and it was still falling. It would be impossible to find a cab. She turned to head for the cross-town bus when she spotted Seamus headed up the stairs, umbrella overhead.

"My Mary wouldn't hear of me letting The O'Brien travel unprotected on a night like this."

6

Her breath came faster. She was close but it was right behind. She crouched
low as she ran, avoiding the limbs that reached out to stop her. The leaves sounded
like explosions under her feet. Too easy to follow her. She paused to catch her breath
but the warm muzzle of the giant beast nudged her, urged her forward. She squeezed
the ruff of its neck in reply and raced on. The clearing was just ahead. Micaela burst
between the oaks into the circle of men and women. She screamed for them to run.
Her grandmother and mother rose from their seats by the fire. They walked toward
her. Her mother, gone all these years, smiled. "I'm glad you've come to take your
rightful place."

Sweat streamed down Micaela's face. She rubbed her eyes
and stretched her body out to touch reality and vanquish the dream
fog. She was safe and very warm in her Upper West Side apartment.
Old buildings were known for their character, but efficient heating
systems did not number among the best of them. It had been so
stifling that she'd shed her clothes.

She untangled herself from the ivory silk sheets and swung her feet over the edge of the California King. She stood naked before the window. The full moon and the glow of the street lights along the West Side Highway made it seem closer to dawn. At times like these she missed Parker, even if he never understood. Of course, how do you describe terror to an architect whose world revolved around the physical reality of space and proportions?

Slipping on a black silk teddy, she walked across the living room. Her five inch stilettos from the night before lay in the middle of the foyer, the beaded clutch tossed on the entry table. A half empty wine goblet sat on the glass and chrome coffee table. In the midst of the sleek leather and modern furniture sat her antique wingback reading chair. Her cat, Grady, curled up on the chair's overstuffed cushion. Nights when she was alone, every night these days, he slept curled at the foot of her bed. The exception being when the nightmares came. He opened his chartreuse eyes then stretched. He stared at the floor before he jumped down. He had apparently decided to follow her into the kitchen.

Micaela turned on the grind and brew. 5:00 A.M. She had about two hours before she needed to leave for Philadelphia. She'd learned early on that work was the best distraction from bad dreams. It had done wonders for her GPA at Penn, not so for her love life.

Coffee poured, she sat at the green and black granite counter and switched on her laptop. Grady jumped up on the counter and nudged her elbow. His black furred cheek tickled her bare arm.

"I'm okay, Grady, just one of the dreams again." The cat's yellow-green eyes questioned her. "Really, I'm okay. But thanks for caring."

She scratched the cat's neck absentmindedly as she shot a quick e-mail to her friend, Nikki, to see if she could cancel their workout at the NYAC at three. Surfing her usual news sites, Micaela saw that a section of the Dorytol pipeline in Iraq had been bombed. Oil prices would spike on the headlines. They would drift back down as analysts got beyond the first paragraph to expected repair times and alternate delivery modes. She called in instructions to the overnight desk to short oil in the O'Brien Family Trust.

She tried to concentrate on business, but her mind drifted back to the dream. It still terrified her as it had since she was thirteen. At the edge of her memory, Micaela knew it was different this time. But how? It was important, but she didn't want to deal with it, not now. Would the time ever come when she could go to sleep without wondering if tonight was nightmare-time? Her computer chirped. Liam's name popped up on the screen followed by his face.

"Liam. I just saw you last night."

"I'm a creature of habit." He looked his usual self: rumpled.

Grady caressed the monitor and meowed. Liam responded in kind with a fair imitation of the cat. Pleased with his response, Grady curled around the laptop and purred like the motor of her Porsche.

"You just caught me. I have a meeting in Philadelphia today." She went to the coffeemaker to pour another cup. When she turned around Liam's eyebrows were raised and he had that crooked grin she usually liked so much, except now. *Shit.*

"Give me a minute." She darted into her bathroom and grabbed a knee-length pink terry robe. She tried for nonchalant as she re-entered camera range.

"So… you're off to the City of Brotherly Love. If they saw your sleepwear, I doubt their reaction would be brotherly."

"Very funny." She scrunched her face in a childish grimace. She was proud of herself. She had stopped short of sticking her tongue out at him. "While I have your attention, you saw the news of the pipeline explosion. I'll send instructions for London. Can you see that they are executed?"

"For you, darlin', 'twould be my extreme pleasure." Liam doffed an invisible cap. "I reviewed the first set of documents for AGF and have some things I want to go over before the meeting, but if you are otherwise occupied…." He moved his head as if trying to peer beyond the kitchen.

"No, I am not occupied." Okay, so she'd been celibate since Parker had left town and had no life. "Your comments on the documents, please."

Liam bent his head as he leafed through some pages. She could still see the creases around his mouth that usually bracketed his grin. He looked back up. That damn gleam was in his eye.

"I wouldn't want to hold you up, 'Caela. Go take your shower. I'll scan my comments and e-mail them to you. We can talk later... when you're more comfortable."

Behind him, she spotted what appeared to be a woman in a white dress shirt. Crap, someone had walked into his office. Deft hands began braiding Liam's hair. For a moment Micaela wondered if it was as soft as it looked. Where was her head? She moved left, out of camera range.

"I've got to go. I'll look through your mark up before Friday."

"Before you cut me off, there's a dinner party at Ambassador Reynolds' residence tonight. If you're free, we could meet early, talk about the documents, and then go to the Embassy."

"Sorry, I've accepted an invitation from Baron Vasilievich to attend the Kirov tonight."

"Very well, then. 'Til Friday." He paused, and then waved the woman behind him off. He appeared alone on the screen. "'Caela, are you all right? You seem a tad off."

"Nothing a good night's sleep wouldn't cure. I'll see you Friday." She hit the power switch on the laptop.

Would he understand about the dream? She shook her head. From all she'd seen, Liam Farrell lived a charmed life. He wouldn't know the first thing about nightmares.

7

Micaela's reflection wavered back into focus. For a moment she thought she had seen someone else in the eighteenth-century Cheval mirror. She had found the full-length looking glass in a small antique shop on her solo trip to London in December. In perfect condition, the cherry wood and carved frame was a match for her bedroom set. She nearly laughed when the salesman had said the mirror, which had come from an Irish Manor house, was waiting for her. That is until the wood had hummed under her touch.

Her image confirmed her decision to wear the navy blue A-line. Simple, not flirty. The scoop neck was not too low, and the hem stopped mid-thigh, just the right amount of cleavage and leg. The blue-on-black brocade waist jacket completed the perfect ensemble for a business evening at the ballet. Micaela sat down at her mahogany vanity and tucked a loose strand back into the French braid. The dark shade of the dress made her eyes more gray than blue. Her mouth twisted in thought; something about the jewelry was too ordinary. She opened the onyx box and removed the gold torc necklace and wafer thin disc earrings. They had been her mother's. After the accident, her grandmother had passed them to Micaela. A touch of blush under her cheekbones and she was satisfied. A shame there was no one to impress.

Her fingers traced the edge of the torc while last night's dream replayed in her head. She still had no idea what she was fleeing in the dream or what her mother's words meant. What place was she supposed to take? She could recite every moment of the nightmare as if it were the alphabet. Why not, she'd had the same one for fourteen years. Until last night it had been unchanged. Then it dawned on her --- the beast had never been there before. She couldn't be certain what kind of animal it was, but she was sure it was there to help.

The doorman rang from the lobby; the Baron's car had arrived. Seven on the dot. She shook her head to clear it, gave one last check in the mirror, and headed out.

The box at the City Center held seven, not counting the security detail, with room for a table in the corner with fruit, cheese, and beverages. In addition to Micaela, the Baron, and Ekaterina, the group included the representatives of investors from South Africa and Japan and their guests. Kat wore yet another sprayed on dress, this one in black. Micaela had started thinking of her as Kat. Not that they were friends, or ever would be, but there was something feral about her. Two dark haired, muscular bodyguards by the door looked like the Cossacks from the throne room last night. Apparently, the mustaches were real. Tonight, instead of sabers, the slight bulge under their jackets marked the location of shoulder holsters. If they went out of their way to make the guns obvious, she wondered what wasn't visible.

The lights dimmed and the curtain rose on *Swan Lake*. Micaela leaned forward, entranced by the splendor of the performance. The grace and physicality of the dancers was primitive and sensuous. The men were all muscle and sinew, the women lithe clouds in motion. During the Second Act, the flock of swans and Odette, the swan princess, danced across the surface of the lake

40

formed from the tears of Odette's parents. An image of her father with tears in his eyes appeared before her. She couldn't recall where or when, but she could hear his voice. "The child must survive."

She turned her face away. Her right hand drifted to her throat to hold back a sob. Ivan reached out in the dark and rested his hand on hers. She pulled away, clasping her hands in her lap. When the lights came up for intermission, her program was a twisted mass. He leaned over, his lips brushing her ear. "Are you all right, Mischa?"

She jumped at his sudden nearness. "I just need a minute. If you'll excuse me." She walked down the deep red hall to the ladies' room. Once there, she ran cool water over her wrists and slowed her breathing. Little tricks she'd learned over the years to calm herself.

The matron handed her a fresh towel. "Can I get you anything else, Miss?"

"No. I'm fine." *Liar.*

The bathroom door opened and Ekaterina strode in. "Ms. O'Brien, we have not been formally introduced. I am Ekaterina Vilkas, Baron Vasilievich's personal assistant." A head nod, no offer of her hand.

"Ah yes… Kat." She took a perverse pleasure in watching Ekaterina's grimace at the informality. "We met at the museum last night. I assume we have you to thank for such a wonderful evening."

Kat turned to the matron. "Leave us."

The poor woman's eyes darted from Kat to Micaela. Whatever she saw in Kat's face caused her to bob her head and retreat.

Kat turned back to Micaela. "Of course, I am responsible. The Baron relies on me for everything. I have his complete trust and those he trusts are amply rewarded."

What the hell, thought Micaela, this bitch comes in here to negotiate a side deal for Ivan. Anger rode in, trampling any sorrow and guilt she had felt. "Does Ivan know we're having this little *tête-à-tête?*"

"I know his every desire and need. It is my pleasure to meet them." Kat's tight smile filled in the blanks.

Micaela leaned back against the edge of the sink in a deliberately casual pose. "Let me be clear on this, Ms. Vilkas. Moran & Boru and, more importantly I, cannot be bought or coerced into manipulating a deal in the Baron's --- or anyone's --- favor."

"Bought? The Baron does not use such crass methods. He does not need your help or cooperation to get what he wants."

"What exactly does the Baron want?'

"You have no idea, do you, Ms. O'Brien?" Kat made "Ms." sound like a four-letter word.

"Enlighten me." Micaela eyed the distance to the door. Just in case.

Kat snorted. "I told him you are not worth the effort. So naive, so American. Not as talented as he thinks you are." She turned her back on Micaela and departed. The door clicked shut behind Kat.

The matron peered around the edge of the door.

"Don't worry," Micaela said, "the wicked witch is gone." As she walked back to the box, she hummed a tune from the Wizard of Oz and wondered where a bucket of water was when you needed it.

Kat was nowhere to be seen. Micaela picked up a mineral water from a small table and walked to the far corner of the box. Ivan stood on the other side with his guests. She would have a few moments of solitude before the performance resumed. Below the balcony, she watched couples, parents and children wander about talking and laughing. In the aisle, a little girl in a tartan plaid skirt twirled around on tiptoe to the delight of those around her.

Ivan appeared beside her. "You are far away, Mischa. I hope you are enjoying the evening."

"Yes, I am. Thank you." Micaela mustered a smile. "I was watching that little girl down there. She reminds me of the first time my parents took me to the ballet." How odd that she'd forgotten about that day until now.

"When was that?" he asked.

42

She looked into his face. He seemed truly interested in a silly childhood story. Either he was a damn fine actor or he had no idea what Kat had just done. She continued her story.

"For my seventh birthday, my parents and grandmother took me to Boston. We had dinner in a fancy restaurant near Quincy Market. I can't remember the name but I had the biggest shrimp I had ever seen. We went to the ballet." The little girl below her was scooped up into a hug by a man who might have been her father. Someone had hugged Micaela like that, too. She remembered her father had stood next to her, smiling.

Ivan took her hand; this time she didn't pull away. His touch was warm, his smile and eyes were soft; a slight blush colored his cheeks. She glanced over his shoulder; the other guests were turned away from her, involved in their own conversation. Did she dare continue to hold his hand in front of other clients? It was an innocent gesture of concern, after all.

"What ballet did you see?" he asked.

Micaela frowned. The memory was right there, just out of reach like so many. Ivan squeezed her hand ever so slightly.

A flash like summer lightning and she knew the answer. "*Swan Lake*, just like tonight. My mother said there were guest dancers from the Soviet Union. It was a big deal. I didn't understand until years later what was happening in Russia at the time."

"Yes. I remember. Dancers from the Kirov and the Bolshoi were here that year. Some chose to remain behind in the United States. The Soviet Union collapsed a year later." A thin satisfied smile curled the edges of his lips.

The house lights flickered and the orchestra tuned up. It was to begin again. She tried to lose herself in the performance, but her focus was on her conversation with Kat. The bitch's remarks rankled her. The reality in Micaela's world was that everyone came to the table with an agenda. Her job was to find the deal that left everyone equally satisfied and equally unhappy, the compromise. The key was what each person really wanted and what they would give up to get it.

Tonight, she was almost sorry that she'd had some success in packing away the metaphysics. All she had from this group was random leaks of auras. She'd been unable to read Ivan this evening. She shook off the thought. She was smart; she knew most men found her attractive. She didn't need any psychic tricks to figure out what Ivan wanted from her, despite what Kat implied.

The reception after the ballet was the usual meet and greet. Kat reappeared to act as hostess. Micaela spent time with the representatives from South Africa and Japan. She was back in her comfort zone as they discussed financial markets and emerging industries.

Her first attempts at conversations with the ballet troupe bordered on painful. She spoke no Russian and most of the dancers spoke only a little heavily accented English. Ivan must have spotted her difficulty. He broke away from a group that included the Ukrainian Ambassador and came to her side. He stood close, his hand resting occasionally on her lower back, as he translated. He whispered simple phrases in her ear and encouraged her to use them. He beamed at the praise and good-natured laughs she received from the dancers for her linguistic bravery. It was more fun than she expected.

For all her responsibilities, Kat still had enough time on her hands to be staring at Micaela whenever she looked her way.

The dancers offered to buy Micaela a drink and were only mildly disappointed when she ordered a mineral water with lime. Ivan clapped the principal dancer on the shoulder and spoke rapidly in Russian. The dancer nodded and bowed toward Micaela.

"What did you say to him, Ivan?" she asked.

"I merely told them that you had to lead a very important meeting in the morning and unlike what they were accustomed to in our homeland, you take your obligations seriously."

She stood by the bar as the vodka flowed and the dancers chatted and laughed among themselves. Some spoke to Ivan but their tone with him was hushed and respectful. She couldn't understand what they said, but caught the sidelong glances her way and the use of her name. It sounded polite and Ivan smiled at the remarks.

As enjoyable as the evening had turned out, getting out of town after the AGF meeting tomorrow would be a welcome break from the controlled chaos of her solitary life. She would stop in to see Peggy and Reece this time. He was still recuperating when she had visited Bridewell over the Christmas holiday. All things considered, Reece had looked strong. Their life was so normal --- Peggy, a kindergarten teacher, Reece the shop teacher, baby due in June. A small part of her envied them... a very small part. Every once in a while, she thought it might be nice to be normal. Then reality set in.

Her musings ended when Ivan showed up inches from her side.

"I have not had the opportunity to tell you how lovely you look tonight. You have made quite an impression on my countrymen." Ivan lifted her glass to the bartender. "May I quench your thirst?"

Like his laugh in the museum, the words sounded more intimate than a simple request. She stepped back until the edge of the bar pressed against her spine. She could feel the eyes in the room watching them. *Safe topics, safe distance.*

"Will you be at the meeting tomorrow?" she asked.

"Unfortunately, I am detained by other matters. We could meet tomorrow evening to review the outcome." His hand brushed her elbow as he rested it on the bar. A shiver sped up her arm and down her spine.

"I'll be going out of town right after the meeting." Although, she thought, she could drive up later, after dinner.

"You have plans, I understand. Another time?" The disappointment in his voice weighed on her.

"Perhaps." She found herself staring into his eyes again, blue-white diamonds, facets of reflections, little mirrors.

He traced the jewelry on her neck. "What an interesting piece. I noticed it during the ballet. It suits you."

"The torc and earrings were a gift from my grandmother. I'm told they have been in the family a long time." She reached for the torc and touched his hand instead.

He caressed the gold. "Magnificent." His fingers drifted from the necklace to her collarbone. "This is a lunula. It predates the torc as a form of jewelry. It is extremely old and the mark of royalty."

That little voice inside told her to step away, but something about him pulled her body closer. A fish on a hook.

He closed the distance between them, his hip pressed against her. "The earrings are equally old, perhaps thousands of years."

His hand travelled up the side of her neck to the earrings. That same little voice screamed warnings at her, while the more primitive part of her mind wondered how his lips would feel if they followed the path of his fingers.

The lunula flared to life. It burned like dry ice against her skin. Ivan pulled his hand back. The sting brought her to her senses and she stepped away.

What the hell am I doing? She retrieved her purse from the bar and took a moment to steady her voice. "I really need to go. We have the meeting in the morning."

Micaela wound her way through the crowd, her face schooled into a practiced smile. She shook hands or nodded her good nights as she passed. Kat caught her eye. Micaela fought the urge to slap the smirk off Kat's face. As Micaela closed the door, she could see Ivan; his mouth smiled but his eyes were narrow slits.

8

Micaela tugged on the glass door to the terrace. She had checked the locks on the doors and windows of her apartment --- twice. Her head throbbed and her collarbone stung. A fretful Grady followed her everywhere. She longed to sit outside and let the crisp February air and glittering stars soothe her. But here she was, twenty-three floors up, and afraid to go outside; afraid someone or something would get in.

It was three o'clock in the morning, too late to call someone. Who would she call anyway? Parker was gone from her life. Her grandmother was certainly asleep. Her only other close friend, Nikki, a police detective, was unavailable. She had texted Micaela earlier to say that cancelling their gym date for tomorrow morning was fine. Nikki had to pull a double shift. They would catch up when Micaela got back from Bridewell.

Liam came to mind. She wasn't sure where he was staying before tomorrow's meeting. She started to call his cell phone, and then hung up. She couldn't call him in the middle of the night with tales of burning jewelry. He would think she was some frightened little girl or some lunatic. She was a grown woman. The boogie man was fiction and there were no monsters under the bed. *Right?*

Micaela stared at her reflection in the Cheval mirror. Her pupils were dilated, her eyes wide. Just for once couldn't the mirror lie? Her skin still burned where the lunula had rested. There would be a mark for sure. She had no idea what had happened. She never lost control. Ivan was attractive but she had been on the verge on throwing herself on him. Maybe he slipped something in her drink. She shook her head. Men that handsome and rich did not need to drug women to get what they wanted.

She had only one choice --- a pot of coffee. When it was ready she curled up with a cup in her wingback chair. Parker had teased her about the chair all through grad school and even more so when she moved into the apartment. Always the architect, he'd said its faded upholstery and overstuffed cushion broke the lines of her sleek, modern living room furniture.

She told him she would not give it up for anyone or anything. It carried some of the few solid memories she had from before the accident. This was the chair she'd sat in with her father in Bridewell and listened to his stories of faeries and kings. She smiled at the thought of her six-year-old self perched in her father's lap. He had told her she was descended from those mythic characters. It had made her feel special and powerful. Together the O'Brien *clann* was invincible, immortal. Tonight, like other times, she thought she found the scent of her father in the chair and felt safe. It reminded her of the pine forest outside Bridewell. Sometimes, when he'd come in from the evening rain, she would tease him that he smelled like a wet dog. She wrapped herself in these memories like a favorite blanket. Grady jumped in her lap and she told him one of her father's stories.

The buzzing of her alarm clock woke her. She felt strangely rested for sleeping upright in a chair for three whole hours. She checked her neck in the bathroom mirror. There on her collarbone where the lunula had rested and below Ivan's touch was a bright red crescent. Her fingers grazed the mark. No pain, no sign of blistering.

48

It looked more like a tattoo than a burn. She slipped the gray silk blouse with the high collar off the hanger. It would cover the mark.

She had just finished loading the dishwasher when the doorbell rang. Through the peephole, the doorman's face was barely visible behind a bouquet of roses. Micaela opened the door, took the flowers, and tipped the doorman. In the kitchen, she laid the two dozen red roses on the counter, took a vase from the cabinet over the refrigerator, and filled it with water. She put the flower filled vase on the coffee table and opened the card.

I look forward to many more evenings like last night.

Ivan

The burn on her neck throbbed. It wouldn't be the first time a male client had tried to use flirtation to influence a deal. She'd had more than her share of shallow attempts at manipulation and thought she was good at spotting it, but as corny as it sounded this time was different. He'd seemed truly attracted to her. She knew she should probably toss the bouquet into the trash, but they smelled like summer in February and each petal was red velvet. It would be a shame to waste perfection.

Maybe after the deal closed.

Until then, there needed to be rules and boundaries. She had to make her position clear. It should be done in person and not by phone message. But the meeting started at nine and he wasn't going to be there, nor would she see him after, so she dialed his contact number. Ivan's voice mail picked up.

"Baron, this is Micaela O'Brien. I received the flowers. I want to thank you for them and for including me as one of your guests at the ballet. I look forward to working with you and your team on the AGF deal." She hoped that sounded suitably professional. She hoped he or Kat got the message. She grabbed her laptop and purse and headed downstairs. At the curb, Seamus stood by the passenger door of the limousine. He would not allow the doorman to open the car door for The O'Brien.

The limousine dodged cars and pedestrians as it carried Micaela east on 50th Street, through Rockefeller Plaza to the Cadwalader Hotel. Seamus was skilled; he made every light. They were, at least, yellow. That's was what she'd swear to in traffic court, if needed.

Massive buildings threw shadows that fought off the dawn, but eventually even granite and concrete yield. Street lights blinked out. Steam clouds billowed from the sidewalk vents, New York fog. Crowds gathered around barricades to catch a glimpse of some celebrity appearing on the early morning news programs. Six-thirty in the morning, midday or midnight, the streets were crowded. New York had no day or night. Whatever your work or sleep habits, you were never alone.

She slipped out of the car in front of the massive brass gates of the five star hotel.

Seamus sniffed. "Would you be wantin' me to accompany you upstairs, Miss?" He had already told her that he thought it was unbecoming a woman of her status to meet a man in his hotel room.

"I'll be fine, Seamus. If I need you, I'll call down. But you know I can take care of myself. While I'm upstairs, why don't you park the limo and go inside for breakfast. Charge it to the Moran and Boru account."

"Wouldn't be seemly, me eating in the dining room. Me being on the job and all."

She had him. "But you'd be closer if I needed you."

"I'll see if I can eat in the staff room, Miss."

She entered through the gates and crossed the cobbled courtyard as Seamus pulled the car around to the parking garage. Inside, the lobby was a whirlpool of suited people arriving and departing. A dark haired man in a black and silver running suit lounged on an oversized sky blue brocade loveseat. An island of serenity in a vortex of bodies, he sipped his coffee and watched the flows around him. Lucky devil must be on vacation. He looked over at her, smiled and nodded as she walked to the elevators.

Floor numbers flashed above Micaela in the elevator. Suite 5501. François had been insistent on the phone yesterday that they breakfast in the suite and not the hotel's restaurant. He had not struck her as a psychopath, so a private meeting in his suite seemed safe enough. Seamus had no worries and would not have to answer to his Mary for anything. She thought about Francois' blue eyes, cleft chin and smile; he was one very handsome man. Better yet, he seemed unfazed by her mental intrusion, even impressed. Good looks aside, she had never met someone who could lock her out like that. How did he do it? Maybe she would just come out and ask him. The conversation could go something like: "François, could you pass me the cream? And while you're at it, how did you shut me down so quickly?" *Oh yeah, that would work.*

Micaela tapped on the suite's door. No answer. She knocked harder and the door swung open under the force of her knuckles.

"François? It's Micaela."

Maybe he was on a conference call or still in the shower. She set her laptop and purse down in the entry foyer. The large vase on the foyer table was filled with fresh flowers. They stirred slightly in a breeze from the open door of the balcony, the sweet smell drifting to her. She looked outside for him. The veranda was deserted. Even this high up you could hear the sounds of the morning traffic. Horns blared, diesel engines hummed and in the distance the wail of a siren. She closed the sliding door and turned toward the suite. She rounded the corner of the foyer into the living room and froze.

The frame of a sofa sat on its side, cushions torn to shreds, wads of stuffing littered the floor. A legless coffee table was wedged into the wall. A pile of broken wood and wire in a corner looked to be the remains of a piano. Long red streaks trailed down the eight foot window ending in a rust brown starburst on the carpet. A leg from the coffee table lay five feet away. The edges splintered where it had been snapped off, the claw foot darker than the rest of the wood. A lone chair stood at the head of a flattened dining room table. Shards of porcelain littered the white carpet.

"François?" The panic clutched at her chest. "Where are you?" The silence was not the answer she wanted. Maybe he was unconscious and couldn't answer. She threaded her way across the living room toward the bedroom. Her foot slipped on a wet patch. A dull thud made her cry out. A piece of end table that had teetered on the edge of an armchair had fallen. She stood as still as possible, straining her ears for any sound other than the pounding of her heart. She thought now would be a good time to be able to willfully find auras.

The living room had not prepared her for the bedroom. Blood was everywhere. It invaded her nose and the metallic taste coated her mouth. It splattered the walls and ceiling. She had been to Reece's family's farm on the reservation outside Bridewell after they had bagged two deer. They had a shed where the deer were hung for gutting and butchering. This was so much worse. But like that day in the shed, she switched to shallow breathing.

The mattress was shredded. The remnants of the sheets, already stiffened with dried blood, lay on the carpet. She spotted an open planner on the nightstand. Spatters of blood dotted the page. Her name and the time of their meeting were circled. It was the only entry on the page.

The smell of blood and other fluids overwhelmed her, cloying and repulsive at the same time. She moved forward toward the bathroom even though everything she knew told her it was a bad idea. She vaguely wondered if this was what shock felt like. If so, it was her best friend right now.

She stood outside the bathroom door. *You can do this, you have to go in. He might need help.* She looked back to the living room and the exit. The voice inside told her she didn't need to do this. François was beyond help and she should get out of there.

Micaela remembered how when she was told she had to do something, she would answer "the only things I have to do are die and pay taxes." She knew that wasn't true. Her father's voice whispered from memory that O'Briens didn't abandon someone in need.

She swallowed the hysterical laugh that tried to force its way out. Her hands started to shake. Her heart pounded in her ears like war drums. Micaela called François's name although she knew there would be no answer, then pushed ahead.

Her senses raced, her thoughts flew like buckshot. Gradually her mind surfaced and reality grabbed hold. On a platform in the center of the bathroom was a massive cream colored granite whirlpool tub. She saw the back of his head first; his wavy brown hair trailed over the head of the tub and one arm lolled over the side. François' body had been arranged in the waterless tub. Brown splotches were scattered over the tub, sink and floor. She moved alongside the tub. Eyes that once flamed blue stared up at her, glassy and cold.

Her gazed drifted down. The scream she'd been holding at bay escaped. François' throat was gone. She could see the vertebrae at the back of his neck, white bone covered with tendrils of muscle and sinew. Micaela's eyes continued on. She grabbed the edge of the tub. His chest was a hollow red cavity framed by ribs. Micaela stumbled back into the bedroom and fell to her knees. Her stockings sank into the bloody carpet. The room swirled around her as she fumbled in her bag for her cell phone. She stared at it for a moment wondering if she could get her fingers to dial 911. Despite the smell, she drew in a deep steadying breath and pressed the numbers.

"Please send help. He's dead." Her voice cracked as she fought the desire to scream again.

"Where are you ma'am? What's your name?" The dispatcher was calm, detached. She sounded so far away.

"Micaela, Micaela O'Brien. The Cadwalader Hotel. Please hurry."

"Are you in a room or in the lobby, Micaela?"

"A room. 5501. It's terrible."

"Are you injured?"

"No. I came in. The piano was crushed. He was in the tub. There's blood everywhere." She looked down at her knees painted russet by the ooze from the carpet.

"Are you sure he's dead? Can you see if he is breathing?"

"He can't breathe."

"Can't? What do you mean, Micaela?"

"He has no lungs."

Micaela heard the rush of air as the dispatcher exhaled. "Oh. Help's on the way, Micaela. I'll stay on the line with you until they arrive."

"I can't stay here, the smell, the blood. I have to get out." Micaela dragged herself to her feet and moved out into the entry foyer. She huddled in the doorway to the balcony, her arms wrapped around her shins, her forehead resting on her knees with her cell phone clutched in her left hand.

9

The squeak of a door hinge made Micaela look up. She peered between her knees to see two pairs of black men's shoes. She followed the legs of a dark blue suit to a gold name tag, the hotel manager it seemed. Next to him was a uniformed officer. The manager's eyes darted toward the suite of rooms, his nose pinched. He made some excuse about handling the arrival of emergency personnel and left. The stripes on the officer's sleeves said he was a sergeant, the hard set of his jaw told Micaela he had not spent his career behind a desk or directing traffic. The sergeant glanced into the living room; a muscle in his cheek started to twitch. He leaned over to reach out to her and she felt herself flinch. He stood up with his back to the living room. "Medical help will be here shortly, Miss."

Micaela pressed the cell phone to her ear, it felt slippery. "There's an officer here now. Thank you, for not leaving me alone."

"It will be all right now, Micaela," said the dispatcher.

"No, I don't think so," she answered.

She stayed on the foyer floor, her face turned toward the balcony door. Several times, the sergeant started to speak then snapped his jaw together. That was fine with Micaela; she didn't know what to say anyway. Finally, a very official looking man in a charcoal suit approached, followed by an entourage of EMTs, officers and photographers. The graying hair at the man's temples was made more prominent by his dark, clean-shaven face. He moved his jacket to display the gold detective shield clipped to his belt and she caught a glimpse of a service revolver. Behind the detective was a familiar face, Dominique "Nikki" Suassuna, her gym buddy and friend. *Safety.*

The detective squatted so his dark brown eyes were level with Micaela's. "Ms. O'Brien, I'm Detective Hendricks. I understand you already know Detective Suassuna. Shall we go somewhere quieter?" Something about the way he said Nikki's name caught Micaela's ear. He was not happy.

Nikki extended a hand to help Micaela stand. Hendricks squinted at them as if searching for some objectionable gesture or word. As they walked to the empty suite across the hall, Hendricks wedged his large muscular frame between the women. His shoulders were tense and back straight. He clearly did not want Nikki on the investigation.

Hendricks held the door open. "If you'll wait here, Ms O'Brien. Detective Suassuna and I need to ask you some questions." He paused in the doorway. "Would you feel more comfortable if you contacted your attorney?"

"I don't think I need one at this point." She didn't know if that was the right answer. Maybe she would regret it later, but she had nothing to hide and didn't want to give the appearance that she did. *Is this how innocent people ended up in jail?* Besides, her attorney was an expert on SEC matters, not murder.

Micaela stood by the large picture window, twisting the edge of the tan drape in her hand. She watched the sun's rays work their way down the shadowed marble face of the department store across the street. A young female officer stood in silence in the doorway. She shifted from one foot to the other, folding and unfolding her arms. She was slim and shorter than Micaela, which put her under five seven. Not very effective at blocking the view. Beyond her, Micaela saw a swarm of officers and EMTs stroll on and off the

56

elevators like extras in a television crime drama. They weren't in a hurry. Why should they be?

She saw Hendricks and Nikki crossing the hall and met them at the door. Hendricks gestured to a small table and two chairs, Micaela shook her head. Shock and fear were converted to energy, so she paced the limits of her cage looking for something to do. She figured hitting something, even a pillow, could be used against her. Nikki sat at the table and took out a spiral notebook.

Micaela faced Hendricks. "Detective Hendricks, what happened in there?"

"I was hoping you could help shed some light on it. How well did you know François Leveque?"

Nikki's eyes were glued to the page as she wrote. Hendricks sat across from Nikki and crossed his legs.

"We had corresponded on a deal we are... were working on. I met him face-to-face for the first time the night before last," Micaela said.

An EMT came in; he must have come from François' suite. Pale, wide-eyed, he looked as bad as Micaela felt. He worked wordlessly, taking Micaela's pulse, checking her pupils, and then he pulled out an alcohol swab and syringe.

Micaela yanked her arm back. "I did not consent to a blood sample, only to answer questions. Why do you need a blood sample anyway?" She looked from Hendricks to Nikki, who didn't make eye contact.

Detective Hendricks waved off the EMT and continued. "Who arranged the meeting this morning?"

"He did. He wanted to meet yesterday morning but I had to be in Philadelphia so we rescheduled for today."

"Can you account for your whereabouts last night?"

"I don't understand, do you think I could do something like that?" She looked at Nikki for support.

Nikki answered. "It's standard procedure. We need to know where everybody who met him was last night."

57

"I was at the City Center in Baron Vasilievich's box. The Kirov performed Swan Lake. After the performance, there was a reception. I must have gotten home about one." Micaela heard her own voice, flat, controlled.

"Someone can verify this?" asked Hendricks.

"The Baron, Ekaterina Vilkas, the Baron's assistant, and guests from South Africa and Japan. I can get you names and numbers. My building has a twenty-four hour doorman and surveillance cameras."

It wasn't all that different from the SEC depositions. In fact, the SEC was tougher, in part because they thought she was using inside information but couldn't prove it. Intuition had not been a valid answer. She doubted the SEC or Hendricks would believe metaphysical gifts.

"Did you touch anything while you were in the room?" Nikki asked.

She squeezed her eyes shut, saw the room and smelled the blood. A trickle of sweat ran down her back. "I grabbed the tub. I thought I was going to lose it. I don't remember touching anything else, but I can't be sure." She searched Hendricks' face for belief, understanding and found nothing. Nikki nodded in what Micaela hoped was support.

Detective Hendricks took Nikki aside; he leaned into her and spoke rapidly. Whatever he was saying, she stood her ground and met his gaze. Nikki glanced quickly at Micaela before she walked out toward the elevator.

"Am I free to go, Detective?" she asked.

"We're almost done. If you will wait here, please." Detective Hendricks headed back into François' suite.

Micaela was left alone except for the young female officer. Her name tag read Officer B. Martin. The poor thing looked like she had just graduated from the Academy. Micaela hoped it wasn't Officer Martin's first assignment. Time dragged on and the claustrophobia grew. Micaela looked at her watch, eight-fifteen. *Damn, the meeting.* She pulled her phone out.

Officer Martin spoke for the first time. "Are you calling your attorney, M'am?"

"My office."

"You can call them later. I'm sure you understand."

"No, you need to understand. In one hour, my conference room will be filled with two dozen people for a meeting that I am supposed to run." She knew she was getting loud, but it felt soooo good.

"Unless you are calling your lawyer, there's nothing I can do, ma'am."

Nikki stepped off the elevator and approached Micaela. "What's going on, Officer Martin?"

"She wants to call her office, Lieutenant Suassuna."

Micaela held her hands out, palms up, in a plea to Nikki. "I have a meeting to run in an hour. I have to cancel or find someone to fill in. I'll even give you my assistant Judy's number and you can call, if that works better."

"I'll take responsibility, officer. Make your call, Micaela. You understand I need to stand here and listen in. Avoid giving any details… ongoing investigation and all that."

"Got it." Micaela called Judy and gave her a vague but convincing reason to cancel. Judy would figure out what was happening as soon as it hit the news, if it hadn't already. Micaela slipped her phone back in her bag.

"Nikki, why are you here? They know we know each other."

She shrugged. "Special circumstances, a request from higher up. Hendricks isn't thrilled."

"That's obvious. What happened to François?"

"It's too early to say."

"But you must have a theory?" Micaela knew that look on her friend's face. Nikki knew something.

"Nothing I can share right now."

59

Micaela watched from the doorway as Nikki ducked under the yellow tape and disappeared into François' suite. Micaela watched officers depart with bags marked 'Evidence'. In one bag she spotted the planner from the desk. She alternated between roaming the suite and slumping against the doorframe. She was beyond exhausted. This suite also had a balcony, so she cracked open the door. A soft breeze that carried a hint of warmth to come drifted in. Imbolc had passed; spring had begun on the Druid calendar.

Nikki returned with a grim-faced Detective Hendricks.

He handed her his card. "Ms. O'Brien, we're done for now. We will need you to come down to the station for fingerprinting and a formal statement. If you think of anything else, please call me."

"Fingerprinting? Am I a suspect?"

"If nothing else, we need to eliminate any prints that belong to you or the victim."

"I can do that. Whatever you need to catch the person… the animal that did this." *I owe François as much. If I'd said something, told him what I saw when I touched him.* "Detective, I need to know. It looks like a war zone in there. How is it that no one heard something and called 911?"

Detective Hendricks said nothing. The silence was broken by the squeak of a gurney being pulled out of the suite, a large green bag atop. Micaela was overwhelmed by the need to see François. Maybe it wasn't him; maybe it was all some cruel hoax, some twisted vision like the sight of Reece on the roadside last Samhain.

She looked at Hendricks. "May I, please?"

"What's one more irregularity?" He glared at Nikki, and then held his hand out to stop the transport. "Ms. O'Brien would like to view the victim."

The victim, he has a name, maybe a family. His sapphire eyes and wavy brown hair were clear in her mind. So was his fear. She should have come yesterday as he'd asked. The EMT unzipped the bag as far as François' chin. Micaela couldn't see his throat, but she didn't need to. She would see it in her nightmares forever. They hadn't closed his eyes; blood was caked in his hair and face.

Micaela nodded, unable to speak. The sound of the zipper closing was deafening. So final. She started to shake, her fragile control gone. The world slipped from focus as her legs gave out. Far away was a strange keening. Arms wrapped around her and pulled her to her feet. *Who was making that sound? Someone tell them to stop.*

She heard Nikki's voice like an echo in a cave. "It's okay, Micaela. You can let it out now." *That's me wailing?*

Micaela found herself out on a balcony, a blanket draped over her shoulders, gulping in the February air. A tall man in a charcoal suit stood in the balcony doorway.

"Why? What kind of animal?" Micaela didn't think she would ever stop shaking.

"We'll find out, I promise." Nikki pressed a glass of water to Micaela's lips.

She tried to drink, but ran for the railing as it all came back up. Through the shimmer of tears, she could see, down the street, the spires of Saint Patrick's Cathedral promising hope and eternal life. In the distance she heard that other detective, *what was his name*, tell someone to see Ms. O'Brien home. And beyond that a familiar lilt, "I'm Seamus, her driver. I'll be taking Miss O'Brien home."

10

Grady's green eyes peered up at Micaela from his post on her chest. He rubbed his cheek against her face and purred.

"You're up." Nikki stood at the foot of the couch, coffee mug in her hand.

Micaela's entire body began to quake. Grady leapt to the back of the sofa, his gaze flickering from Nikki to Micaela.

"Nikki, please tell me it was a bad dream."

"I wish I could."

Micaela rolled off the couch and scrambled for the bathroom. She choked and gagged through dry heaves; you don't really throw up when you haven't eaten in… she didn't even know what time it was. She sat on the marble floor and stared at the blood on her stockings and skirt edge.

Nikki passed Micaela a damp washcloth which she spread over her face.

"Seamus stayed with you until I got here. I would have helped you out of your clothes, but you were in no shape," Nikki said. "I found a sheet and managed to cover the couch to protect it from anything on your clothes."

"How long have I been asleep?"

"Since about three o'clock yesterday afternoon. It's two o'clock Saturday morning."

"I was supposed to be at Grandma's by now."

"It's okay. She called last night. I told her what I could, the rest she'd seen on the late night national news. She said to call when you were able. She's sweet."

"She's the best." Grandma was a rock. For the first time in a long time, Micaela ached for Bridewell. She slid her back up the bathroom wall until she was upright and shuffled to the living room. Nikki followed, her arms half raised, encircling Micaela ready to catch her. She made it as far as the wingback chair and curled up in a fetal position.

"Can I get you something?" Nikki tucked a blanket around Micaela.

"Answers."

"I'm trying." Nikki perched on the edge of the coffee table. "Do you remember anything else that would help? Anyone who Leveque might have had a problem with?"

Micaela thought about the words Liam seemed to have with François at the Museum. It didn't seem possible, but after yesterday, who was she to decide?

"Nikki, are you here as my friend or on official police business?"

"Detective Hendricks asked me the same thing."

"What did you say?"

Nikki locked eyes with her. "I told him that I had three months of accumulated vacation time and today would be a good time to start taking it."

Micaela uncurled. "So everything we talk about is off the record?"

"Yes."

"Really?"

"Trust me on this. I know exactly what I'm doing." Nikki headed for the kitchen. "Why don't you take a shower, you'll feel better. I'll fix something light. Then we can talk."

Micaela's thigh high stockings crackled as she pulled them off, coppery flakes fluttered to the tile. She knew smells would wash away; she wasn't so sure of the guilt. The caked blood dissolved and ran down her shins creating swirls like the shower scene in *Psycho*. François' matted brown hair filled her mind. His fear and need to speak haunted her. She had gone to Catechism as a kid trying to fit in with the world outside the Druid community. There she had learned about the sins of commission and sins of omission. It was why, in the Catholic Church in town, people prayed for forgiveness for "what they had done and what they had failed to do". She may have failed in the 'to do' department before François was dead but she would not fail him after death. She would find his killer. Her tears mixed with the soap, water, and blood.

Stepping out of the shower, she stared at herself in the bathroom mirror. Her red-rimmed eyes sat atop dark circles. She didn't look like someone who had just slept eleven hours. She sat on the edge of her bed and laid back. *Just for a minute.*

She woke to a bright blue sky and the smell of coffee and warm bread. Micaela walked out of her room to a steaming mug, a stack of toast, and various jars of jams and spreads on the dining room table. She sat across the table from Nikki and nibbled at the toast, unsure it would stay down.

"Do you believe NYPD can find François' killer?" Micaela asked.

"If I did, I wouldn't be on vacation right now. Everything I know says this is outside their jurisdiction."

"And you have contacts they don't?" They had never really talked about Nikki's work. There had always been an unwritten rule during their workouts that they wouldn't talk shop.

"I have access to sources the NYPD doesn't." Nikki grabbed a slice of toast and smeared hazelnut spread on it.

"Why not share with them?"

"My sources are less than orthodox, even by New York standards."

"We… I need to find his killer. I'd like any help you and your sources can give." Micaela raised the mug to her lips and took a tentative sip. It stayed down, too. So far, so good.

"That works for me." Nikki pulled a pad out of her messenger bag. "I had to leave all my notes behind. Let's start at the beginning; fill in any additional details you might have remembered."

Micaela filled her in on the private bank, AGF, and the show at the Met. She omitted her sensing of François' fears; her vague impressions wouldn't help the investigation.

"Did you see Leveque talk to anyone?" Nikki asked.

"I'm sure he talked to a lot of people, we all did. I saw him speak to Liam Farrell, Ethan Lowell, Ambassador Reynolds, and of course Baron Vasilievich. The Baron came into the Impressionist Gallery while François and I were there." Micaela went into the kitchen to pour another cup. François' murder was so brutal that she couldn't imagine Ivan doing it. In fact, the only one that had left the box was Ekaterina. She was a bitch, but that kind of violence… she might break a nail.

"I know where to find the Ambassador. I need contact information for the rest again," said Nikki.

Micaela pulled up the distribution list for the AGF deal on her laptop and sent it to the printer. "I don't have Lowell's contact info, but I can get it from the office. His company, First Colony, is a client of Moran & Boru's Boston office."

"Micaela, I know this has been tough but, given how upset you were, I have to ask. Was there a personal relationship between you and François?"

"No. It's just that---" Micaela looked down, the toast was bread crumbs."I feel responsible."

"Why?" Nikki set the pen aside. She twirled a double-headed axe pendant that hung around her neck between her fingers.

"He tried to talk to me about something that night at the Met. He wanted to meet the next day, I postponed."

Nikki pushed her pad to the side. "You don't know that things would have turned out any differently."

"I know."

Nikki filled a travel mug of coffee for herself and then tucked the pad in her messenger bag. "I'm going to head home and freshen up. I need to talk to the others, see if they can add anything. Will you be okay?"

"Yeah. I need to get ready for next week and figure out when the AGF meeting will be. Nikki, what will happen to François?"

"There'll be an autopsy. Then, I guess someone will arrange for his body to be sent to France."

"Who handles this? I want to help, if I can. It's the least I can do."

"I'll find out. Are you sure you're all right?" Nikki hand was on the doorknob.

"I will be. It gets better, doesn't it?"

"It never goes away, but, eventually, you learn to live with it." Nikki closed the door behind her.

Micaela wasn't so sure.

11

Micaela filled her day with details and activity. She called her grandmother and arranged to come up later the following week. She rescheduled the AGF meeting for two weeks from Wednesday in Brussels and spoke to François' boss, Henri Montbelliard. She offered to see that things were handled right on this side of the Atlantic. François had no family other than Montbelliard and colleagues at La Tène. Montbelliard said he would consider it and get back to her. By four, she was ready for a run to burn off the rest of the tension. She left her cell phone and MP3 player home, wanting only the solitude of a run along the river.

After her run, she stepped off the elevator and heard the muted ring of her phone beyond her apartment door. By the time she got inside the message light was flashing. The first message was from Grandma. François' murder had made CNN and a cameraman had filmed Micaela being escorted out of the hotel to a waiting black sedan. There had been no mention of Micaela's name. The next message was from her assistant, Judy, checking on her. Twenty-three years older than Micaela and a transplant from Moran & Boru's Boston office, Judy was a self-appointed combination of mother hen and pit bull.

The third was from Ivan. He had also heard the news and delayed his departure for Russia. He thought it was a bad idea for her to sit at home. If she had no other plans, she should meet him at Très Couteaux at seven for dinner. After all, his message said, she had to eat. She peered into the refrigerator, leftover bagels and week-old Chinese takeout. He was right, of course.

After a torturous trip down the Westside Highway, Micaela entered the restaurant. The maitre d' informed her that the Baron was already seated. He checked her leather coat and escorted her through the sea of white linen, flashing silverware, and shimmering crystal. Ivan was not alone; Kat was seated on his right. On her right sat a man that Micaela thought looked like one of the security guards from the box at the ballet. He did not introduce himself.

She wasn't up for Kat's crap, but there was no retreat now. After a wistful glance toward the exit, Micaela cracked her neck and steeled herself for what had just become a working dinner. Ivan stood and pulled out the chair to his left for her. At least she had a nice view of the river.

"My apologies for being late, Baron."

He arched an eyebrow and lifted one corner of his mouth in a smile. "Baron?"

"I mean, Ivan, it's nice to see you again." In a strange way she was glad to be with him. He was calm, solid.

"I wish it could have been under more pleasurable circumstances." He signaled for a server. "Would you care for wine or a cocktail?"

"A glass of cabernet and a water. Thank you." She turned to Kat. "Kat, I'm glad you could join us." Micaela smoothed her napkin onto her lap.

"I am happy I could be here for you. You must be traumatized. Poor thing."

"It was difficult, but I'm fine. I appreciate your concern, Kat."

The fourth chair was occupied by a dark-haired, broad-shouldered man who draped his arm across the back of Kat's chair.

Micaela sipped her wine and stared out at the Brooklyn Bridge and the Promenade beyond. Red brake lights on the cars blinked their warnings as they crossed the river. Her mind was for a moment a blessed blank, the hum of table conversation and the clatter of plates just static.

"Micaela? Are you with us?" Ivan's voice brought her back.

"I'm sorry, you were saying?"

"I was asking if the police had any new information on Monsieur Leveque's murder?"

"Nothing I'm aware of. Of course, I'd be the last to know." Micaela shrugged.

"Why is that?" He held the stem of his wine glass between his long fingers. The burgundy liquid swirled against the crystal.

"I got the feeling they believe I or my firm were somehow involved."

Kat laughed. "You? How ridiculous."

Ivan's long golden lashes did little to soften the steel glint in his eyes. A cold wind seemed to pass between him and Kat. It brushed Micaela's skin and raised the hair under the long sleeves of her turtleneck.

Servers arrived with their dinners. The dance of plates and pepper mills, the cascade of water glass refills was enough distraction to break the tension for the moment. Micaela had ordered veal Marsala, Kat's filet mignon was rare. The mystery man had ordered the same as Kat. Ivan played with a dark soup that looked like beef broth, maybe borscht.

A mocking smile played on Kat's lips. "Micaela, I understand you grew up in a small mountain village in Massachusetts?"

"I spent part of my childhood there."

"Do you still have family there?"

"No one that I see often." Micaela stared into Kat's grass green eyes. No one had eyes that color, Micaela thought. They must be contacts.

Kat continued probing. "You were orphaned, too. Such a shame your parents cannot be here to celebrate your successes."

"I know they are pleased with what I have done so far --- wherever they are." How did you explain the Otherworld to people from cultures based in modern religions?

"I would not have thought you were so spiritual." Kat's smile mocked.

It was time to change subjects. She turned to Ivan.

"Ivan, all I know about you is what I've read in the media. They say you are the financial tsar of Russia and a supporter of the arts around the world."

"I was raised to believe that money and power cannot be squandered." His pale blue eyes glittered in the candlelight like the lights of the bridge. "You are also quite successful for one so young. What is your secret?"

"I have no secrets, just hard work and a good education. *You* are the mystery. A line here and there in the business and society page, but beyond that… nothing."

"Don't you find that people with secrets are much more interesting?" He raised the soup spoon to his lips.

"There is something to be said for people who are exactly what they seem." She took a bite of her veal. One should never talk with one's mouth full, especially if one needed time to think.

"The veal is delicious. Would you like a taste?" Micaela pushed her plate a little closer to Ivan.

"No, thank you. I have an issue that severely limits what I consume, hence the broth." He pushed the bowl away.

"How terrible. I would never… I mean, you look…." *What, not starved, healthy, attractive?*

"It is nothing really, a minor inconvenience." He covered her hand with his.

70

"How do you manage when you travel? The entertaining you must do?" Micaela's hands, usually so pale, looked bronzed next to his.

"Over the years, I have adapted. I am not without resources."

His thumb felt like the beat of a butterfly's wings as it moved across the back of her hand. She eased her hand away. The blackness had reappeared, the red splotches larger.

"Ivan, we are involved in a business transaction together. I'm sure you would agree that it would be inappropriate to cross certain boundaries or to even give the appearance of it."

"I understand. Some in our business are more concerned with perception than reality. Your honor and reputation are as important to me as your peace of mind. I shall not publicly compromise that." He pulled his hand back.

Kat dabbed her mouth. Behind the napkin, Micaela caught a glimpse of Kat's smile.

It would have to do. And since Micaela would see that he was never alone with her, he would not compromise her honor in private.

After dinner, Ivan suggested a walk through the Seaport. Kat walked ahead of them accompanied by her dinner companion. Micaela had overheard Kat call him Sergei.

It was a chilly evening and the wind blew in from the river, but Micaela was comfortable in her coat, the peacock blue turtleneck, and navy wool skirt she'd worn. Maybe she should offer her leather coat to Kat. All Kat was wearing was a silver dress that barely covered her lingerie and displayed her long athletic legs. Micaela knew that she could never carry that look off. Based on the faces on the approaching men and some of the women, the February air had its predictable effect on Kat. Sergei put a protective arm around her, which she shrugged off.

Ivan grasped her elbow and turned her to face him. He threw a disparaging glance at Kat. "You are beautiful. Do not compare yourself to your lessers."

"How did you know what I was thinking?" Micaela asked.

71

He ran a cool finger down the creases between her eyebrows. "I have known one like you. You think too hard and wear it on your face."

As she moved to step away, the air went still and soundless.

"Ah, Mischa, have I broken the rule already?" Ivan glanced around. "No, it would seem we are alone."

The street was deserted. Impossible! Crowds just don't vanish from the streets of New York. First the colors, then the lunula, now this. The visions and flashes were worse than anything she remembered from her childhood. She looked around for the gate with the sign that said 'Welcome to Madness'.

From the roof of the Seaport, Micaela heard the warning caw of a raven. The remnants of the burn from the lunula throbbed on her collarbone while a shiver of energy ran down her spine. She blinked and the crowd had returned.

"Are you well, Mischa?" His concern was obvious.

"I'm okay. Going out seemed like a better idea earlier."

"I shall hail a cab for you." Ivan walked beside her as they joined Kat and Sergei on South Street.

Kat stood within inches of Ivan. "Baron, perhaps Ms. O'Brien would care to join us at the Club. I'm sure she would find Johannes fascinating."

"I'm not quite ready for an evening out." *And when I do go out, it will be not be with Johannes, whoever he was, or anyone else Kat introduces me to,* Micaela thought.

At the waiting cab, she shook Ivan's hand. *Keep it professional.* "Thank you for dinner. I shall see you in Brussels."

"Until Brussels. Be well, Mischa." He closed the taxi door behind her.

Out the rear window of the cab, Micaela saw Ivan's hand raised in farewell. He turned and vanished into the shadows of an alley. Kat and Sergei walked toward Chinatown. Micaela didn't know of any hot clubs there, but she wasn't the expert.

Above their heads, a raven launched from the Seaport roof.

72

12

Just after noon on Sunday, Nikki rapped on Micaela's door. "I figured you hadn't eaten." Nikki laid out bagels, cream cheese, and lox on the table.

Micaela poured beans into the grinder of the coffeemaker. "So where do we stand?"

"I've spoken to everyone you gave me and a few additional names I picked up along the way."

"Did you find anything out?"

"I found out you didn't tell me that Liam and Ethan had words with François that night."

Micaela banged around in the cabinet. There were clean coffee mugs somewhere. "I was across the room. I couldn't hear what they were saying." *That sounded lame.*

"Well, Liam was at the Ambassador's dinner until one, then at a pub in Tribeca, with lots of witnesses, until four. The video cameras at his hotel showed him coming in alone and not leaving again. Lowell says he drove back to Boston after the Museum. I'm trying to verify his whereabouts the next night."

Relief flooded Micaela. She'd known it wasn't possible that Liam was involved. "So that leaves us?"

"Nowhere. I called a buddy of mine on the force who's working the investigation. They say they are following up on a promising lead from Interpol. But off the record, they don't know anything more than we do." Nikki pulled a steamed tuna filet from the bottom of the shopping bag and crumbled it into Grady's bowl.

"Your friend wouldn't give you any more information?"

"No, but I also have friends at Interpol. I'll see what I can get directly from them. The next step is to look at the surveillance videos and check for any tampering the police might have missed."

"How are you going to get access?"

"A different friend." In response to Micaela's raised eyebrows, Nikki said, "Best if you don't ask."

"Access aside, wouldn't the police catch any tampering?"

"Not if they didn't know what they were looking for."

Liam was in the clear. The coffee smelled delicious again and the lox were mouth-watering. She spread cream cheese and layered lox on an everything bagel. They ate and cleaned up in silence. She walked Nikki to the elevator.

"Have they released François' body yet?"

"The Coroner's Office says they will be releasing the body to Campbell and Winston Funeral Home tomorrow."

"Call me at my office when that happens."

"Will do." Nikki held the elevator door open. "Micaela, I know you are used to making things happen, but this is a different world. Go slow."

Micaela's heels clicked across the marble floor toward the elevator that would take her to the offices of Moran & Boru. The lobby was quiet. She had cut herself some slack and come in at ten this Monday, instead of her usual seven o'clock. Of course she'd pay for the extra sleep when she got to her desk.

The elevator door opened on the thirtieth floor where Judy, her assistant, stood sentry, hands on her hips.

"A Detective Hendricks is here. I told him he needed an appointment. He said you'd make time. I figured he could cool his heels in the conference room. Pushy cop."

Micaela smiled and shook her head. "Judy, we need to work on your assertiveness. You are far too meek. How long has he been in there?"

Judy sniffed at her humor. "About an hour. Mr. Moran is waiting for you in his office. You're to go there first."

"Did you at least offer him a coffee?"

"Not in this lifetime." Judy turned on her heel and headed for her desk, muttering not so softly under her breath.

Micaela took the left-hand hallway so she didn't pass the conference room. Brian Moran, senior partner at Moran and Boru, mentor and friend of her father, came out from behind his desk.

"Are you sure you're ready to come back? You could leave down the service elevator, I'll tell Hendricks you're still not up to talking."

"Sitting at home makes it worse and who's to say he won't show up at my door?"

"Micaela, you don't always have to out tough the rest of us," Brian said

"It's not about tough, Brian. It's about distraction. Let's get this over with."

"Fair enough." He returned to his high-backed leather chair behind the mahogany desk.

A man rose from the burgundy sofa. He wore the standard-issue double-breasted navy suit, dark framed glasses, and close cropped graying hair. Brian introduced him. "Micaela, this is Jonathan Sutcliffe. He heads the criminal law department at Skeffington and Morgan. I asked him to come over as soon as Detective Hendricks showed up on our doorstep."

Micaela sat in one of the chairs. "Is this really necessary?"

Sutcliffe answered for him. "Consider it our usual abundance of caution. I have information that the police are currently acting on

75

an Interpol tip that would link François Leveque's murder with this firm, you, and another of our clients."

There was no point asking him how he came by this information; it's why they paid him and his firm a seven figure retainer.

Brian leaned back in his chair, his fingers steepled against his chin, his feet propped on the mahogany desk. It was Brian's 'I'm thinking but not worried' position and Micaela appreciated the vote of confidence.

"Details?" he asked.

Sutcliffe pulled out a folder and opened it on the coffee table. "Interpol believes that Leveque was involved in some sort of alternative belief system group. That's their generic term for everything from the New Age feel-good stuff to Satanists. Certain members of this group, including Leveque, are rumored to have progressed from using drugs to mimic visions, to dealing drugs and ultimately weapons."

Micaela shook her head. She found it hard to accept the image of François as a drug dealer or gunrunner, but what did she really know about him? He had definitely been afraid of something or someone. She looked at Brian. He valued her intuition about people. It had made the firm millions and saved them from more than one bad situation. Had she missed this one?

"I don't know, Brian, he didn't strike me that way. But, for the sake of argument, let's assume the police are right about the guns and drugs, how do they tie it to the firm or me?" she asked.

"We don't know exactly. Which is why Sutcliffe is going into that conference room with you." Brian took his feet off the desk.

As they walked down the hall, Sutcliffe coached her. "This will be similar to your meetings with investigators from the SEC. Say nothing, unless you clear it with me. Our goal is to let him talk, to see what he does and doesn't know."

The preliminary discussion in the conference room was a repetition of the earlier of questions at the hotel. Then Detective Hendricks changed direction, as expected.

"Ms. O'Brien, do you know an Ethan Lowell?"

Sutcliffe leaned over to discuss her answer before she finally answered, "I met him once at the opening at the Met."

"You have had no other dealings with Lowell or First Colony Shipping?"

Again, Sutcliffe consulted with her before she spoke. "I know the company name. They are handled from our Boston office. I have had no personal dealings with the firm." That was technically true; First Colony had declined to participate in AGF and she had not met with Lowell about that decision or any other deals.

"As a child, do you remember your father meeting with anyone from that company in your home?" Hendricks leaned back in his chair, his eyes scanning between Micaela and Sutcliffe.

Micaela waved Sutcliffe off. "My father has been dead fourteen years, what does this have to do with him?"

Hendricks pulled a photo from his folder showing of the bits and pieces of charred wreckage. "Yes, quite tragic. A plane explosion, mid-air. I understand you were the only survivor, the miracle child. Never did figure out how it happened."

She stiffened. *Son of a bitch.* "What do you hope to accomplish, Detective?"

Sutcliffe made a show of putting his hand on Micaela's elbow to help her stand. Not necessary, unless he was afraid she'd take a swing at Hendricks. That was an option.

"Detective Hendricks, unless you have specific questions for Ms. O'Brien regarding the current matter and not past personal tragedies, we are done here."

"I'm sure there will be additional questions." Hendricks stood. "I understand that Mr. Leveque's employer has requested that you handle the arrangements for the return of the body to France. That is very generous of you."

"I am glad to help. Someone needs to do the honorable thing, Detective." Micaela extended her hand. Hendricks declined to take it.

Micaela returned to her office and dove into her e-mail inbox; deleting, responding, and forwarding others to Judy. A copy of an e-mail had arrived from Henri Montbelliard, François' boss, requesting that the French Embassy defer all details to Micaela. She printed multiple copies and strode down the hall to Brian's office. She tossed Sutcliffe's copy onto the coffee table.

"How did Hendricks know before I did?"

"Relax, Micaela. He doesn't have enough information to get a wiretap or search warrant. He was clearly fishing. My guess is this was leaked by someone at La Tène or in the Ambassador's office." Sutcliffe tucked the email into his folder.

"Let us know when you have more than a guess, Sutcliffe. Brian, I'll be gone the rest of the day, it seems I have arrangements to see to." She started for the door. "I'll be here for the aerospace closing tomorrow morning, and then I'll be at the wake."

13

The scent of the flowers drifted down the hall, that overpowering sweetness unique to funeral parlors. She knew François' spirit was not in the room and had most likely moved on, but it felt wrong to leave his passing unmarked, to leave him alone. In the front row, a solitary figure sat, his head bent. From the rear, Micaela wasn't sure if he was someone she should know. She left him to his prayers or thoughts.

The last wake she had been to was Mr. Ryan, her swim coach and husband to her dance teacher. But that had been a real Irish wake, complete with whiskey toasts from a small bar at the back of the room and familiar faces. Tonight, she wandered the almost empty room and read the small florist cards tucked in the arrangements from the participants in the AGF deal. There were others from people she didn't know, including a local rugby team.

On a side table was an exquisite bouquet of delicate white lilies and red roses. The card read: First Colony Shipping. She had reviewed everything she could on Ethan Lowell and First Colony on the Internet last night… which wasn't much. Hendricks' line of questioning hinted at a possible connection between François and First Colony.

Of course, she knew the man in the front row. She turned to face him.

"The flowers are acceptable, don't you think, Ms. O'Brien?"

"They are lovely, Mr. Lowell. I hope you weren't here for long. I planned to arrive earlier, but a business meeting ran longer than I'd hoped."

"I arrived shortly after six. Please do not concern yourself; being alone does not bother me."

Micaela sat on one of the striped damask couches set against the wall. She looked not at the casket but at the rows of folding chairs bereft of mourners. Lowell turned a folding chair to face her.

"Have you been in the city since the opening, Mr. Lowell?"

"I returned from Boston as soon as I received word of the arrangements you had made." His hands rested on his knees, his back military straight and his shoulders broad and squared.

"It is very considerate of you to make the trip. You must have known François well."

"We worked together over the years on various projects. François was an honorable man. He represented Montbelliard well."

She watched Lowell's face as he turned away. It was still, his eyes ahead to the casket. The only movement was a small twitch on the left side along the scar that ran down his cheek and disappeared under his jaw. His shoulders sagged.

"I am sorry for your loss. I didn't know him as well. François and I met for the first time at the opening." Under normal circumstances, Micaela would have touched his hand in support.

His cornflower blue eyes turned to her. Beautiful, unreadable. "I am told you found him."

All she could do was nod. They stared at each other, neither knowing where to go from there. She wasn't interested in reliving those moments.

He straightened his shoulders. "François and Liam had been after me to reconsider participating in AGF. Perhaps now I need to rethink my position."

80

"We have rescheduled the meeting for two weeks from tomorrow in Brussels. Please call my office, if you change your mind. I can add you to the distribution list."

"Thank you. Maybe we will meet again. After all, your firm and mine have a long history."

What was it Machiavelli had said…*keep your friends close and your enemies closer*. She smiled. "One, I hope, we can continue."

Lowell stood. "I must also be going. I'm expected back in Boston. Please take my card, Ms. O'Brien. If I can be of any help, call. The number is my private line. If I don't pick up, press zero to reach my assistant. I shall tell Connie that your calls are a priority."

Her fingertips brushed his as she accepted the card. No colors, no aura, and no hint that he might be involved in any of the things that circled around François death. But wasn't that what you always heard on the news: "he seemed like such a nice guy."

She sat alone until she couldn't procrastinate any longer. She approached the casket and spoke to a space above the closed box. "I'm so sorry. I wish you could tell me what happened. Who did this to you? If we had been able to talk… if I'd known what you were afraid of… I could have protected you."

Nikki spoke from behind. "I'm not sure you could have prevented this."

"I could have tried. I should have saved him." Micaela turned, her hands clenched. Liam stood behind Nikki. He stepped toward Micaela, his hand held out.

"You can't change what is past, only what will come, 'Caela. We're here to help you honor his passing."

Liam stood on Micaela's right. He gently lifted the lid of the casket. Micaela gripped the rail of the kneeler and exhaled slowly. The mortician had worked magic. Nikki came up to Micaela's left and took her hand. Nikki whispered words in a strange and lyrical language. Micaela was fairly sure it wasn't Portuguese, so she assumed it was Nikki's tribal tongue. When she was finished, Nikki stepped back.

Micaela retreated when Liam took a small vial from the pocket of his jacket. She knew the ritual that was coming. Her grandmother had performed it for her grandfather. But not for her parents: no bodies, no ritual. Which had been all right with Micaela, she wanted no part of silly superstitions. It saved no one.

Liam opened the vial and put three drops on François' lips. Micaela knew the liquid was sacred well water. He turned to Micaela and put his hand out to her. "It is better if both halves, male and female, help him on his journey to the Otherworld."

Micaela stared at François' face. She would do this for François. She took Liam's hand and joined him in the words.

"Come spirits
Carry your brother on the wind
Carry your brother on the sunlight
Carry your brother on the waters
Take him across to the bright land
Take him across moor and meadow
Take him across a calm sea
Take him across a blissful ocean
Take him across the open land
Take him across the western threshold."

Liam closed the casket. "Go easy to the land of the ancestors. Let the waters carry you across to the Blessed Isles there your family and loved ones await." The actions spoke to her, to memories of tradition and duty. It was clear Liam respected François enough to be here and help his soul on its journey. Liam turned Micaela to face the room. During the ritual a dozen people had arrived and stood waiting to pay their respects, some faces she recognized from the Met. Kat's pet bodyguard Sergei stood against the rear wall. One by one they approached the casket and paid their respects before approaching Micaela to offer condolences and thanks.

None of the pieces fit. How could the François that brought these people here be the same person that Hendricks tried to link to darker dealings? Why would someone have brutally murdered François? Her intuition kept telling her Hendricks was on the wrong trail. But intuition wasn't proof for anyone, including, she had to admit, herself.

When everyone else had left, Nikki and Micaela walked out. Liam lagged behind reading the names in the guest register. Micaela paused under the funeral home's awning. A soft rain had begun.

"I'm glad you came, Nikki. You didn't have to." Micaela hugged her friend.

"You've been through hell these last few days." Nikki's hand made small circles on Micaela's back, the way you would soothe a child. Micaela's throat tightened. Then through that, she felt the hum of energy. Was it coming from Nikki or nearby?

Liam caught up with them on the sidewalk. Micaela watched him slip a sheet of paper to Nikki. "I'm going to a place I know to eat, drink, and celebrate François' life. Will the both of you join me?"

Micaela had grown up in the tradition. It is hard for some to understand that what seemed like a boisterous party was the coming together of a community or *clann*. You met to mourn, tell stories, and remember a person's life. As the cab sped down the FDR, she wondered why she was going. She had no stories to tell except the horror of his death. Maybe, it would be enough to listen.

14

Down a narrow cobblestone alley in Tribeca was the heavy oak door of the Salmon Run Inn. It was carved with fish and deer and the worn name of the Salmon and Buck Hunting Society. It looked like the remnants of an old speakeasy. As she entered, Micaela eyed the ancient wood bar, faux stained glass lights, and the stuffed and mounted animals on the walls, including the namesake salmon. She wasn't sure if she was still in New York or had just been transported to Lafferty's Pub outside Bridewell.

"How did you find this place, Liam?"

"A friend from Armagh put me on to it years ago. You may meet her tonight. A damn sight better than your standard chi-chi New York wine bar."

"I happen to like some of those chi-chi wine bars." She thought that a more sophisticated setting would have been a more appropriate way to remember François.

"François and I shared more than a few here." *Had he just read her mind?*

His eyes twinkled at her shock. He led her past the students in NYU sweatshirts, artists with sketchpads open beside them, and other locals nestled up against the elbow-worn bar. Nikki drifted toward the pool table. Her smile was all charm, but her eyes scanned the room. She was in cop mode. Micaela knew well enough that if someone knew something about François that would help, Nikki would get it from them.

"Devlin, pints for the lady and myself and a round for the rest. Sorry 'Caela, no oak-aged Chardonnay here, but Devlin does a fine pour."

"Tis said I do, *An Tiarna* Farrell." Devlin bowed his head to Liam.

Micaela turned to the old-fashioned jukebox and skimmed the music selection. After the last four months of computer video-conferencing, she had looked forward to meeting Liam face to face. She had never considered the possibility it would include a wake.

Liam rested the pints on top of the jukebox and leaned in. Energy flowed off him in waves so real she thought she could touch them. No colors, just amazing heat. It was warm and familiar like a fire on a winter night. Micaela leaned away before she was washed away in it. She reached into her purse for quarters and studied the song list.

"Have you found anything to your liking, 'Caela?" He inched closer so that his breath warmed the back of her neck.

"It's better than I expected." She fed the coins into the slot and quickly punched in several numbers.

She followed Liam as he wound his way toward the pool table. He exchanged greetings of *"Dia duit... Dias Muire duit"* with patrons. When they had reached the group by the pool table, the game stopped and all eyes turned to Liam.

He raised his glass. "To our friend, François, may his name, his laugh and his courage be always remembered." The group replied, "To François." From the end of the bar, Devlin added, "As close to Irish as a Frenchman can get." A cheer and laughter rose from the crowd.

The crowd resumed their conversations. Micaela couldn't make out every word, but amidst the laughter she heard François' name over and over. None of this fit with the picture the police were

85

painting. What was she missing? She needed to talk to Nikki. Micaela and Liam made their way to the pool table in time to see Nikki sink the eight ball. Game over, someone re-racked the balls; Liam passed the cue to Micaela.

"Your break, 'Caela."

"I haven't played in years."

Liam's eyes mocked her. "Not up to a challenge?"

Micaela snatched the cue from him and chalked it. As she drew the stick back, she locked eyes with Liam and smiled. The strike went off perfectly, sinking the six and the ten in the corner pockets.

Micaela proceeded to drop the next four balls. Devlin put a fresh pint on the rail for Liam; she'd barely touched her first one. She hadn't had this much fun since she was twelve shooting pool in the back room of Lafferty's. She knew she could run the table.

Micaela moved around the corner to set up her next shot and found herself pressed up against Liam. He was deliciously warm. She slipped the shot and scratched. Accusations against Liam for inappropriate use of his charm came from the crowd.

Liam faced the group and threw his hands up in surrender. "I would not have any of you think me less than honorable… the game to the lady."

"You concede to save your ego." Micaela tossed the cue at him and laughed. "I had you, Mr. Farrell."

"That you did." He bowed to her. "Come sit by the fire while I nurse my wounded pride."

Micaela followed him to a back corner, where a few tables surrounded by comfortable armchairs waited. She chose a table near the small fire with a view of the bar and the pool table. She hadn't noticed the last time she was there if, after all these years, Lafferty's still had its pool table. Did they still hold *seisiúins* in their back room by the fire complete with pipes, tin whistles, bodhrans and Lafferty, himself, on fiddle? Next time she would venture further than the corner booth.

86

"Liam, what did Devlin call you? I know it was Irish," she said.

"Gaelic actually. You don't speak it?"

"No, my grandmother keeps trying to teach me, but I'm hopeless with languages."

Liam raised his glass. "To your grandmother's effort then, *Slainte.*"

"*Slainte,*" she replied.

Liam took a sip of stout. The firelight shimmered off the golden strands in his chestnut hair. Devlin and several others gathered round. Liam began the stories. "Ah Devlin, I was remembering the night those two rival rugby teams showed up here and started to brawl. François was more than happy to jump in as an extra bouncer."

Devlin laughed. "You should have seen him. He strong-armed a hooker and tossed him onto the sidewalk, or maybe all the way into the street. He put one very large forward into the hospital."

"A hooker?" Micaela asked.

"It's a rugby position." Devlin raised his eyebrows as if to say, "What did you think?"

Liam patted Micaela's arm. "Well now, before you get worked up… the forward had charged François and, in self-defense, he cold-cocked him. No charges were pressed. I don't think the guy would admit he'd been knocked out by a Frenchman in a silk shirt."

Devlin continued. "Then there was the time that young buck from Jersey challenged the Frenchie to match him shots of Paddy's Irish whiskey. After the sixth round, François slipped me a note to serve the young man watered down cola. The young-un couldn't tell the difference at that point. But the hangover was the better for it the next day."

Tuxedos, brawls, drinking games, his fear. Micaela raised her glass. "I met François only once and he made quite the first impression. What I have heard tonight makes me wish I'd had the time to discover the real François."

87

Liam returned the toast. "To discovery."

A band of five musicians entered and began to tune up. Devlin and several of the men shifted the pool table to the side of the room. Liam set his glass down and eyed Micaela's Brooks Brothers suit and jade silk blouse.

"You're a tad overdone for a *seisiúin*." He removed the clip in her hair, his fingers liberating her auburn waves. He tilted his head and grinned. "It's a start."

Micaela glared, ready to be angry. *But that grin and those eyes, damned Irish charm.* The best she could manage was, "You are something else, Liam Farrell."

He stretched and stared into the fire, something moved behind his eyes. "'Tis true."

The music began and dancers took the floor. Devlin escorted an elderly woman into the room. She was greeted with a round of cheers from the group and offers to dance. She finally accepted Devlin's arm and sparkled in a flawless reel. A tall red headed man grabbed Nikki's arm and dragged her into the mix.

The dance ended and the band began the air *Inisheer*. Devlin and the old woman made their way to where Liam and Micaela sat.

"So you are Liam Farrell." Her eyes glittered with excitement.

"Aye, himself."

Micaela marveled at how thick his accent had become since they'd walked into the pub. She could hear her own rhythms change, too, reverting to the music of conversations heard at the dinner table as a child.

The woman bowed her head to Liam. "'Tis an honor, Mr. Farrell."

Liam took the woman's hands in his. He pressed his forehead to them. "Aine Harkins of Armagh, it's I who am honored."

"A charmer, just like all the Farrells." Aine laughed and turned to Micaela. "And who might this be?"

"Micaela O'Brien, M'am," she answered. This slight woman, no more than five-one, glowed with a golden aura that required respect, even from those who couldn't see the colors.

"The daughter of Donnachadh and Maura O'Brien? Your grandmother is Una Rourke?"

Micaela's heart skipped. "You knew my parents?"

"Your grandmother and I studied together. I had the pleasure of meeting your parents once or twice and, of course, I heard tell." Aine nodded. " 'Tis right you found her, Liam."

Micaela pulled another chair into their circle. "Will you join us? Please."

"I suppose this old woman can stay up past her bedtime once in a while." Aine looked at Devlin. "Now go on with you. See to that niece of mine. You wouldn't want to leave her to the likes of some of these."

Devlin bowed. "Your wish is my command."

"He's rather sweet on my Nora." Aine patted Micaela's hand. "Sometimes the young ones need a little push."

Micaela smiled. Aine sounded just like her grandmother.

Several women in tight jeans and t-shirts descended on Liam, wheedling for a dance. Clearly, those young ones didn't need a little push. Micaela watched as Liam acquiesced and took charge of a reel with grace and strength. A crew of men formed up beside and behind him. She found herself staring at Liam. Micaela had some experience with the dance and he was nothing short of breathtaking.

The music stopped and Liam was swept to the bar by the crowd. He looked back and shrugged at his inability to break away. Aine and Micaela sat by the fire and talked. Micaela wasn't sure she would call it talking though. Aine asked Micaela questions about her family and work, and then moved on to her personal life. Maybe it was the resemblance to her grandmother but Micaela found herself oversharing.

"So, is there anyone special in your life?"

89

"I'd been seeing Parker since graduate school. We're great friends. He's away on a long term assignment."

"He's not the one, is he?

"Things are going well with us, we…" She paused. "No, I guess not. I don't know if there is 'the one' out there for everyone." Especially, she thought, one who would understand her nightmares and her metaphysical issues.

"I'll tell you what I told my niece: when *you* know who you are, it will be easier to find the one." The music began again. Aine turned her attention to it. Her wrist and hand flicked with an invisible tipper as she drummed along with the bodhran.

The tempo and volume slowed and the room hushed. A tall man in construction boots, dirt soiled jeans, and a baseball cap stepped up in front of the musicians and began to sing *Ireland's Call*. His voice was the sound of a tenor angel. Soon the bar vibrated as men and women draped arms around each other and joined in. Liam stood alone in the middle of the crowd at the bar singing. From his side of the room, he raised his glass to Micaela. In the midst of the voices, Micaela could hear the Irish. She and Aine moved to the edge of the circle that formed on the dance around the tenor.

Micaela looked across the dance floor. She stifled a gasp and stepped back from the circle. François stood on the other side of the circle. He wasn't exactly solid, more like a mirage shimmering on the horizon. His lips moved as he sang along. She looked around the room; everyone seemed oblivious to his presence.

Her surprise was replaced with curiosity. The spirit world was as much a part of her childhood as the New England Patriots or the Boston Red Sox. She made her way toward his spirit; it never occurred to her to run the other way.

Nothing like this had happened to her since her trip to Gettysburg with her tenth grade American History class. She had opened Pandora's Box last Samhain and now all kinds of psychic shit was spilling out. This was one more thing to deal with.

She was about three feet away when François turned, smiled, put two fingers to his lips, blew her a kiss, and then vanished.

She whispered after him, "*Au revoir, mon ami.* I will bring whoever did that to you to justice. You have my word."

"I would expect nothing less. The word of the The O'Brien is law. His death will not go unavenged." Micaela turned to see Aine walking back toward the table. She had seen François, too. Micaela moved alongside her.

"Well it's time for this old crone to head home." Aine retrieved her shawl from the back of the chair. She took Micaela's hands in hers and pressed her forehead to Micaela's hands as Liam had done to her.

Another unbidden memory surfaced for Micaela of people in a pub in Ireland greeting her mother the same way.

"Aine, there is no need for this. I should be the one paying respect to your wisdom."

"Wisdom is the result of many lifetimes and a long path."

"Path? I don't understand."

"You will, in time. I hope one day you will visit Nora and me in our little shop across the street. I would like to hear how you are doing."

"I will come to see you… soon." Micaela needed to know what she meant by the things she had said. The woman spoke in riddles.

Patrons made way for Aine as she hobbled to the door leaning on a gnarled walking stick. She was followed by a young woman, presumably her niece, Nora. Liam hugged Aine. They exchanged words.

Liam returned and flopped into the chair. "I'm done with being Himself for tonight."

Nikki returned from the pool table and picked up her bag.

"I'm going to head out. I'm expecting a call from one of my contacts in about an hour. I'll follow up with you both tomorrow."

Nikki gave Micaela a quick hug. There was that hum of energy again, no more than the vibration of a cell phone, but there.

Micaela and Liam were surrounded by regulars wanting to buy them a drink. She overheard several remarks on the way Aine had treated her. Others pulled back, put distance between themselves and her. She'd thought for a moment that she could relax and be herself here. Wrong again. She chatted politely with those who dared approach her. Eventually, the crowd wandered back to the bar.

"So, 'Caela," he said. "Tell me, where did you learn to shoot pool?" The dimple on his right cheek deepened.

Micaela talked about Lafferty's pub and the seisiúins. And when the topic turned to the dance, she even told him about her lessons with Mrs. Ryan.

"Someday you all have to meet my Grandma Una. Nikki's already met her, sort of. Una raised me after my parents died." Micaela fell silent. Her parents would have liked Nikki and Liam.

Liam asked. "I notice you call your grandmother by her given name."

"It's not meant as disrespect. I've always called her that. It's what everyone calls her. My parents and Una never really treated me like a child. Mrs. Ryan used to call me an old soul."

"It's just an unusual thing for a child." Liam shrugged.

"I know, but my childhood was not the usual kind."

"Really now? What was so different, besides the name thing?"

"Nothing I want to talk about." She stood up. "I should be going. Tomorrow's a busy day."

"The night is still young. Please let me get you a drink, perhaps you'll dance with me."

"I need sleep." She tilted her head toward a group of the ladies at the bar. "But if you still have the energy, there's a whole group still ready to go."

"That hasn't been my type in years." He scowled as he slipped on his long black duster. "I'll see you home."

"I'm fine." She pulled on her wool coat and slung her bag over her shoulder.

"I'm an old-fashioned guy when it comes to a young woman out alone at one in the morning."

"You don't need to interrupt your evening." She had been taking care of herself since she was fourteen and gone off to Ashwood Prep. It had worked fine for her.

"So, now it's a crime in New York to accept a courtesy from a gentleman?"

Micaela turned and led the way to the door. She had seen several new sides of Liam today. Overprotective was not one of her favorite revelations. She was not some helpless lass.   On the sidewalk, Liam walked beside her with his hands stuffed in his pockets. They hailed a cab at Church and Warren Streets and rode in silence to the Upper West Side. The taxi left them in front of her building. The night had turned chilly and the rain had changed to sleet.

Liam stood so far from Micaela that she felt contagious. "I'll be heading back to London Thursday morning. From there, I'll be on to Knowth." He was getting drenched. "I'll call you on the computer as usual."

He looked down, water dripped from his hair. She pictured him sitting at her feet while she toweled his hair dry. *Damn, why couldn't she stay pissed at him?*

"I'm sorry I was rude at the pub. Did you want to come up and dry off or have a cup of coffee?"

Liam stepped back. "It's nearly two. As you made clear, you need your sleep. It's just as well, it wouldn't be right." He turned and left without even a handshake.

Micaela stared after him. They worked together; there had to be boundaries. *Right?*

It was still dark the next morning when Micaela arrived at Campbell and Winston. Mr. Edgar Winston III was waiting. He was not your classic undertaker. Round face with sparkling eyes that waited to laugh. Given his white hair and wide girth, she thought he made a better Santa than Grim Reaper. He did wear the obligatory black suit but accompanied it with a lavender shirt topped by a pink, purple, and silver tie.

"Ms. O'Brien, the French Embassy called. There have been some paperwork issues and they are unsure when the transport will be cleared. Ambassador's Reynolds office also called to say that she is working on it, but is not hopeful of an immediate resolution."

"Can we arrange something else? Private transportation?" She ran mentally through the list of corporate planes in the area. Knowth, First Colony, there were others but she didn't know the owners well enough. Was Interpol or Hendricks the source of the delay, she wondered.

"A private plane is …well… a gray area, but not impossible." His grin was more conspiratorial than sympathetic.

Micaela reached for her phone. No answer from Liam. She reached Ivan, but his plane was already over California on its way to St. Petersburg. He offered to turn the plane around. Micaela appreciated his generous offer, but assured him there must be another option. In her wallet was Lowell's card. He had offered his help. It still wasn't clear in her mind that he wasn't involved in François' murder, but she was out of options. She dialed the number; when it rolled to voicemail, she hit zero. His assistant, Connie, picked up. Micaela explained the situation. Connie was professional and friendly. She told Micaela that Mr. Lowell was in a meeting, but promised to do everything possible and call Micaela back within thirty minutes.

Twenty minutes later, Micaela's phone rang. Connie had clearance for François' body to be transported on Lowell's private jet from Teterboro Airport. The commercial jet was already en route to New Jersey from Boston. It would be fueled and ready for departure in two hours. If Micaela wanted to accompany the hearse to the airport, she would arrange for a car to get her and return her to the location of her choosing.

Two hours later, Micaela stood on the tarmac of Teterboro. The Gulfstream 650 sat on the runway, bathed in the morning sun. Even from the outside she could see that the plane had been modified. It had four windows on each forward side instead of the usual eight, creating a larger cargo area. The crew wore full uniforms and black arm bands. They lined up at the lift and handled François' casket with care and respect. The Captain thanked Micaela for her efforts.

As the plane disappeared over the eastern horizon on its journey across the Atlantic, she whispered, "Let the waters carry you across to the Blessed Isles."

The limousine was waiting.

15

Micaela took Thursday and Friday off. She needed a long weekend home to see her grandmother and sit by the creek. Then she would begin again. Once across the George Washington Bridge on Wednesday evening, she opted for the longer but more leisurely ride. It would take her far to the east of Bridewell and meant a later arrival, but would give her time to unwind. She cranked up the music and merged onto the Old Post Road. Route 1 had transformed over the years; gas stations changed brands, a diner closed, victim to a nearby chain restaurant, old porch roofs sagged a little more. Traffic was light as she rolled along in the cocoon of her car.

A stomach rumble reminded her that she hadn't eaten since lunch. The dashboard clock read 10:00 as the Patriot Diner came into view. A full lot marked it as a safe bet for good food. A black Hummer pulled into the lot behind her and continued to the back lot where diners usually provided larger spaces for RVs, and trucks. Micaela parked in an open spot between two motorcycles, leaving ample room between them and her Porsche, in case the bikes tipped over.

She tucked herself into a corner booth and ordered a chicken wrap and Diet Coke. She watched the usual diner crowd: truckers at the counter, teenagers laughing over mounds of cheese fries, a family travelling north to catch some late season skiing, and an assortment of nondescript patrons.

She had just finished the last of her sandwich when she felt a tingle of energy. She glanced around to see if she could pinpoint the source, but it was gone. She dismissed it as one of those random events she'd had of late. She'd made progress in corralling the psychic events, but would sometimes experience these little pings in public places. They never felt intentional and she had always assumed it was the echo of her own energy bouncing back from an unwitting receptor like sonar.

She left and then pulled into a nearby Starbucks for the required caffeine break. What looked like the same Hummer from the diner fell in behind her as she pulled back onto the highway. Route 1 opened up to two lanes and, determined to make up lost time, Micaela pulled into the left lane. The Hummer moved over as well. She adjusted her mirror until she could see the silhouette of the driver. The Hummer moved up to tailgate. Micaela sped up, so did the Hummer. *What an asshole.* She moved into the right lane and the Hummer followed, still close on her bumper. Her pulse accelerated as her focus switched between the road ahead and the car behind. Traffic vanished as Route 1 merged into a single lane again and civilization thinned. The Hummer loomed in her mirror. Micaela lurched forward on the impact as it rammed her rear bumper. *What the hell.*

It was near midnight and the road was deserted. She had no idea where the nearest police station was or if it would even be manned at this hour. The Hummer closed on her bumper again. The image of François laying in that tub rose up in her mind. Her heart raced and she gripped the steering wheel. Her knuckles gleamed white in the darkness. Whoever was in the Hummer had set their sights on her.

She hit the speakerphone button and gave a voice command for 911. The operator from a nearby small town said she would send the next available cruiser, but there had been a brawl at a local bar with shots fired. The operator asked what kind of car Micaela was in. When she heard it was a Porsche Cayman, she actually snorted and asked why Micaela didn't just outrun the slower Hummer. Micaela retorted that she wanted them caught, she needed answers. She watched the headlights of the Hummer close in again. The dispatcher told Micaela a cruiser was ten minutes away. *Shit.* She could be dead in a ditch by then. She hung up.

Micaela's next voice call was Nikki's cell number. She was miles away in the city but at least someone would know. Micaela inched her car up to try to get a plate number for her. No front plate. When Nikki picked up Micaela gave her location and a description of the vehicle. She could hear Nikki relaying information to someone.

"Nikki, I've given you all I know. I'm heading for…"

"You're headed for the Cape, right?"

What was Nikki talking about? She knew Micaela was headed west to Bridewell?

"But, I… "

"Listen, Micaela, I'm trying to get a better fix on your wireless signal. You know how sometimes signals overlap and mix."

Micaela paused. Her mind raced in overdrive. Overlap, mix. Nikki was trying to tell her that someone could be listening in.

"Yeah, I know what you mean. I'll call you when I get somewhere with a better signal."

Micaela hung up. Hopefully Nikki had gotten a fix on her location and one of her mysterious friends would pick up the Hummer and catch a break in the case. The Hummer smacked her bumper again. Micaela opened up the engine. The Porsche's turbo roared to life and the distance between them opened. Micaela glanced at the Hummer in the rearview mirror. Two separate single headlights emerged like twin Cyclopes from either side of the vehicle and sped forward. Her new pursuers passed under the glow of a street light; racing cycles. She would have bet money they were the same ones she had admired at the diner, sleek animals of black and chrome.

Whoever was behind this wasn't stupid. They knew that, if the element of surprise was lost, she would outrun the slower vehicle. This was Plan B. But racing cycles couldn't force her off the road. That left her with one frightening option --- they were armed.

The exit signs flew by. She had driven these roads for hours at a time as a teenager and thought she could still drive them with her eyes closed. She pulled off at the exit for the decommissioned Rock Lake Army Base. The riders followed her. She kept track of them in her mirrors. Crouched low over the bikes, she could not tell the riders from the machines.

Panic could mean death. She reached deep for the focus she had mastered over the years. At Ashwood Hall, they had taught horseback riding. Of course, it was dressage. On the sly, Tex Crowley, the stable manager, had taught them to ride rodeo. Her favorite part was the barrel races, the union of rider and horse. One false move, one lapse of concentration, and rider and horse could go down, maybe never to get up. Tonight, she had more horsepower to control.

She increased her speed on the straightaway; her pursuers kept pace. She braked around the gentle curve that followed and repeated the pattern on the next stretch. In the third straightaway, Micaela accelerated more, pushing the speedometer past 120 mph. The third curve outside the military base was a hairpin.

She threw one last glance into the rearview. "Come on guys, keep up."

Micaela floored it, pushing the Porsche to its maximum in speed and handling. Nice and tight, she drifted around the curve. She felt herself lean into the turn, the same way she had with her horse. Her laptop bag slid across the back seat and smacked against the door.

One of the cyclists wiped out in a shower of sparks into the trees and the chain link fence that surrounded the base. The second rider hung in as Micaela sped on. The interchange for Routes 1, 95 and 395 loomed ahead of her. She deliberately slowed so that the cyclist was about twenty feet behind. White dashes bled into solid. The motorcycle was less than ten feet behind. The solid line pointed to the concrete barricades between the highways. She hit the brakes, the motorcycle veered left to avoid slamming into the Porsche's rear. Micaela jerked the wheel to the right and accelerated across the divide onto Route 1. The rider's reflexes failed. He scraped along the concrete and spun out in the lanes on the Route 95 side.

She swerved under the overpass and onto Old Mill Road. She meandered without headlights until sure she had lost her last pursuer. She turned the lights back on before she attracted attention of a State Trooper or worse. She considered calling Nikki or, more importantly, her grandmother. But *they could* be listening.

Micaela detoured around the east side of Providence and part of the way to the Cape before looping back west and home to Bridewell. She continued monitoring her rearview mirror for any signs of the cyclists. There were no vehicles behind her until after the Pokanoket Tribal Lands. From there on, she spotted cars and pickups in the mirror, but none came too close and they turned off onto local streets after less than a mile. Her only other company for the remainder of the drive was a large bird so black that it stood out in relief against the starlit sky like an ebony kite.

It was almost four in the morning when Micaela turned into Una's driveway. The three-acre front yard was a barricade of trees and shrubs so dense that the house and the back fifteen acres were invisible from the road. As a child, this had created an island of solitude and peace for her. Now, as she drove through this small forest, phantoms moved between the trees and monsters were everywhere. Micaela prayed no one had followed her here. She would not bring this to her grandmother's doorstep.

16

The curtain of forest parted to a house ablaze in electric illumination. Motion detecting spotlights shone from the corners of the house, and beyond the trees the barn was lit up. Her grandmother's SUV was surrounded by cars and vans Micaela didn't recognize. She pulled up alongside a midnight blue Shelby Mustang. As far as she knew none of Grandma's friends drove a muscle car.

She cut the engine and rested her forehead against the steering wheel. The fear that she'd held at bay rose and beads of sweat formed on her forehead. Tremors in her right leg made her wonder if she would walk or crawl to the house.

She raised her head to see a long black feather on the dash. She had no idea how it had gotten there, but she wasn't going to leave it behind. It hummed with life in her hand as she tucked it into her laptop case. In the glow of the spotlight, she saw a large black bird perched on the gable of her parents' bedroom. The raven ruffled its feathers and tucked its head beneath its wing to sleep.

She grabbed her briefcase and laptop in one hand and opened the car door. Una stood in the halo of the porch light, relief washing over her face. Micaela bounded up the three front steps in one stride and dropped her bags. She hugged her grandmother and kissed her cheeks. They walked into the house, Micaela's arm around Una's shoulders, and Una's arm around Micaela's waist. Micaela wondered who was leaning on whom.

She stopped in the timeless parlor. Una never called it a living room because she said she wondered what that made the rest of the rooms. Comfortable furniture with floral upholstery and overstuffed cushions, large bookcases filled with well-loved books, a server along the wall to the upstairs that held Una's best Irish whiskey and Waterford tumblers. The single change, since Micaela was a child, was a new rocking chair that had replaced the wingback chair she had taken to Penn, Harvard, and then New York. A wood fire crackled in the fireplace. The sharp smell of the burning peat in the fireplace mixed with the sweet smell of baking bread and the smokiness of bacon drifting from the kitchen.

"Grandma, it's a bit early for breakfast."

"It filled the time. People get hungry waiting." Her grandmother nodded toward the kitchen. "They wanted to give us a moment, but I know they're just as anxious to see you."

Liam's silhouette filled the archway to the kitchen.

"Thank Aoife, you're fine."

Liam's fingers grazed Micaela's cheek, as if confirming she was solid. The heat flowed off him as it had at the Salmon Run, but now it was soothing like a soak in a hot tub.

She laid her hand over his. "How did you find out? Let me guess, it was you Nikki was talking to when I called."

Nikki set down a pile of plates and wrapped her arm around Micaela. "We were all worried."

Micaela frowned. "I didn't think it was safe to call from my cell phone. I wasn't sure if the phones were tapped here. Then, I drove around for a while to make sure no one was following me."

"We are monitoring all the lines and surveillance equipment is in place." Nikki stepped aside so Micaela could get to the kitchen.

"It took you long enough." Reece leaned against the kitchen sink. That old boyish grin had returned. He looked taller and more muscular than she'd remembered. Of course, her most vivid recent memory was of him was covered in blood and being carried off the side of the mountain.

Micaela headed straight to Reece. "You look great. Peggy must be thrilled. Are you still in physical therapy?"

"No, therapy has been done for a while. The whole thing has been hard on Peg, but she's tough. Hell of a way to start married life, huh?"

Micaela narrowed her eyes to her best scowl. "With a baby on the way, I hope you've given up hunting."

"I've cut back." He lifted one shoulder in a shrug. "Can we eat now? I'm starving."

Micaela held Reece's hand as they went to the table. Her almost big brother was here and well, and she had made it home. The night was looking up. She sat between Nikki and Reece with Una and Liam across the table. Micaela filled the group in on the Hummer and the two motorcycles.

Reece set his fork down. "Chief Running Deer told me to tell you that you're a damn fine driver."

"I didn't see anyone following me."

"We picked you up just before the tribal lands. Our people switched off every half mile or so."

"How did the Pokanoket get involved?"

Nikki answered. "I phoned Liam who called Chief Running Deer. I let Una know what was going on and that we were on our way."

"Did anyone happen to call the police?"

Liam's eyes roamed around the table. "We thought it would be better that we handle this. We had local backup, don't worry."

"Local backup, I assume that's Bridewell PD and the Massachusetts State Troopers."

Reece grimaced. "Not exactly."

"Explain 'not exactly'." Micaela saw Una's face; it said "take a deep breath, child'. That was not about to happen.

"Everything's under control." Liam reached for Micaela.

Micaela slammed her mug down; coffee splattered across the table into Liam's eyes. "If anything happens to my grandmother because you decided to play Rambo, you will never know peace."

Una patted Micaela's shoulder. "I'm fine, dear. They brought lots of help. Besides, who would trouble themselves with an old woman?"

Reece cleared his throat. "After he called us, we had people all over the property in fifteen minutes. No one was getting near the house, Micaela."

"After I called the Chief, I called Ethan." Liam looked ready to duck.

"Ethan Lowell, why the hell did you involve him?" She dug her nails into the table.

"This is his turf, too. We have to respect that." Reece was all business. "Our people kept an eye on you from the Tribal Lands to here. There are another dozen of my people positioned on the property. Ethan has six of his guards inserted into our patrols."

"So those were the shadows I saw as I drove in? Eighteen people for as many acres. It doesn't seem like enough."

"I contacted the Sons of Danu." Liam refilled Micaela's coffee. "They sent another two dozen. We wouldn't let anything happen to Una."

"The Sons of Danu. They're a bunch of old men sitting around Lafferty's telling stories."

"Do you think I would let harm come to you or Una?" Liam's voice was a low growl. "You can't fix everything on your own."

Reece pushed away from the table. "I'm going out to check on the guards. Care to join me, Liam? Nothing like a night patrol to clear your head."

Micaela felt Liam's anger scorch through the room as he strode out the door. Una turned to Micaela and started to speak.

Micaela held her hand up. "Don't defend him. He tells me I can't handle things alone, but it was him who decided that we could manage without the police. He put you in jeopardy."

She picked up her coffee and moved toward the back porch without waiting for Una's response. As Micaela stepped out the door, a tall redheaded man with a small machine gun emerged from the trees.

"It's Sean Murphy, Micaela. If you must take the air, *An Tiarna* prefers that you sit in the shadows. No porch light, please."

"Tell Liam, that I'm sure Himself knows what's best. How about I make his job easier by going to bed. I wouldn't want to trouble *An Tiarna*." Micaela wheeled around and slammed the porch door. So she was to be a prisoner in her own house, was she?

As she marched through the kitchen, Nikki called after her. "He's just worried about you."

Micaela collided with Lowell in the dark parlor. His hands reached out to stop her before they both ended up on their asses. He held her at a distance. "Where's the fire?"

"Shit, what are you doing here?"

He released her and stepped back. "I was invited to help. Liam has briefed me on your pursuers. I have sent some of my people out to search for them."

"How convenient for you." She saw the confusion in his face and watched him stiffen.

"If a friend called on you for help, Micaela, wouldn't you do everything in your power?"

"I didn't realize we had reached the level of friend. You've put yourself and your people at risk for someone you hardly know." *Unless you needed to cover your tracks.*

"I respect Liam and consider Byrne Connor a friend. My family has had long dealings with them and with Moran and Boru. It would have been less than honorable to do otherwise." His words were clipped and strained.

She took a deep breath. Her intuition told her that he was sincere, so either Detective Hendricks was wrong, or Lowell was one damn fine actor.

105

"I'm not sure I understand any of this, but I guess I owe you for the use of your plane and this. Can I at least get you something to eat or some coffee?"

"I would like that, but it's late and commitments in Boston require that I return. My people will remain. Other members of my security staff will be here soon to relieve those on the ground."

She looked at the clock on the mantel, five o'clock, nearly dawn. When she looked back, Lowell was gone.

17

Micaela dreamt of the motorcyclists. They wore no helmets and their red eyes glowed in animal faces. It was too dark to tell what kind. As dreams and visions will do, the scene shifted to François vanishing into the woods outside Una's house. She chased after him, calling his name. He turned to face her, his throat was gone, but he started to speak, "Stay away from… " One of the motorcyclists leapt from the woods cutting off his words. Again.

Her dream had shown her what she had not voiced. Whoever had killed François was the one after her yesterday. Saying it, even to herself, made it more terrifying. She had seen what they had done to François. The air in her room felt warm and thick like syrup. She pulled back the white lace curtains and cranked open the old-fashioned windows. The skies were crystal clear and the three-quarter moon hung in the brightening sky. A large dog loped across the lawn and into the brush. Moments later, Nikki followed. So many people out there, so she and Una could be safe in here.

Micaela turned around to her childhood bedroom. The walls were still the pale rose color she had picked out when she was twelve. The shelves above her old desk were lined with the porcelain horses, unicorns, and mermaids she had collected on her travels with her parents. She began rearranging the figures to erase the gap where a silver frame with a picture of her on horseback in Ireland, her parents by her side, had rested.

Micaela opened her closet and rummaged around on the shelf that hung above her clothes. Would it still be there? She had put it up there when she was thirteen. Then, she had stood on a stool to reach the shelf. Now, on tiptoe, she reached in the darkness to the back for the carved wooden box. She carried it to her desk and lifted the lid. It was filled with treasures of a childhood lost, seashells from trips to the Cape, a medal she'd won on the Junior High Swim Team, a picture of her at six standing next to her first pony, a small bird's nest she had found in the woods, and the silver framed photo. She returned the photo to its place.

At the bottom of the box was the velvet bag her father had given her when she was seven. It was for magical things, he'd said. He was always one for fantastic tales. She remembered exploring the woods with her mother and gathering flowers and herbs for her to put in her crane bag. Remnants of lavender, figwort and maypops still crunched in the bag along with a piece of brown fire agate she had found in the eddy pool of the creek. Once in a while when the door of her mind opened, good memories that had vanished after the accident would be found.

She reached into her briefcase and pulled out the black feather from her car. A voice inside told her it belonged in the pouch. She tucked Da's crane bag under her pillow and stretched out. Maybe, its magic would help her sleep.

In what seemed like moments, Micaela woke to sunlight streaming across the floor. A breeze fluttered the curtains and carried birdsong. Through the web of winter bare branches she could see the old barn she'd kept her horse in. It was so serene, like that moment in a bad horror movie right before the monster came out of the swamp and ate everyone. Liam and a group of men and women walked out

108

from a stand of ash trees. He looked up at her and nodded. His hair flowed loose around his shoulders, more red than brown in the late morning light. He hadn't changed clothes, probably hadn't slept.

She slipped on yoga pants, pulled a sweater over her "I Love New York" t-shirt, tied her mop of hair into a ponytail and headed downstairs. The kitchen was empty. She poured two cups of coffee and sliced off a hunk of brown bread. She hoped Liam liked butter and marmalade since that's what he was getting. By the time she opened the back door, he was on the porch.

"Breakfast?"

"Love some." Liam sat beside her on the top step.

"I'm sorry I lost my temper last night. It's just the thought of something happening to Una... I owe you an apology." She stared out at the woods, catching a glimpse of one of the guards.

"You had a rough night. Actually, a rough week."

"Still. I was an ungrateful bitch."

Liam broke off a piece of his bread and passed it to her. "What matters is that Una was protected and you're okay for now."

"For now? You think they'll try again."

Liam's eyes followed things in the woods that Micaela couldn't see. "Probably. There's been no sign of them, but we'll rotate the guard until we're sure."

"I can't stay here forever; I have work to do. I need to find François' killer."

"And we will. But not before a second cup of coffee." Liam headed into the kitchen.

Micaela shouted after him. "Would it be okay if I went down to the creek?"

"Only if I can join you." He returned with steaming mugs. They walked in silence down the path. Liam never stopped scanning the woods. Occasionally he nodded to a bush, acknowledging some unseen presence.

She sat under a weeping willow at the edge of an eddy pool. It had been her favorite spot since she was a little girl. She had come here alone since her mother died, to think, to wonder, to try and remember all the things that she had forgotten that day. Today as always, she watched the water swirl and twist its way in and out. Between the worn stones, the small fry darted in search of food. Liam scattered the last of the brown bread on the surface. The tiny fish swarmed in a flash of silvery feeding frenzy.

"It was horrible, Liam."

Micaela leaned forward. The details of François' murder were slowly becoming clearer. It had happened so fast, a blur of images that was now taking shape. In the reflection of the water, she saw Liam start to reach out to her. He pulled back, his elbows on his knees and his hands clasped in front of him.

"There are things that people should never witness. I'm sorry you had to see that, 'Caela."

The words tumbled out of Micaela. "The edges of François' neck and chest were jagged. They were torn, not cut. Once, when I was younger, I found a fawn on the other side of the creek. It was dead, torn up just like François was. Reece said it was wild dogs. That tourists sometimes dumped their dogs out here when they didn't want them anymore. I know that Animal Control once captured a coyote on Columbia's campus, but there are no coyotes inside a five star hotel. Whoever did this is a monster."

Thinking of Reece raised images of his injuries last Samhain. He had survived. François had not. She stole a glance at Liam. His eyes were squeezed shut and his knuckles white. She reached out and placed her hand on top of his hands. He flinched. His eyes widened and filled with pain.

"I'm sorry. I didn't realize how much it upset you," she said.

"It's not you, 'Caela. It's me. I'm tired, on edge." He had wrapped his arms around himself.

She patted the mossy earth beside her. "Why don't you stretch out here? This was my favorite nap spot as a kid. I'll stand guard for a change. Grandma always said the fairies watched over

110

me when I slept." She scooted over and leaned against a weeping willow.

He smiled her favorite crooked grin. "The fairies? Is that what Una told you?"

"Not exactly. Her precise term was Sidhe."

"Well, if I have you and the Sidhe watching, I suppose I could rest my eyes for just a minute."

Before she could count to ten, Liam's slow rhythmic breathing marked his slumber. Her eyes roamed the underbrush Una had said was the Sidhe's hiding place. Bright green fiddlehead ferns pushed up through the soft earth. She looked for her childhood imaginary friend, the girl with leaves for hair.

The music of the creek as it bubbled over the stones helped Micaela think.   What did she know? First, François had been afraid and now he was dead. Second, someone believed she possessed information that was enough of a threat to want to run her off the road. The only connection she knew for sure was the AGF deal. Detective Hendricks seemed to be fishing around for some other connection between Ethan Lowell, her father, and some alternative belief system. Well, her family, clinging to Druid beliefs and the "Old Way", fit that bill. She leaned her head back against the trunk of the willow, the tips of its fronds danced on the surface of the water as a bright green oak leaf drifted by on the creeks current. Maybe the information she'd asked Judy to send would get her closer to the truth.

Liam moaned in his sleep. His fingers clenched and flexed. Micaela moved closer and brushed his hair back. His hand locked around her forearm in a crushing grip. He bolted upright. His amber colored eyes glared at her. With a small shake of his head, he seemed to find her face.

"Micaela, I'm sorry. Did I hurt you?"

She massaged her arm. "I guess I shouldn't sneak up on you, even asleep."

He took her hand and pushed the sleeve of her Aran sweater up, gently probing her arm. "Nothing feels broken."

"I'm fine, Liam. Really. You were having a bad dream."

"How long was I asleep?"

"About an hour. Maybe you should go up to the house and get some more sleep."

"Later. I need to check in with the guard." Liam ran his fingers through the unruly waves. "I promised Una I would talk to her about the gathering tonight in the Grove."

"That's sweet of you, but you don't have to go." They started toward the house.

"It has been a long time since anyone from home has been here. I am now, so it is my place to go. You should be there, too. There will be plans set for Beltaine."

"Grandma can't get me to go. What makes you think you can?"

"I'd feel better if you were both together."

"There is a small army out there. I can wait at the house."

"Stubborn woman. Would you at least go to the Céilí afterwards? There's no place safer for you than among your own."

Shit. The Céilí at the Community Center. In the middle of everything she'd forgotten. Grandma had donated money to them for a new children's library. It was to be dedicated to her parents.

"You're right. Tell Grandma, I'll be at the dance."

"Now if, you'd just come to the...." He draped his arm around her shoulders.

"Don't push your luck." She shrugged him off.

At the foot of the path, Micaela and Liam were met by a man and a woman. Both had shoulder holsters and, at their waists, leather belts with very lethal knives sheathed in them. They fell into step behind Liam and Micaela as they walked to the porch.

Liam took up a position on the railing; Micaela sat on the wicker sofa. Their guards stood on either side of the stairs. They reminded Micaela of Ivan's Cossacks.

"Liam, the guards are all pretty heavily armed, yet you walk around without guards or weapons. Is that wise?"

"Don't worry about me. Now, if you'll excuse me, I need to be sure everything is in place for tonight. And then." He winked at her. "I have orders from The O'Brien, Herself, to get some sleep."

18

Two red and blue overnight boxes sat on the table when
Micaela walked into Una's kitchen. The first, a medium size package
bore Judy's name, the second and larger came from Moran & Boru's
Boston office. She took the boxes into the parlor and set them next to
the coffee table. Judy's package contained some internal memos
covering instructions from First Colony regarding investments and
risk preferences. She read through the details. Everything was in
perfect order and nothing appeared inconsistent with market
conditions. The files contained newspaper clippings and press
releases that covered the awarding of major shipping contracts over
the last decade. No terrorist groups, questionable government
contracts or pirates. In short, no smoking gun.

The oldest document in Judy's pile was a letter from an old
Boston law firm, dated ten years prior, designating Ethan Lowell heir
to his Uncle Jeremiah Lowell's estate and, as such, sole owner of
First Colony and Director of the Mather-Lowell Trust. He would
have been in his early twenties at the time. She'd turned to the pile
from the Boston office when the screen door clicked shut.

"Didn't mean to disturb you. You're doing work?" Nikki
stood next to the sofa.

"Yes and no. My assistant sent me copies of everything we have on Ethan Lowell and First Colony. She had a friend in our Boston office forward what they had."

"You're looking for…?"

"I'm not sure. Before my little driving adventure with the motorcyclists, Detective Hendricks came to my office. He started off with the same stuff, but then he started asking about Lowell, First Colony and my father."

"Your father?" Nikki sat cross-legged next to the coffee table.

"I don't get that connection either. According to our records, Lowell took over First Colony ten years ago. My father's been dead for sixteen. But then, Lowell's everywhere I go. I don't believe in coincidences."

"Don't you think we should bring Liam into the loop?" Nikki pulled a folder from the Boston box.

"Not yet."

"Okay. So what have you got?" Nikki asked.

"Nothing. The New York files are pretty standard. I was just about to go through the Boston material. Hendricks thinks Lowell is involved. I keep getting mixed signals. But if Hendricks is right…." Micaela fell back against the sofa cushions.

"No wonder you were pissed when he was here last night."

"What kind of mixed signals? About who?" Reece came in from the kitchen carrying a sandwich and a large glass of milk.

Nikki answered. "NYPD thinks Ethan is involved in François' murder. Micaela isn't sure. But he and his people are here."

Reece's face twisted in thought. "Ethan can be a lot of things, but what happened to François… not his style."

Micaela tossed a financial summary of First Colony to Reece. "In my world, people with this kind of money buy any style they want."

"In my world and I thought yours, too, there are things beyond the numbers, beyond appearances." Reece pulled up to his full height, which seemed taller than she remembered.

"And what world is that? Some alternate reality, new age place where you measure people by the color of their aura? Well guess what, he doesn't have one."

Nikki's and Reece's mouths dropped open. Liam came through the front door. "Who has no aura? And how would you know, 'Caela?"

Damn. "No one has an aura. It's a bunch of crap to make people think they can understand someone by the colors they give off — like some lava lamp from the sixties," she said.

"I didn't know you were a student of such things. Perhaps you could educate me. What color is my aura?" Liam perched himself on the edge of Una's server.

"If there were such a thing, it would be brown since you like to lay it on thick."

"And I thought it was the gray-green of the Blarney Stone. Have you by chance had the opportunity to kiss it?"

Micaela launched a sofa pillow at Liam's head. "Insufferable."

"That's what my Ma always says. Why so interested in Ethan?"

"Some man I barely know is lurking around my grandmother's house, professing to protect her. I have a right to be curious."

Liam sat on the thrown pillow, picked up one of the First Colony files, and started leafing through it. Micaela had been so pissed that she'd forgotten Reece and Nikki were in the room. Had she been angry with Liam or herself for shooting her mouth off about auras? Nikki moved to the rocking chair by the fire. She had that relaxed look that Grady, her cat, had when he feigned disinterest but watched everything.

116

Liam set one folder down and picked up another. "Ethan's hardly lurking, 'Caela. He came to help protect you and Una."

"Why? What's in it for him? From what I see here, he's the ultimate capitalist and not one to go out of his way for public recognition. There has to be some profit in it for him."

Reece sighed. "Let me try. Micaela, this is Ethan's territory, much in the same way that the Pokanoket and the Navajo have their tribal lands. While not all our lands are on the reservation, the Nations know what is theirs."

"So is this some kind of feudal system? Lord of the Manor and all that?"

Reece held his hands out to Liam in a plea. "Liam, help me out here."

"Ethan comes from an old family, old traditions, not unlike your own or any of ours. We were raised to do the right thing, the honorable thing. When I called, he didn't hesitate. Ethan... and the rest of the Lowells... have known us and our families for a long time. There are connections that go a long way back and debts owed on both sides."

Micaela rubbed her forehead trying to push all the pieces into place. "Then, why is Detective Hendricks asking about him in the same conversation about François' murder? And why is he asking about First Colony and my father?"

"Ethan had no reason to want François dead," said Liam.

"Jonathan Sutcliffe, the firm's criminal attorney, says Interpol thinks François and some others were mixed up in running guns and drugs. Then, Hendricks asks about First Colony. Connect the dots. Interpol and Hendricks believe that Lowell's company is part of that."

Nikki leaned forward in the rocker, her eyebrows pulled together in a frown. "Liam, if they can show the drugs and guns connection for François and La Tène, then using First Colony as a shipper doesn't sound so far-fetched."

Liam shook his head. "No, it's impossible."

"Why?" Micaela asked.

Liam answered, "Neither François or Ethan would do this. It violates all the rules of conduct."

"Rules of conduct. Whose rules?"

"The same ones your family has followed, Micaela. The reason you are the person you are today."

She turned toward Liam. "The person I am today. Two weeks ago, I was on my way to partner, life was good. Now, I'm living a bloody nightmare. Someone tries to run me off the road and several dozen members of a private army are on patrol outside. Tell me... who am I?"

Nikki twisted her long black hair into a ponytail. "Gentlemen, I think Micaela needs some answers. If you're going to stay, grab a file and make yourself useful."

Micaela read page after page of company history waiting for some revelation to leap out at her. Liam sat on the floor, his shoulder against Micaela's knee as he leafed through files. She supposed she could have moved her legs out of the way. Nikki had pulled out her own laptop. Reece had a pile of folders in front of him.

Moran & Boru's relationship with First Colony and its predecessor, Lowell Ship Builders, went back to Moran & Boru's founding in the early nineteenth century. Her firm had supplied letters of credit to secure transatlantic cargo for Lowell. There was no evidence that any of this cargo included human trafficking or anything illegal or immoral.

Micaela laid down the last file. "I can't find anything in here. The only guns they seem to have run were during wartime. Pick a war, they always bet on the winning side. There is nothing out of the ordinary for a company this old, other than a propensity to have owners who are named Jeremiah, Benjamin or Ethan."

Nikki rubbed the back of her neck. "I've searched all the modern maritime records and haven't come up with anything that looks remotely illegal. If this is all Interpol has, they haven't a leg to stand on."

"There must be something they're hanging their hat on, something solid enough to send Detective Hendricks on his fishing trip."

Nikki packed up her laptop. "I'll check with my connections at Interpol and a friend, well more like family, in the Portuguese Embassy. It will take a few days, at least."

Micaela and Nikki pushed all the files under the server by the stairwell. Micaela kept one folder out. It contained memos and handwritten notes from her father about meetings with First Colony. There was no earth-shattering information, just his words in his own hand. The walnut mantel clock struck two.

"Liam, I'm sorry. I was the one who told you to get some sleep," Micaela said.

Nikki held a finger to her lips and beckoned Micaela and Reece to follow her out to the kitchen. Liam had fallen asleep, his head resting against the sofa. Micaela took the quilt from the back of the sofa and carefully draped it over him. She wanted to get him off the floor and at least onto the sofa, but had learned the hard way not to do anything that would startle him from his sleep. As she headed into the kitchen, she thought, just maybe, she should take a ride into Boston, check out First Colony's headquarters and Ethan Lowell. Alone.

19

Micaela watched from the kitchen window as Una and Liam walked through the fading sunlight toward the Grove. They wanted to be there before sunset to light the fire. Several of the guards, mostly women, slipped into parallel paths. Nikki had gone out to meet one of her sources. As Micaela headed into the parlor, she knew the rest of the guards were out there, unseen and all-seeing.

Micaela traced her fingers over the leather book bindings on the shelves beside the fireplace, looking for something to pass the time. She pulled her old copy of House of Seven Gables down and curled up in the armchair in front of the fire. She had begun to doze when the front door hinge squeaked. She jumped out of the chair, the book crashing to the ground.

"I didn't mean to startle you." Lowell crossed the room. He looked ready for a night out. The black jeans and burgundy turtleneck showed every muscle. This was a man who knew the difference between toned and monstrous. Micaela realized she was staring and turned back to the fire. First, Ivan's effect on her, now Lowell's. Granted she hadn't been with a man since she and Parker had parted four months ago, but this was ridiculous. She had better control than that.

He sat in the rocker on the other side of the fire. "I hope I'm not overdressed. Una had mentioned a dedication and a dance tonight."

"No, you look perfect. I mean fine."

Micaela focused on his face. That wasn't much help. His blue eyes glittered in the firelight, his face and lips looked slightly flushed as if he had just finished running. The thin scar that ran down the left side of his face glowed in the firelight. Rather than mar his appearance, it took a face that might have bordered on pretty and gave it just the right injection of dangerous.

"If it's not too nosy, how did you get that scar?" She hoped it explained her staring at his face.

"In a duel, defending a fair maid's honor."

"You could have just said it was none of my business."

"Would it have been more believable if I said I got it in a barroom brawl?" He traced the scar with his index finger.

"Maybe… no, not really." She reached down to pick up her book. He beat her to it and her hand wrapped around his instead of the cover. He slid his hand out without releasing the book. Micaela was inches from him.

"Thanks. I've got it." Micaela waited for him to let go.

"You are quite welcome." He eased to a standing position with the fluid motion of a dancer.

She was past knowing what to think about the man. Her instincts told her he had not killed François, yet her conversation with Hendricks had planted just enough doubt. She had no tangible proof either way. In the pit of her stomach was the feeling that the only thing believable about him was his well-heeled Boston accent.

Lowell stood by the server. She had not seen him cross the room. The boxes of documents were inches from his black leather boots and the file of her father's papers in his hands. He couldn't possibly read. The only light was from the fireplace and a small reading lamp next to her chair.

"When I arrived, one of my people said you were in here... reading. I was surprised to find you unprotected." He leafed through the file. His eyes directed at the papers.

"You don't consider the dozen or so guards outside protection?" She snapped off the reading light, just in case. "Actually, it was nice to have a few moments to myself."

"And I disrupted your solitude. You didn't attend the gathering with your grandmother?"

"Does everyone know about that?"

"We all do our homework." He returned the file to the table. "We all have histories, don't we? Although our stories are sometimes more interesting to outsiders."

"I've never gone to the gathering." She hoped he didn't notice the box.

"If it's not too nosy?" A mocking smile played across his lips.

Fair was fair. "I was supposed to go to my first council meeting the Samhain after my thirteenth birthday. For people like my grandmother, Samhain is the start of the Celtic New Year. They believe that on Samhain the boundaries between this world and the otherworld are the thinnest. They think it's possible to pass between the worlds in either direction."

His voice softened. "What happened?"

"I wanted no part of it. My parents had died that summer. They weren't coming back." She was glad to be enveloped by darkness.

"It must have been a difficult time."

"I got through it."

She heard the rumble of a throat clearing before she saw Liam come in from the kitchen. "Hope I haven't interrupted," he said.

Lowell turned and was nose to nose with Liam. Lowell's smile was all innocence. "Not at all, we were just getting to know one another while we waited. It did not seem wise that she be alone."

122

"How thoughtful." The air around Liam swirled red with heat that rebounded just inches from Lowell.

She stepped between the men. "Are we leaving or not? The party starts in twenty minutes."

Lowell offered her his arm. "Shall we?"

She heard Liam grind his teeth as she strode out, leaving the two men to follow behind.

Nikki had gotten back just in time for the fun and was standing by the cars. She looked from Liam to Ethan to Micaela. "So Micaela, who are you riding with?"

She fished her keys from her pocket and tossed them to Nikki. "Shotgun."

Micaela raced around to the passenger side of the Porsche and climbed in, while Nikki retrieved a large duffel bag from her Mustang and put it behind the passenger seat.

"I'm honored. I get to drive your baby." The engine roared to life. "Ooooh."

Micaela wiggled her fingers in farewell at the boys. "Do they ever grow up?"

Nikki faked a sigh. "Eventually. Then again…"

"How long is eventually?" She thought about Ivan. He was so secure in himself. He wanted a partner, not a servant.

"For some, centuries. For others, lifetimes." Nikki put the Porsche into first. "That would be Liam's Jag ahead. The Ferrari behind us is Ethan's."

All they needed were flashing lights. Nothing like keeping a low profile, Micaela thought. She looked at Nikki's duffel behind the driver's seat. "These your dancing shoes?"

"No, just some equipment."

Micaela twisted around and unzipped the bag. Just equipment? It was an arsenal. The duffel contained several pistols, a rifle, numerous knives and one large, shiny machete.

"Looks like you're prepared for anything."

"Almost. I left the rest at the house." Nikki checked the mirrors and scanned the tree line on the side of the road.

"The machete looks like silver. I didn't think that would be the first metal of choice." Micaela laughed.

Nikki turned onto Cerwiden Street. "Silver is soft, so it's a layer of silver over titanium. People assume I use it for some strange Amazonian ritual."

"Will you teach me?"

"Teach you what, strange rituals?"

"For starters, the guns." It was time, Micaela thought, that she took her self-defense to a new level.

"Why?"

"After the other night, I need to be able to defend myself better."

"It's not the answer you think it is. But, I suppose it can't hurt. We'll need somewhere safe to teach you." Nikki turned the Porsche into the parking lot of the community center.

"I have a friend who owns a range on the other side of town." Micaela had been absent from Bridewell for so long she wondered if Ansgar still considered her a friend.

"Will your friend be there tonight?"

"Oh, he'll be there."

"Introduce me."

Harold Dorset and Una met the group at the door. Mr. Dorset had been the swim coach when she was in eighth grade. He had insisted on this tour. It came complete with a perky blond junior reporter and a photographer from the Bridewell Gazette.

The group began in the reading room. A sign at the entrance announced the Dennis and Maura O'Brien Reading Center. The local Yankees couldn't get their tongue around Donnachadh so her father became Dennis. Large cushions designed to look like rocks and logs surrounded the fire pit her grandmother had requested. The center of the pit contained a glass-enclosed gas fireplace. Micaela surveyed the ceiling and the rest of the room. The state of the art fire suppression system was in place. Not exactly the real thing, but a safe compromise. Cases filled with books were scattered around the room and against the walls. One entire section bore a plaque with Moran & Boru's name. A pleasant surprise were the plaques from Knowth and First Colony. Sofas and oversized bean bag chairs created inviting spaces to curl up in.

"Mrs. Rourke, Miss O'Brien, can I get a picture with Mr. Dorset? You and your group could sit by the fire pit?" the photographer asked.

Micaela's first inclination was a resounding no, she'd had more than enough attention from the Bridewell Gazette and others after her parents had died. But tonight was important to her grandmother.

"One picture." She turned to Liam and the rest. "I hope you don't mind."

Lowell addressed the reporter. "Perhaps, instead of just a group of adults from out of town, it would be better if we brought some of the young people in from the dance. They could sit in the circle with Mr. Dorset while Mrs. Rourke read to them."

As they set up the picture, Una whispered to Micaela, "Harold Dorset is planning a run for mayor."

That explained the photographer and Dorset's enthusiasm over the photo-op suggestion. It was interesting to watch blue-blooded Dorset cozy up to the Irish vote. What would be next, she wondered, kissing Pokanoket babies?

After the photo, they continued toward the community room. Liam stopped in front of the large trophy cases that lined one wall.

"There are a few here that belong to you, Micaela," he said.

Micaela tried to keep moving, but Dorset stopped beside Liam. "Micaela was a star of the swim team, a natural, and our mermaid."

125

"I tried not to embarrass myself," she said.

In truth, swimming was her salvation that year. Under a cap and goggles, people couldn't tell one swimmer from the next. She enjoyed the anonymous rhythm of it, the soundless cocoon of the water. She would swim endless laps just to be alone.

She peeked through the cracked window of the swinging door to the pool.

Mr. Dorset held it open. "Go ahead, take a look around."

Lowell eyed the dilapidated bleachers and regulation pool. "So Micaela, did you sink or float?"

"Only a descendant of Cotton Mather would ask that." She let the door swing shut in his face.

She walked alone among the lockers. They were in worse condition than the bleachers, missing doors, holes where locks used to be. She skipped a tour of the showers. Mr. Dorset was standing by the diving blocks when she came out.

"Micaela, you know that I am running for mayor, but this isn't about that. I hope you remember how passionate I am about this program. Your grandmother was very generous in her donation for the reading room and it is probably not the time to do this, but you're here. We are woefully underfunded. The program may have to shut down."

She'd had her issues with the good people of Bridewell in the past. Dorset, even then, had sought to use her notoriety to publicize the program. But the young people who swam in this pool now hadn't been part of that; she wouldn't punish them.

"Mr. Dorset, send a proposal to my office in New York." She handed him her card. "I will review it and get back to you… after the election." They continued through the gym and on to a hall full of strangers who thought they were friends. She slipped her arm though Una's and pushed the door open.

126

20

The entire town, or at least her entire childhood, was in the hall. Applause greeted Micaela and Una's entrance, cameras flashed. She was thirteen again, stepping off the plane at Bridewell Airport. The miracle child, the sole survivor of that terrible explosion.

Lafferty and his fellow musicians began playing as Micaela and Una entered. Liam, Nikki and Lowell hung back until the initial roar had died down. The night belonged to Una, so Micaela stepped to the side and tried unsuccessfully to fade away. Nikki and Lowell had melted into the crowd. Liam was only inches away. She grabbed his arm. "Save me."

"With pleasure. After you and Una have said your piece."

She rolled her eyes at him then made her way to the front of the room. She had underdressed deliberately in black jeans, an emerald green tailored blouse, and low-heeled black suede boots, hoping to be invisible. Now, she stood beside Una and Harold Dorset. After his introductory remarks that included some of his personal memories of her parents and, of course, how proud they would be of their Micaela, he turned the microphone over to Una.

"You all know me and have heard me tell stories and harangue you to support this project for too long. I want you to know how much your contributions are appreciated, but it's time," she turned to Micaela, "that you heard from the next generation."

Micaela took a deep breath and looked out over the crowd of strangers with familiar faces from a distant past. In the middle stood people who had, suddenly and strangely, become part of her present: Liam, Nikki, and Lowell. She raised her hand and touched the crane bag nestled against her chest, a piece of her parents.

"All of you know my grandmother, and many of you knew my parents. Maura and Donnachadh left their mark on all of us. I feel them with me every day." She reached out for Una's hand. "When I was a little girl, my Da would sit me on his lap in front of our fire. He would read to me and tell me stories he had learned from his Da. The chair we sat in then, now sits in my living room." She smiled at Una. "I mean... my parlor in New York. Many of you sit in similar chairs or on couches with your children and grandchildren. My grandmother asked for the fire pit reading circle, not to replace what you do at home, but to give you a place where you can come together as a community, as our ancestors did around a fire. It is the shared stories, the time together that makes us *clann*."

Liam's soft smile and nod caught her in the throat. She squeezed her eyes together. *No tears.*

"I have one last request." She motioned for Ansgar and Mrs. Ryan to come and stand beside her. "I had a chance to see the pool tonight. I know I told Mr. Dorset that I wouldn't get back to him for a while. I lied." She shrugged. Laughter rippled through the crowd.

"I would like to ask your support, tonight, to start a new program to make refurbishing the pool the next project. In addition, I propose that the pool and swim team be dedicated to the late Brendan Ryan. For the few who have not heard, it was Mr. Ryan who first taught me to swim, which saved my life every time I fell into the lake." Louder laughter greeted her remark from those who remembered that it was Ansgar who often helped her off the dock.

"That pool was my refuge when I most needed one."

Mrs. Ryan's eyes glistened. Micaela lost her next thought as Una embraced her. The hall filled with applause. After the hugs and handshakes had been exchanged, Liam steered her toward the side door. Alcohol was not allowed inside the hall, but eighteen inches beyond the side door was perfectly acceptable.

A group of young men and women milled around what looked like an ordinary hot dog truck but actually dispensed adult refreshment tonight. The fact that it was February in the Berkshires only meant bragging rights about who stayed out the longest and wore the lightest sweater or shorts. She received a dozen offers of stout. If it took the chill off as much as everyone promised, she'd be in shorts and a t-shirt by the third round. She began re-introducing herself to people she'd known in grade school but didn't recognize now. After all these years of trying to make herself a stranger, they made it easy to come home.   She spotted Ansgar in the group and introduced him to Nikki. Micaela left them at the start of a heated but friendly discussion about the pros and cons of a catalogue of weapons.

The largest group was the Son and Daughters of Danu. Micaela stood at the edge of their circle. "I want to thank all of you for the protection and peace of mind you have given to me and my grandmother these last few days."

Sean Murphy, her red-headed, machine gun toting guard, stepped forward. In the floodlights, his freckles stood out like brown stars across his cheeks. *He was way too young to be playing soldier.*

"It is a privilege that we have had for centuries. We are honored and blessed to have two generations of Priestesses in our midst. Who also happen to be damn fine people." Sean raised his glass. "*Slainte.*"

Micaela raised her glass in silent return. She didn't want to know what Sean meant about Priestesses. What was the rule: Don't ask the question unless you want the answer. She talked to some in the group; others only wanted to hug her or touch her arm. She could feel their auras starting to light up. There were too many people in one place and half a stout had weakened her control. She moved toward Lowell and his small group. He was still an aural blank.

"Are these your people, Mr. Lowell?"

"Most of them. Each of us left a part of our contingent at the house. Standard procedure."

"Standard procedure? You sound like this is an everyday event."

"I have a military background and my own security needs." Lowell's gazed flickered over his men and into the trees beyond. Two of the men peeled off and vanished into the woods. There had been no mention of a military background in her files.

"Did you serve in Iraq or Afghanistan?"

"No, an earlier conflict." He bowed to her. "If you will excuse me."

She caught a glimpse of weariness in his face that spoke less of lost sleep than of battles fought, and death seen. Liam circled around from the other side of the group. Micaela watched as the women curtsied and the men bowed to him. She heard many call him *An Tiarna*. Micaela intercepted him on his path to the refreshment truck.

"What does *An Tiarna* mean?"

"Just a holdover from the old days when the Farrells were important people." He offered her a stout. "That was a fine talk you gave. I do believe there's hope for you."

"I wasn't aware I was so hopeless." She waved off the stout.

"There are those who think you are all work and no play. Not me, of course. No one with a black teddy like yours could be all work." Liam sipped from his glass. A hint of a grin peeked from the edges.

The video call. She turned away from the floodlights to hide the blush and moved into the relative safety of the hall. The music began again. Liam had followed her in. He held out his hand.

"I don't dance anymore."

"Don't or won't?"

"This is a bad idea. It's been years." She saw Mrs. Ryan watching her, eyebrows raised in question.

"Just follow my lead. It's like riding a bicycle."

She took his hand. "You haven't seen me on a bicycle."

They stepped out to join the group of dancers. Una, sitting beside Chief Deerfield, looked over to them and nodded. Micaela tripped once and almost retreated to the sidelines but Liam's hand squeezed hard and they continued.

Liam was a master of the Sean-nós, an older form than the step dancing most people recognized. It was more fluid and, unfortunately for her, more improvisational. She watched him in a futile effort to anticipate his moves. Hopefully, Lafferty and the other musicians would need to wet their whistles soon and end her humiliation.

The tempo increased. Her body vibrated to the uilleann pipes, her pulse kept time to the beat of the bodhran. She felt herself slip away as the room faded. When she looked around, Liam still held her hand but they were in a large ballroom where candlelight shimmered off the crystal teardrops of chandeliers. The women were swathed in ankle length dresses of satin and brocade in a rainbow of colors. Some of the men wore *clann* tartans or *lein-croich* while others were attired in formal waistcoats. Micaela looked at her own knee-length evergreen satin dress. It would be scandalously short anywhere but on this dance floor. The corseted top with its embroidered edges in silver and gold made the dance and her cleavage more dramatic.

Her steps became sure and strong. She mirrored and challenged Liam's in the Sean-nós, confident and relaxed. She didn't need to think; the dance flowed through her like a river. She was certain that she and Liam, along with the dozens of others who watched them dance, were guests of the Lord of the Manor. At the edge of the circle, a tall man with storm gray eyes and wavy black hair stood waiting. Was he the Lord of the Manor? She was supposed to know but she couldn't remember.

The music stopped and Liam and Micaela acknowledged the applause with a bow. When she raised her eyes she was back in the hall of the Community Center. Her friends and neighbors ringed the floor. They stamped their feet and clapped. She and Liam stood alone on the floor. The music had ended in this time, too, but the man with the gray eyes was nowhere to be seen. She pulled her hand from Liam's hoping he wouldn't feel the tremble. *No such luck.*

"Do you need some water, 'Caela?"

"No, just some air."

Outside the door she sank onto an empty bench cloaked in the shadows. People came and went from the hall. They nodded but kept a respectful distance. She saw Liam standing in the doorway talking to Sean but watching her.

Nikki slid in beside her. "You okay?"

"Either everything is catching up with me or I'm losing my mind." Micaela stretched her legs out and stared out at Mount Greylock rising behind the trees.

"You're not any crazier than the rest of us."

"Thanks, that makes me feel so much better."

"Good, now that we've settled the question of your relative sanity. You said you wanted to learn to handle a gun. So, here's the plan. You, Ansgar, and I will hit the pistol range at seven tomorrow morning."

"What about Liam?"

"Hopefully, he'll sleep in. Are you sure this will make you feel safer?"

"I don't know. My life is… had been pretty under control until…" she frowned trying to decide when the turn had happened. "Last Samhain."

As soon as it slipped out she regretted it. *When had she lost the ability to think before speaking?*

Nikki opened her mouth to say something, but snapped it shut when Micaela stood.

"It's getting late, Nikki. I think I'll call it a night. Seven A.M. will be here before we know it. I'll tell Liam you're out here and can vouch for my sanity now."

"I'll bring the car around." Nikki headed to the parking lot. Micaela noticed the bulge at the small of Nikki's back. She had cut

Nikki off, but she was about to ask about last Samhain. How would Micaela explain the attack on Reece and her involvement in the search? Avoidance and retreat, the preferred approach of cowards.

Back in the hall, she said her goodnights. Liam was at her side. She could hear the whispers of what a fine pair they made. As difficult people went, she had to admit she was the worst of the pair.

"I'll be right behind you on the way home." He walked her to the car. "Will you join me on the front porch for a nightcap?"

He shifted from one foot to the other and wiped the palms of his hands on his jacket. Of course, after what had happened on the dance floor, her palms were sweating, too.

"Una keeps the best whiskey in the side table by the stairs. I'll bring the glasses. Will anyone else be joining us?"

"Not unless you want them to."

21

Something had clicked for her tonight, so loud someone else must have heard. For the first time, since she was a little girl, she had felt like part of the community. A place had opened, but with it had come that other community, a vision of another place and time, and she was just as certain that those people were hers, too. They knew each other well. Her relationship with Liam and the gray-eyed man touched deeper than the rest, more intimate. In that lifetime, she and Liam were lovers. In that time, they had left the hall and slipped off to make love. She wasn't sure what her involvement with the gray-eyed man was, but it was intense. The sensations were no less real and had travelled back to this time. Her body had responded to unseen touches from a distant past. Had Liam seen the same thing? Was that why he was so nervous?

Nikki drove and chatted away about the Céilí, Ansgar, and the pistol range, mostly small talk. Micaela was grateful her participation was not required in the conversation. Despite the chill, she opened the car window. The air was filled with the earth scents of early spring, and the sweet smell of last autumn's leaves returning to the ground. She couldn't see it, but out there the last of the snowdrops, the flowers of Imbolc, blanketed the forest floor. It was said that the first Priestess to come to America had planted bulbs taken from the Lucan Forest in these woods.

She tried to distract herself with thoughts of the work that waited in New York. The rescheduled first meeting for the AGF deal in Brussels was ten days away and she was behind in preparations. As the lead banker for the deal, she had to grab the reins. So tomorrow, she would get up early, when the house was quiet, and revisit the original agenda. After the gun range, she would sit with her Bluetooth in her ear, lead counsel on the other end, and the first draft of documents in front of her. They would go through them page by page for potential negotiation issues.

She had a plan and was on solid familiar ground until Lowell opened the car door for her. Everyone else was headed inside, including Nikki. Liam's shadow was framed in the parlor window.

"Never say you cannot dance. Your performance was excellent tonight." He extended his hand to her, as if she were alighting from her carriage.

"Trust me, it was a once in a lifetime experience. It will not happen again."

"A pity."

"I want to thank you for being here. I still don't understand why you did this."

"I thought we had covered this ground. And after what I saw tonight, although you may not admit it, you have a deep understanding of honor and your duty to your community. I can only conclude that I have done something to cause you to doubt me."

"I suppose I'm not accustomed to relative strangers putting themselves and their people's lives on the line for me and mine." Since she had been a teenager, there had always been an agenda.

"Then why do you think I am here? What ulterior motive could I have?" His anger flowed over her like molten lava, a dark side that flashed through his stiff New England formality.

She talked on, hoping to defuse the situation. "I'm not sure who you are and that makes me uncomfortable. When I was younger, people tried to come into my life offering friendship and help. But in the end, they had their own purposes. I'm not big on 'trust me'."

"You seem rather trusting of them." Lowell nodded to the shadows behind the curtains.

"I've known Nikki for years, Liam for a while, too." *More than one lifetime maybe.*

"Then I can only hope that I have the longevity to earn your confidence. But it will have to wait, other demands require my attention. Until tomorrow evening, I bid you adieu. My people will remain."

"On that point. Since there has been no activity for the last two days, I believe the guards are no longer necessary. I would like to personally thank your people. But I think it is time they return to their regular jobs and homes. I'm sure they have better things to do."

"Am I also dismissed from your home?"

In the darkness, a chorus of dogs sang to the moon. "It's my grandmother's home."

"This is the home of your spirit, Micaela. If you say I am not welcome, then I am bound by that."

The polite, proper Micaela told her she was being rude, but the practical Micaela wanted him gone until she was sure about him. He wasn't what he seemed. Without pushing too hard she tried to find his aura, with no success.

"You have been the perfect gentleman. I see no reason to banish you."

"But you would prefer I not come here."

"I don't know. Too much has happened recently. I don't want to detain you from your business obligations. We will be fine here." She was stammering.

"You have been through much. I will take your uncertainty as a sign of hope that I may gain your good graces." He bowed.

She stared at her feet not knowing how to respond. When she looked up, he was gone. Not turned and walked away, but gone, as in poof. She needed that nightcap.

Liam stood in front of the fire, holding two Waterford crystal tumblers filled with three fingers of amber liquid. In the firelight, his eyes looked the same color as the whiskey. Nikki and Una were nowhere to be seen.

"The night has cooled, 'Caela. Do you still want to sit outside?"

"Sure, let me grab a sweater." She opened the hall closet and grabbed the same Aran Isle sweater she'd worn to the creek, and then met him on the porch.

He handed her the glass but didn't let go; his fingers grazed the pulse in her wrist. "You were amazing at the Céilí."

"It was overwhelming, especially the dance." There, she'd said it.

His hand drifted up her arm. "Everyone was enchanted by you."

"I had an excellent partner. To be honest, I was never very good at the Sean-nós. Mrs. Ryan always said I was too stiff, couldn't relax."

"You should relax more often."

His hand cupped her cheek. He put his own glass down on the railing and cradled her face in both hands as he leaned into her. He tasted of the smoky whiskey. She tried to put her glass down and heard it roll away on the ground below. She touched his lips with her tongue. A moan rumbled deep in his throat, his kiss became more urgent, as his tongue traced along her teeth. His fingers slid back and laced through her hair as she wrapped her arms around him. She searched for the edge of his sweater and reached her hands under, searching for flesh. She wanted to drink him down, to press her skin, even it was only her hands, against him. A fragment of a vision surfaced from that other life of the two of them wrapped around each other, the lines between their bodies melded into one pulsing need.

They pulled apart, gasping like two drowning people breaking the surface. Liam held her to his chest. His heart pounded against her cheek. She ran her fingers down his spine and was rewarded with a delicious shudder from him. Could they sneak up to her room?

Like a shift in the wind, he stiffened. "Sorry. I'm not like this."

"You didn't force yourself on me."

The pain she had seen at the creek was back in his eyes. "Trust me, 'Caela, I'm not your type. This was a mistake." He tossed back the rest of his whiskey and headed up toward the barn.

22

Liam, Nikki and Una were halfway through breakfast when Micaela came into the kitchen the next morning. Nikki scratched away on a pad.

"… I'll go over this with Ethan this evening."

Micaela pulled up a chair. "He won't be back. I told him it was time, I… we got back to a normal routine."

Nikki's eyebrows headed north.

Liam set down his mug. "I'm not saying you're wrong, 'Caela, just perhaps, a little discussion first."

"What would you have liked to discuss?" Her palms pressed into the wooden trestle table. "The fact that the police seem to be fishing for a connection between Lowell and François' murder? Have you ever seen his temper?"

"You do have a way of bringing out the best in some of us, 'Caela." Liam's arms were folded across his chest, the same one she had pressed her head against last night.

"Some manage to put away their best pretty quickly." She stabbed a sausage from the platter while she counted to ten. "My point is the crisis has passed and I can't stay here forever. It's time. I have things to do this week before the Brussels meeting."

Liam stared into his mug. "Agreed. But you'll have to make amends to Ethan for refusing his help."

"When I'm damn sure he didn't kill François, I'll kiss his ring or anything else he wants if that's what it takes."

Liam took his coffee and headed upstairs muttering, "Stubborn woman."

Nikki poured more coffee for her. "What's up Micaela? This isn't just about Ethan."

"All kinds of crazy shit, that's what's up."

"You seemed fine at the Community Center until after you danced with Liam. Which was amazing, by the way."

"That wasn't me dancing. Let me rephrase. I don't know how else to describe it, I think I was hallucinating." Damn, she'd rather talk about visions than kisses. How messed up was she?

"Tell me what you saw."

"It was nothing, forget it." Micaela started clearing the table.

"Micaela, we've been friends for a couple of years now, but you never asked why your Brazilian friend who worked for Interpol is now working homicide for the NYPD."

Micaela stood at the kitchen sink. The Waterford tumblers from last night sat at the bottom of the basin. They needed to be handled carefully.

"Everyone has a right to their secrets and to decide when they want to share them, if ever." The tumblers could wait.

"Kind of like you?"

"Low blow. Okay, so what's a nice Brazilian girl like you doing in New York carrying around a small arsenal?"

Nikki stood and leaned against the counter next to the sink. "At home, I was part of a special squad, the kind they don't talk about. We were gifted with talents most humans don't have. Some of us could see things that others couldn't."

"Psychics?"

"Some. Others had different talents. From there, I was recruited by Interpol to help start a similar group."

140

"How did you end up in New York?" Micaela sat back down at the table.

"There was an accident and it was better if I tried to drop off the radar. I had a friend in the NYPD. We had worked a case together once. He's just a nice cop from a regular family, whose father happens to be the Police Commissioner. I asked him to help get me a job. I knew New York had no special squads. I thought I could just be a cop."

"When we were at the hotel with Detective Hendricks, you mentioned that you were there by special request."

"Who knew the Assistant Commissioner in charge of homicide would turn out to be a pagan and gifted? He sees the potential of a special squad and the Commissioner is open-minded. But he has no idea what he's getting into."

"Hendricks looked angry that you were there."

"He found out about my special assignments. He is a fundamentalist Christian. Anyone with a gift, in his mind, is a devil worshipper."

"In Massachusetts, we know a little about people who jump to those conclusions. I can see why you wouldn't want to draw attention to yourself."

"No, I may not take out a full page ad in the New York Times. But, what I'm trying to tell you is that it's okay to see things, lots of us do."

Micaela fussed with the Waterford.

"When you're ready to talk, I'm here." Nikki grabbed her duffel bag from under the kitchen table. "In the meantime, let's go play."

"One more coffee, please."

"That's why they make travel mugs."

Ansgar met them in the front office of the range. Nikki picked out four different pistols for Micaela to try.

Two hours later, Micaela called a time out. "I asked for a lesson, not torture. There are aches in muscles I didn't know I had."

"You'll get used to it." Ansgar packed up all the guns except the H&K. "It's like when you swam. You work the same muscles in different ways. They hurt at first. But, you keep at it. By the way, Dorset asked me to help coach the team. Care to drop in to give the team some pointers?"

"Maybe, send me the schedule and I'll see what I can do."

Nikki slid her own Glock into its shoulder holster and slipped her leather jacket back on. "You did fine for your first time out, Micaela."

"I'll be safe as long as my attacker is the size of a barn." But they hadn't been. They were black clothed figures on black cycles moving at over a hundred miles an hour. The real question was, if it came down to it, could she pull the trigger?

Nikki patted her on the back. Micaela fought the urge to wince. Goddess, her muscles were already screaming in protest.

"Keep at it." Nikki said. "Give the H&K one more try, so we're sure."

Micaela massaged her right forearm, but she picked up the H&K and fired at a fresh target. She finished the second round of trials and headed for the car.

"What's next?"

"Once we decide on the best fit, I can get you through the permitting process. We'll have it all sorted out by the time we get back from Brussels."

"We?"

"You didn't think I'd leave you with just Liam to look after you?" Nikki had her phone out. "I'll send a text to a dealer I know in Jersey. We can stop in before we leave for Brussels and try on grips to set a size."

Micaela grinned at the thought of browsing through an imaginary gun department at Brooks Brothers. Did handguns come in pinstripes?

Liam was coming out of the woods as they pulled in. Nikki unloaded the bag and headed inside. Liam looked more rested than he had in days.

"You kids have fun?"

Micaela rubbed her biceps. "I'll let you know when I can move my arms again."

"You'll be fine. About last night…" He chewed at his bottom lip.

"It was all just a bit too much for both of us, I guess. And you were right, I should have talked to you and Nikki before I dismissed Lowell and his people."

"As long as everyone is safe."

"Were you just up at the barn?"

"With everyone heading home, I wanted to make sure we didn't leave Una with a mess."

"Everyone was comfortable up there?"

"It was good enough for our purposes. It's a nice sized space." He set his bag next to the Jag.

"You stayed with them."

"I wouldn't ask my people to do anything I wouldn't. The barn is actually in pretty good shape."

Micaela looked out to the east end of the property. With most of trees bare, you could see the barn from the front porch. A dozen or more people moved in and out of the wide doors loading gear into vans and jeeps.

"I haven't been up there in a while. I kept my horse there up until graduate school."

143

"You ride? A nice gentle canter, I suppose." He cocked a mocking eyebrow at her.

"I'll have you know, I got my first pony when I was six. When I went to prep school, they taught us dressage. The stable master was a retired rodeo rider and taught a couple of us how to barrel race." She could feel the smile creep across her face. "One summer, after we got our driver's licenses, three of us entered an amateur rodeo competition in West Virginia. We took first, second and third. They didn't invite us back."

"Why don't you keep horses anymore?"

"Life got in the way, graduate school, work. Ogham, my last horse, was getting up in years. I donated him to a camp about ten miles from here that teaches special needs kids to ride."

"Ice Maiden O'Brien has a heart. Wait until I tell them back at the office."

"Don't ruin my reputation. I work hard at it." She faked a smile. Did he think her so frozen last night? "I guess you'll be heading out?"

"The Knowth plane is waiting at the Bridewell Airport. I'll bring the plane back for you and Nikki next Monday."

"I've already booked a commercial flight."

"You know I'm not convinced this is over. Nikki can transport things on the Knowth plane that wouldn't make it through regular airport security. There will be other passengers on the plane from Clovis who are friends." He took her hand. "Cancel your flight, please."

She nodded. She wanted to protest that she could take care of herself, but it would have been a lie. He headed down the driveway to his Jag, as she walked back to the front porch.

Micaela packed all the files on Lowell to take with her. She would ship the Boston files back interoffice. On second thought, she could take them back personally and while there take in some sights, like Lowell Manor or the First Colony headquarters. Nikki insisted on riding back to the city with her.

144

Una set out a light lunch for them, which consisted of roasted chicken, mashed potatoes, asparagus and fresh baked apple pie. Talk at the table was simple; their mouths were too full.

As Nikki passed her the last of the dishes, Micaela whispered to Nikki, "Can you give me a few minutes alone with my grandmother?"

"Take as long as you need."

Micaela pulled out a dish towel and started drying. Una stood beside her putting dishes away in the cabinets.

"You've been through a lot the last few weeks." Una headed for the stove.

"More than anyone knows." Micaela hung the soggy towel beside the sink.

"I'll put a kettle on. It's time we talked."

Micaela set out the cups. "It's past time. I should have talked to you after Samhain and what happened with Reece."

"You weren't ready. No one, including your parents, could ever get you to do something until you decided." The shrill whistle declared the water was boiling.

"You were there that night on the mountain… in the cave. The entire Grove Circle, I could hear and feel you."

"You are one of us. We gave you support."

"Since then, I've tried," she said, her voice catching in her throat, "to put it away, to shut it out."

"I know. We'll give you space and will help where we can." Una set a plate of her raspberry thumbprint cookies down. A childhood favorite of Micaela's.

"Right after Samhain, I would occasionally see some people's auras. I meditated, read up on it, worked out, martial arts. I had it all contained." The teaspoon clinked against the inside of the cup as she stirred in honey. "At least I thought so."

"Things have changed, we've felt it."

"Then, after François was murdered, I saw his spirit at a pub in New York. Last night at the Céilí, when Liam and I were on the dance floor, I was somewhere else, some time else." Her hands trembled but she felt relief.

"Aine called me about the Salmon Run. I felt you leave last night."

Micaela ran her fingers through her hair, pulling it back from her face. "I can't control it anymore, Grandma. What do I do?"

"When you were a little girl and learning to sail at the Cape, what did your father tell you to do?"

She remembered a long forgotten night on the sailboat with her parents and friends. They had let her steer, the wind was high, small whitecaps glowed in the moonlight.

"He said, 'Don't fight the currents or the wind, use them.'"

"Are you stronger than the elements? Stronger than Lir?"

Micaela shook her head.

Una continued. "You can't fight yourself. I'm here to help, so is the rest of the Grove, as is Aine."

"I don't know where to begin. So much has happened, I feel like I'm running out of time."

"You have much to learn. The first lessons are to remember the stories and trust your intuition. You carry the knowledge. You'll know what to do. Now, get back to New York, you have a lot of work ahead of you. I'm always just a phone call away."

23

"Did you guard the place while I was gone, Grady?" The cat's chartreuse eyes stared at her from the glass and brass console by the door. "I'm sure Beatrice took good care of you while I was gone."

Micaela grabbed the stack of mail and sorted it in vague overlapping piles on the table: garbage, shred, and keep. The silence was deafening; she opened the south terrace door and turned on the sound system. Horns honked and sirens screamed on the street below; too much noise, she closed the door. She needed to unpack and get ready for work in the morning.

Next to her bed was a new vase overflowing with fresh pink and red roses. Their fragrance filled the room and their petals were scattered across her bed. A card read: With affection, Ivan.

How had he arranged this? She picked up her cell phone and scrolled through her contacts for AGF. It was just after eight at night, so it would be just after three tomorrow morning in Saint Petersburg. She dialed Ivan's number to leave a message. She wasn't sure who was more surprised: her because he answered, or Ivan because she had called.

"Mischa, is everything okay?"

"It's been a crazy couple of days, but I'm fine. I wanted to thank you for the roses. How did you get them arranged with the petals and all?"

"Beatrice is a very sweet woman."

Her housekeeper, Beatrice, fiftyish, energetic, devote Catholic, had been cleaning Micaela's apartment for the last three years. She fussed over Grady, bringing choice leftovers from her family dinner table. Protective did not begin to describe Beatrice. But Micaela knew that Ivan had a certain charm.

"Remind me to talk to her about letting strangers in."

"I had hoped we had moved past strangers." He sounded hurt.

"Of course we have. Listen, Ivan, I don't want to go into details, but be careful. Do you have security?"

"In Russia, it is like putting on a coat in winter. I am flattered that my safety concerns you, but what has caused the worry I hear in your voice?"

"I think whoever killed François tried to run me off the road this past weekend." The other end of the phone was quiet. She wasn't sure he was still there. He finally let out a breath.

"You were not harmed?"

"No. I'm fine." She moved aside enough of the petals so that she could lie on the bed.

"Perhaps they were only trying to frighten you?"

"But for Liam and the others, they might have succeeded in doing more than scare me."

"Tell me what I can do?"

"Be careful. There are all kinds of people looking into it. We don't know if it has to do with our deal or something unrelated. I suppose I should call the other members, it's just… "

"You are not sure who to trust. In that case, I am doubly honored that you called me. Let me take care of contacting the others. I will say nothing of your travail, and perhaps I will learn something in my conversations with them."

She did trust him. He had set her psychic alarms off at the beginning but since then he had been kind and respectful. He treated her like an equal and hadn't charged in to rescue the poor damsel in distress. She knew he was romancing her, but she was starting to think it was just about her.

"Ivan, I feel like I owe you an apology. I jumped to certain conclusions in the beginning."

"Then, let us start over. Ms. O'Brien, I am Ivan Vasilievich and I would be honored if you would allow me to call on you."

"That would be nice." She couldn't help but smile.

She heard a soft knock on her door. She checked through the peephole. Shaking her head and laughing, she opened the door. Ivan stood on the other side, a cell phone to his ear.

"May I hang up now, Mischa?"

"I hadn't expected you to call on me so soon. Please, come in." She swept her hand out to invite him in. "I thought you were in Saint Petersburg."

"I returned this morning for a meeting and dinner at the Embassy. I was just pulling away when you called. It was but a quick trip across Central Park. My apologies, I allowed my concern to overrule my manners."

"I'm glad you're here. I've been out of town, so there isn't much in the refrigerator. Can I offer you tea or coffee?"

"Just a small glass of red wine, if you have it. I have spent the last hours at one of those tedious Embassy dinners that required I keep my wits about me."

Micaela opened a new bottle and set it out to breathe, then took an open bottle of Pinot Noir from the wine locker and poured two glasses.

Ivan stood by the North balcony door. "Your views of the river must be wonderful. How did you find such an apartment?"

"My parents purchased it before I was born. It passed to me when they died."

Ivan moved to the sofa. "I understand you were a quite young when that happened."

Micaela sat down next to him. "I was thirteen."

The sorrow in Ivan's eyes echoed her own pain. He wrapped her in his arms, and pulled her close. "I have lost people I cared deeply for. The pain never truly goes away."

His fingers massaged the tension from her back. He laid his cheek against hers. She felt him slowly inhale. As he exhaled, the warmth of it washed over her. His lips touched her throat.

She awoke on the couch the next morning, blinding sunlight in her eyes. She knew she had been drained by the events of the previous days, but to fall asleep on Ivan was beyond comprehension and courtesy. She would have to call him, find a way to make amends. She stood up slowly. Her neck hurt. Sleeping on the couch had not helped her stiffness from the gun range. A hot shower, a mug of coffee and some ibuprofen and she'd be right as rain. The day was cold, so she wrapped a scarf around her neck. No point inviting a sore throat when you already felt like crap.

How would she make it up him? He probably had no interest in seeing her again after last night. She tried to drink the coffee and felt nauseous. Maybe some toast. She had no time to be sick.

Micaela stopped at her office to drop off the New York files to Judy and pick up messages. Judy followed Micaela into her office. "Detective Hendricks has called several times, Ms. O'Brien. I continue to tell him that you are out of town and unreachable."

Micaela sat in her chair, overcome by weariness. She fought the urge to put her head on her desk and take a nap. "Judy, we've know each other most of my life. You worked for my father. I think you can call me Micaela, don't you?"

"You're right, I have known you most of your life, Micaela, and I have never seen you look so tired. Are you sick?"

"It's been a long few weeks and I think it caught up with me last night. I fell asleep on the couch, it stinks for sleeping."

"Well get some rest, please."

"Tonight, I promise."

She opened her e-mail hoping to see a message from Ivan. Nothing. She picked up her phone and dialed his number. She wasn't sure if he was still in New York or over the Atlantic. Her call went to his voicemail. She needed him and hoped last night had not killed their relationship. She left her cell number and headed out. She had one more stop before she headed for Boston.

The small silver bell on the brass hook tinkled as Micaela crossed the threshold of the Singing Stone Irish Shoppe. She made her way through the racks of cream colored wool sweaters and brightly colored shawls. Shelves displayed the traditional Irish crystal and china patterns found on most bridal registries and popular with tourists. Deeper into the store, the ordinary merchandise was replaced by a rich variety of handcrafted pieces of pottery, carved figures, jewelry, hand-blown glass, and metalwork. Musical instruments, whistles, pipes, and bodhrans lined one wall waiting for eager hands to take them up.

"Make yourself to home, Micaela. I'll be finished in a jiff." Aine stood at the register ringing up the purchases of a gray-haired middle-aged woman in a tartan cape. Behind the wooden register were rows of unlabelled jars that held seeds and dried herbs. Micaela recognized a few from Una's kitchen.

The woman, her purchase complete, came over to Micaela and grasped her hand. "It's an honor to meet to you. I can't wait to tell my husband that I met The O'Brien."

A clear vision flashed before Micaela's eyes. This smiling woman spent night after night staring at her ceiling beyond distraction worrying about her son overseas. Micaela could also see

151

the woman's son in a desert camp somewhere. The words spilled out before she could stop them.

"Please don't worry about Tim. He'll be home soon. He'll have some troubles but he'll be fine." She clamped her hand over her own mouth to stem the flow.

The woman kissed both Micaela's cheeks, tears shimmered in her eyes. "Thank the Goddess." Tim's mother was on her cell phone within seconds of walking out of the shop.

Micaela turned to Aine. "What have I done?"

"You gave one of your people good news." She came out from behind the counter. "Come in the back, we'll have tea."

"But if I'm wrong?"

"Did it feel wrong to you?"

"I don't know that I felt anything other than a compulsion to speak."

"We can work on that." Aine locked the front door and turned the sign over to "Closed".

She led Micaela down a long narrow corridor. There were two small rooms along the right side. On the left was a larger meeting room. Aine stopped and took a key from her skirt pocket and unlocked a door to a smaller room. A steaming teapot, two china cups and saucers and a plate of shortbread cookies were already on a side table.

Aine poured. "I'm glad you came, I'm just sorry Nora isn't here. But you two will meet one day."

"It was you I wanted to talk to. The night we met, you said some things that didn't make sense." A light prickling like an army of ants crawled over her skin; the energy level in this room was strong.

Aine moved the tea and plate of cookies to a larger table at the center of the room. A purple candle, set in the center of a spiral clay holder, flickered.

"Let us see what the cards will share." She held out the Tarot.

Micaela shuffled the deck as she had been taught years ago and selected ten cards, which Aine laid out in the Celtic Cross. The first card was the Tower. Soldiers tumbled out of the collapsing and burning structure.

She tapped the card. "The card of warfare. Your situation is critical, a crisis is coming. It is crossed by the Fool. You will need to step out of your normal ways because of this, something hard for you to do. Your past includes both the ten of wands and the four of pentacles. It speaks to a heavy burden that you carry and large pieces of yourself locked away."

Micaela stood to refill her tea. "I'm to believe that some random assortment of cards reveals all this? You know my grandmother, you know my past."

"The nine of wands in the ninth position tells me that you fear the return of something or someone that was over." Aine's fingers moved through the air less than an inch above the cards.

Micaela sat down and chewed at her lower lip. She stared at the cards, unwilling to meet the old woman's eyes. "It's getting worse. I use to be able to control it, avoid it."

Aine leaned over the cards. "You will need to choose soon. Do this with an eye not only to the past that you dwell on, but to your destiny. There are many around who will help you. The Earth Mother, the Goddess, is in your cards, but that is no surprise. I also see at least one man strong in emotions who will be there for you."

"You're creating more questions than answers."

"It is your job to seek the answers. But that has been the way of the teaching since our people began."

"That's the second time you've said that. I have no people." In her mind, she could hear her father's and mother's voices as they sat around the dinner table with Una and talked about their people, the *clann*. She had echoed these words at the Community Center.

"Even as you say it, you taste the lie." Aine returned her gaze to the cards. "The final outcome card is Death."

153

"I'm going to die?" Ivan's voice whispered to her, indistinct words of comfort in Russian. He had received her voicemail. She loosened her scarf and rubbed her neck.

Aine slid the card across the table. "Most of us die eventually. That is not the meaning. It is the card of transformation. It says that your life as you know it will end."

"I need you to tell me how to get my old life back." Micaela fingered the card.

"Which old life, Micaela, daughter of Donnachadh and Maura?"

Micaela's shoulders sagged. Again, Ivan's voice whispered in her head, he would come and all would be well. Warmth flooded through her. She sat up and smiled. "A new life wouldn't be so bad. In fact, it will be all right. Thank you."

Aine reached across the table, grabbed Micaela's chin and tugged the scarf down further. "I knew I felt something, a darkness, when you came in. Now I am sure. We have no time to lose."

"What are you talking about?" Micaela tried to pull away. Aine's grip tightened.

"Of course you would not remember. Come." Aine took Micaela's hand and dragged her upstairs to the kitchen of what appeared to be her home. She pulled a tall stool in front of the sink. She pushed Micaela onto it with her back to the basin. Aine reached into a cabinet and pulled a small bottle of water from a cabinet.

"Brigid's water. Tilt your head back. This should release its hold on you, or, at least, weaken it. I do not know how powerful it is. This will sting at first, but like the cause, you will not recall the cure."

More like a flamethrower than a sting. Micaela felt the first rush of the water on her throat and over her own screams she heard the first words of Aine's incantation. She struggled against the magic. Ivan would make it right.

154

24

Micaela sat across from Aine at the kitchen table and finished her tea. After the card reading, they had somehow ended up in the upstairs apartment. Odd she couldn't recall how. But, it had been a nice visit filled with small talk about Una and events in Bridewell. And as she waved goodbye to Aine, she felt better than she had all day. A Tarot card peeked out of her purse.

Minutes later, she sped north to Boston on Interstate 95 with more questions, no answers. She dropped the files off at Moran & Boru's State Street office by three o'clock. Her quick visit turned into an hour of hellos to people she worked with now or who knew her father then. Mike Duffy, a floor trader with a shock of white hair and an ever present smile wrapped around an unlit cigar, remembered her father and was more than willing to talk about First Colony.

"We've done business with First Colony since the early days of the firm. Folks say Mr. Boru met the Lowells when he came here from Dublin over two hundred years ago. Your father was in charge of the First Colony account and met with Jeremiah Lowell, now and again. Ethan Lowell must have been a boy and away at school. I do remember him saying that Jeremiah was coming out to Bridewell once. I can't remember where you and your mother would have been. Didn't hear much of Lowell until after Jeremiah retired. He doesn't really come round here. I guess, with your father gone and all…"

"Thanks, Duff. If I ever stand still long enough, I owe you a dinner at Durgin Park."

"Make it the Black Rose and you have a date." He kissed her on the cheek. "You're the picture of your mother, but, lass, you have your father's eyes. Such focus."

First Colony's offices were two blocks east on State Street. A young blonde receptionist with a headset wrapped around her right ear sat behind a tasteful modern cherry counter. Like the rest of the furniture in the lobby, it was all curved edges and flat surfaces. Behind the desk, a vivid seascape with an eighteenth-century schooner in full sail under a clear blue sky was a contrast to the lightning flashes of buttons on the multi-line phone in front of the girl. After the fifth pink message slip, she looked up at Micaela.

"May I help you?" She plucked an earbud from her left ear, music drifted out to Micaela. Modern multi-tasking.

"Mr. Lowell, please." Micaela looked through the double glass doors that led to the offices. From what she could see, they were like any major corporation, ordinary walnut furniture, neutral beige carpets, and stock artwork on the walls. Quite subdued given the wealth of the Lowells.

"Mr. Lowell hasn't arrived yet. Is he expecting you?"

"Not really. I was in town and thought I would stop in."

"He should be here any time now. Excuse me..." She punched a button on the oversized phone bank. "First Colony Shipping. How may I direct your call? No, Mr. Lowell isn't in yet, may I transfer you to his voicemail?" She forwarded the call and looked back up. "Sorry for the interruption."

"Isn't it almost quitting time?" Micaela glanced at her watch; it was already five.

"For most of us, except Mr. Lowell, that is. He's out all day at meetings or inspecting his ships, and doesn't arrive until evening. Then, he and his assistant will work most of the night. Do you want to wait?"

"No, I have another appointment." It was almost the truth.

"Can I tell Mr. Lowell who stopped by?"

She pulled a card from her wallet. "Tell him Ms. O'Brien was here."

The receptionist read the card. "Moran & Boru? He'll be so sorry he missed you. I overhead him talking about some new banker at your firm, a woman. Oh… it must have been you. I'll be sure he knows you were here."

The red eye of the surveillance camera winked at Micaela from above the seascape. Somehow, she thought, it wouldn't be necessary.

Her next appointment was Lowell Manor, a half hour outside Boston. She wasn't sure what she expected. Maybe some perverse satisfaction by intruding on his space, the way he had invaded Bridewell. She parked near the gate. Fort Lowell might be a better name for the compound. The twelve foot iron gates, bluestone walls, and long winding driveway made it impossible to see the house. Through the bars of the gate, she glimpsed a whitewashed two story stable, larger that Una's house. A plaque on the gate designated Lowell Manor, an historic home, built in 1785 on the site of an earlier 1671 structure.

She had to get a better look. She walked along the perimeter and looked for a chink in the defenses. Her breath was a swirl in the late February night air. The Lowell Estate appeared to be several dozen acres, all enclosed by an endless wall. She returned to the gate and squeezed her face up to the bars for a final look, like some tourist. A single light glowed in the stables.

"Wouldn't it be easier to press the buzzer, Ms. O'Brien?" Lowell's arm brushed across her shoulder as he swiped a security card in the stainless steel pad.

She jumped sideways. Where had he come from? "I was curious about where you lived."

"The house is open to the public one Saturday each month. You could contact the Boston Area Historical Society for a season pass. It includes The Mount and the other vintage homes." His lips curled in a smile as his eyes mocked her.

A green light appeared over the camera lens in security pad and a disembodied female voice crackled over the speaker. "Mr. Lowell?"

"Yes, Connie. It would seem Ms. O'Brien has dropped in for an unexpected visit." He turned to Micaela. "It would be easier for you if you pulled your car up, or we could ride in the cart." An electric golf cart sat just inside the walls. The gates swung open and lantern lights flickered on along the walk. He bowed and swept his arm ahead for her to enter. If he was in any way responsible for François' murder, following him was a really bad idea.

Lowell eyed her with curiosity. "Having second thoughts about a tour? Or is it the guide?"

She could turn around and get in her car. But she'd come this far, why leave without some sense of who he was? He had spent all that time in Bridewell, had wandered the grounds while she slept. He'd had ample opportunity to finish what had been started by the motorcyclists, if they worked for him. She followed him through the gates and studied him as he moved. His wide shoulders tapered into a narrow waist set off by the tailored suit he wore. He walked with the ease and grace of old money. Sure of his position in the world.

They rode in the golf cart past the stables where low pines gave way to a wide expanse of lawn that ended at a stark forecourt. The only plants were two bare rose vines that climbed the side walls of the court. In the gloom, she wasn't sure they would bloom in the spring. In the center, water spilled from one basin to the next of a three-tiered fountain. Obscured by the fountain was a narrow oak door with gas-fed lanterns on either side. This was not a house that welcomed uninvited guests.

The door swung open to the silhouette of a woman that Micaela assumed was Connie. She wasn't the bookish type that Micaela expected. Instead she was petite, about five foot three, with

158

shoulder length brunette hair, brown eyes, an upturned nose, and an athletic build.

"Mr. Lowell." She turned and extended her hand to Micaela. "Ms. O'Brien, such a nice surprise."

"I'm sorry." Micaela felt the heat of the embarrassment in her face. "I assumed you were on your way to your office."

Lowell led her into the foyer. "Normally, we would be, but I couldn't leave your curiosity unsatisfied."

"I shall call the office, Mr. Lowell, and tell them not to expect us tonight." Connie disappeared through a panel that swung inward on the left side of the vaulted grotto style foyer.

Lowell led Micaela up a curved staircase. The walls were lined with eighteenth century masterpieces. She recognized a Benjamin West, a Stuart, and a Trumball. They entered a long gallery. One side was covered with mirrors that even at night brought the moon and starlight inside through the long windows that covered the opposing wall. She placed her purse in a corner and walked over to a Georgian side table where a silver tea set gleamed.

"To answer your question, yes, it is a Revere. The tourists are quite taken with the collection." He leaned against a marble pedestal.

"I can see why. This is magnificent." She reached out but stopped.

"Feel free. Revere meant it as an everyday service, although the art of afternoon tea has been lost. Would you care to see the rest of the house?"

Her curiosity continued to overwhelm her caution. Grady would probably have some cat thoughts on that. In a side parlor, a grand piano appeared ready for a performance. Sheet music rested on it.

"Do you play or is this for show?"

He sat on the bench and let his fingers stray across the keys. "It relaxes me sometimes. Other times, it makes me remember."

"I should go. I intruded."

159

"As I recall, you did not try to climb the wall; I opened the gate and invited you in. But perhaps, I arrived too soon." He cocked an eyebrow at her.

"Okay, I was checking out your house… from the outside. You've been to mine." Goddess, she sounded like a five-year-old in the schoolyard.

"I have not visited your home in New York."

"In Bridewell, remember."

"As I recall you do not live there, only visit your grandmother." His tone challenged her.

"It's my home, too." *When had it become home again?*

He smiled. "So I thought. Let me show you the rest of the public space."

"Public?"

"Do you think I actually live in this museum? The contents are beautiful and steeped in history. But they are ineffective for modern living."

"So, you and Connie live under the stairs?"

"No, various doors lead to more suitable accommodations within the house and on the grounds. Come, let me show you the upstairs quarters. It is late, perhaps you should select a room to spend the night, or Connie could make a hotel reservation."

Connie emerged, as if summoned, from behind a panel in the wall. She handed Lowell a stack of phone messages which he shoved unread into his jacket pocket.

"I can make my own arrangements," Micaela said.

"As you wish." His nod was a gesture that fit the house and its history. "The Hawthorne Room is ready to receive guests. It includes a first edition of Seven Gables for your reading pleasure."

Connie pursed her lips, fighting a smile. Micaela wondered how much he shared with her. Connie turned and disappeared through a swinging door. Beyond the door, Micaela could see a corridor that ended in a sparkling stainless steel kitchen.

Micaela and Lowell climbed the stairs where the artwork continued. These pieces were later additions from the Hudson River School of the early nineteenth century. The next floor contained the private living space and he led her into what must have been the master bedroom. A fireplace lined with blue delft tiles filled one wall. In the center of the room was a cherry four poster bed as narrow as a modern full-sized bed, but longer.

"The Lowells were tall by comparison to their peers. This bed was built by the same craftsman who constructed Tom Jefferson's bed. Would you like to try it out?"

She looked from him to the bed. "Hardly."

"Most tourists want to at least sit on it. Although we rope off the doorway to keep them out, once in a while one will slip under for a photo."

A single rose stood in a slender vase on the nightstand. Ivan's voice, fainter than before, whispered to her not be alone with Lowell. "I'm sure you have things to do, I don't want to keep you," she said.

Lowell leaned against one of the posts of the bed, his arms folded across his chest. He might be mistaken for part of the exhibit, except for the modern European cut silk suit. The navy jacket brought out his cornflower blue eyes. "You dislike me, don't you?"

"I don't know you well enough to dislike you." She stepped closer to the hall.

"You've done a good deal of research on me and my history."

"So you saw the boxes at my grandmother's house. Yes, I looked into your background. You came out of nowhere and took up guard duty at my house."

"I thought I had explained my allegiance to Liam and the Nation already." His jaw was so tight she was amazed he could still speak.

"And your relationship with François?"

"Perhaps we should discuss this in the parlor." He didn't give her time to answer. He was in the doorway and headed for the stairs to the first floor.

161

The move out of a bedroom was fine with her. Lowell was the soul of restraint, calm, even-toned, but she had grown up with first-hand experience of what happens when that stoic New England surface was scratched.

A fire crackled in the hearth. Opposite the fireplace was a wall of French doors that opened onto a stone veranda that seemed to reach across the entire rear of the mansion. He handed her a glass. "Port, it has always had medicinal value. Good for the nerves."

She held the tall glass in her hand, the fragrance of the ruby vintage drifted up. She took a polite sip. This was not the time to over-indulge and unleash her so-called gifts.

He faced her from in front of the fire. "What has my relationship with François to do with your negative opinion of me? I understand how traumatic it was for you to find him. His death has been painful for me. I considered him a friend." He lifted his glass to his lips.

"I understand that you were also business partners."

"I do business with many that you know, your own firm included."

She set her glass down and spoke softly, trying for a curious rather than accusatory tone. "Some have implied that one of his business dealings may have ended in his murder. Were you aware of anyone with whom François had a falling out?"

"Serious enough to want to kill him in that manner?" He moved away from her and lowered himself onto a loveseat. His face was still. "No one leaps to mind. I am aware that the police think I am somehow involved. And yet you sit here with me."

"I'm not sure what to think. The things said about François don't feel right. But I didn't know him any better than I know you. The facts are he was murdered, someone tried to run me off the road, and then you arrived to help."

"I did not kill François. I will grant that you have no reason to believe me. But you are smart enough to realize that if I had and I wanted you captured or killed, I have had ample opportunity, including right now."

His words echoed her earlier thoughts. Her eyes flicked to all possible exits. When she looked back he was inches away. She hadn't seen or heard him move. He held her upper arms the way he had in Una's parlor, a brush of fingers.

"I cannot prove a negative." His tone was earnest, almost pleading. "But I can earn your trust and when the real killer is found, and then you will be sure."

There was a light tap on the door. Connie entered with a tablet in her hand. He stepped away from Micaela, his hands clasped behind his back.

"I'm sorry to interrupt, Mr. Lowell, but you'll want to see this." Connie handed the computer to him, who glanced at the screen then passed it to Micaela.

"Do you recognize this man?" he asked.

"That's Detective Hendricks from the New York Police Department. Why is he in Boston?"

"Apparently on the same sightseeing tour you took. Connie, please open the gate for the gentleman." He watched over her shoulder as Hendricks started down the same path around the stables.

Did Hendricks follow her here? Had he been watching her all along? She looked into Ethan Lowell's cold eyes. Did he think this was a setup? Long minutes of silence passed before she opened her mouth to speak. A bell rang, cutting off her words.

Lowell pressed his finger to her lips cutting off her words. He took Micaela by the elbow and led her to the veranda. He whispered as they walked. "Go now. Whatever this detective believes happened, I do not want him to think you are involved. I would recommend that you exit on foot through the rear gate. It is about a half mile walk. The path is not well lit, but Connie will give you a low voltage flashlight. It will give you enough light without attracting attention. You will excuse me if I do not accompany you, but it seems I am about to have another unexpected visitor."

163

"But my car is out front."

Connie handed her the keys and purse. "I had already moved it to the rear of the property. You really should be more careful where you leave your purse."

Connie walked her to the edge of the veranda. "At the foot of the stairs, turn left and then continue down the lime walk. The hedge will hide you from view. At the end of the walk, follow the garden wall to the next path at the back. It will take you to your car. Follow the service road until you reach the main road."

"Thank you."

Connie whispered, "You must believe this, he and François were close. The Lowells' ties to Montbelliard's are long and deep. Ethan could not have killed him." She handed Micaela the promised flashlight. "Go now and be careful."

25

The gravel path crunched under her feet, so Micaela moved to the grassy edge where her footsteps would not be heard. The moon was shrouded in clouds and shed no light to guide her. Once through the garden, the path curved left, away from the house lights. Someday, she would like to see what appeared to be a magnificent historic landscape in sunlight. She switched on the flashlight and searched for the way to her car, alert for any unusual noise.

A shiver of energy trailed down her spine. She trained the tiny flashlight to either side of the path. On the right side of the path, beyond the dim beam, she made out the silhouette of headstones and a mausoleum. The family cemetery... *great, more spirits*. She started to do the sensible thing and turn away, when she heard a whisper. Not a human whisper, at least not a living one. Human voices travelled to the ear, this voice reverberated in her skull. Things just kept getting better.

She picked her way between the headstones and neatly trimmed shrubs to the locked gate of the mausoleum. A newer stone beside the crypt marked the passing, ten years prior, of Jeremiah Lowell. A half dozen small plaques and a larger one edged the doorway like apartment mailboxes outlined the gate.

On the left were the names of several young Lowells from the 1740's; none had survived past their fifth birthday. Above them was a larger plaque that read:

In Memoriam

Ethan Mather Lowell

Beloved Son and Patriot,

Born June 11, 1748. Lost in battle October 24, 1779.

On the right side of the crypt door were plaques for another Jeremiah Lowell, 1715- 1785, below that Prudence Mather Lowell, 1725-1781. The voice again, this time stronger and definitely female.

"My son."

"Prudence?"

"Micaela, you must care for my son."

Great, they knew her name. "Prudence, your Ethan is beyond my care. He is waiting for you in the Otherworld."

"My Ethan, so alone, so lost."

Was that it? She thought the Ethan in the house was her own long dead son. Is that why she clung to this spot? The plaque read In Memoriam. He had most likely died in some remote battle. His body never recovered, never buried with the family. Alone and lost.

"I'm not sure how I can help find your Ethan so you can find peace."

"I am beyond your assistance. Help him."

"I'll try." She could feel Prudence's departure.

Micaela drove back to Moran & Boru's Beacon Hill townhouse. She knew Ethan would handle the Hendricks problem. Prudence was another matter. Micaela never made promises she couldn't keep. But how to keep this one?

26

"You were in Boston two nights ago." Hendricks marched into Micaela's office. He'd be even more pissed if he knew Nikki was in the next office. When she had found out about the little side trip to Boston, Nikki had appointed herself Micaela's full-time bodyguard.

"We have an office there. That's not unusual." She placed the roses Ivan had sent her on the credenza behind her desk. She was glad he wasn't upset she had fallen asleep the other night. She slipped the card into her pocket; there was no need for anyone to know they were from him.

"Is that office in Lowell Manor?"

Keep it close to the truth. "You piqued my curiosity. I ran into Mr. Lowell and he invited me in."

"You were in there for a long time."

"Isn't Boston a little out of your jurisdiction, Detective Hendricks?"

"I also happened to be in the neighborhood. If you aren't involved, Ms. O'Brien, then you are in way over your head."

"So you have implied, but you've yet to supply any evidence."

"These are not your standard issue criminals, they don't leave evidence you'd recognize. Although… given your own history, maybe you might."

She swiveled around in her chair and fussed with the newest delivery of roses form Ivan. The delicate fragrance calmed her and helped her resist the urge to snap back at Hendricks. She turned back to face him. "Let's not dance around. You followed me to Boston, showed up at my office with no questions, just vague accusations. Aren't you concerned I could file a harassment complaint?"

"I'm sure you and your friend, Detective Suassuna, have the right connections."

"As I said, get to the point. I have a flight to Brussels and I haven't packed yet."

"There are things, creatures in this world that operate outside the rules of nature. They are pure evil, the Devil's servants." His eyes had taken on the glow that you see in 'true believers' that knew the difference between right and wrong. As they defined it.

She looked deeper for his aura and saw him flinch when she touched it. So that was it, he was a sensitive in major denial and deep in his own fear of himself. She felt a pang of sympathy.

"To begin with, Detective, being a New York City cop does not make you an expert on the rules of nature. And frankly, that crap about servants of the Devil has been overused. I get called one at least once a month simply because I work on Wall Street."

Hendricks cocked his head to the side. "Can you really be that naïve?"

Kat had called her naïve at the Met, too. Not that either opinion would keep her up at night.

"Not naïve, only logical and practical. I have never put stock in things I can't see or touch." What had Aine said about tasting the lie?

"For someone, who by all reports shouldn't be alive, you have very little faith."

"I do, just not the way you define it."

168

She had always believed in her own ability to create a plan and control the outcome, but she'd been groping around in the dark a lot these days.

He shook his head as if she were a misguided child and rose from the chair. "When the time comes, you know how to reach me."

She watched from the hallway until the elevator door closed behind him. Nikki joined her outside her office.

"He has some strange ideas and he's persistent," Micaela said.

"But a damn good cop."

27

Micaela dozed for the first hours of the flight to Brussels. When she woke, Rebecca Black Owl of Clovis Corp. stared at her from across the cream colored leather captain's chairs that were part of the plane's furnishings. She was petit, not more than five foot two, with a glistening sheet of black hair to her waist, arched cheekbones, and caramel eyes. Liam and Nikki lounged on chairs and sofas at the other end of the cabin with members of Rebecca's staff. A steward set a plate of warm croissants, jams, and mugs of coffee on the café table between them.

"You are well chosen, Micaela O'Brien, to be the one to lead us in this endeavor." Rebecca idly stirred her coffee.

"Not lead, organize." Micaela rested her palms on her thighs and stilled her breathing. There was something about this woman.

"You are too modest. There is an aura of power about you." Creases of a frown marked Rebecca's face. "But there is also a shadow at the edge of your mind. Someone seeks entry."

Rebecca's eyes became deep black drowning pools. Micaela felt herself pulled into the vortex; she pushed herself back from the edge.

"I'm not sure what that was about Ms. Black Owl, but don't try it again." What would she do if Rebecca did try again? Shoot her in psychic self-defense, an unlikely defense strategy in court.

"You are powerful when prepared. Whoever seeks to own you relies on the element of surprise. You must not let your guard down. Use your totem animal, the wolf, to protect you."

"My mother said the horse was one of mine, and you are saying the wolf is another. The old ways say I should have four totems, one for each gate of the circle. That is, if you believe that sort of thing."

"And you, what do you think?" Rebecca returned Micaela's gaze with pale brown eyes.

"Six months ago, I would have said all this mystical stuff was ridiculous." She really wanted to say bullshit, but good manners prevailed.

"And now?"

Micaela swiveled around and stared out the window. She struggled for the words to describe what she believed now. The first hint of sunrise over the mid-Atlantic glowed on the eastern horizon. Brussels and her real job lay beyond it. She turned back to Rebecca.

"Things have changed."

"So they have and so they will." Rebecca rose from her seat. "If you will excuse us. My staff and I have business matters to attend to before we land. I shall see you at the dinner reception tomorrow evening."

Between crossing time zones and a refueling stop in London, they landed at two in the afternoon the following day. Rebecca remained in the private rear compartment with her staff. Liam stayed behind to call Byrne Connor, who had remained in Dublin instead of attending the meeting; Liam would join them for dinner. A limousine, courtesy of Knowth, transported Micaela and Nikki to the Metropole Hotel.

In the lobby, Micaela set her carry-on and suit bag down; her laptop stayed over her shoulder. Rebecca Black Owl's push at her aura had fanned the embers of Micaela's powers. Mists garbed in nineteenth and twentieth century clothes floated past like tourists moving through Grand Central Station on a leisurely Sunday. Some of the phantasms turned to stare at her, amazed she could see them. Some tried to speak.

"This is magnificent. The lives that passed through here. The history."

Nikki's eyes roamed over the lobby. "That's not my particular area of expertise, but it is a beautiful building. A shame we're only here for two nights."

Micaela knew her friend scanned for human threats, not the high vaulted ceilings, curlicue brass-railed balconies, creamy marble, and oak panels. After what Nikki had revealed back in Bridewell, Micaela wondered if she could see the prior hotel guests as well.

A black silk suit and a gold nametag with a mouth pinched in disapproval skittered across the lobby on an intercept course. He snapped his fingers at a bellhop and pointed to Micaela and Nikki's luggage. A small muscle under his right eye twitched. The lobby specters jumped out of his way for him, except for a ghostly bellhop who dutifully reached for their bags, alongside his living counterpart.

She gave a small shake of her head and whispered, "Non, merci." The specter and the flesh and blood version both bowed and stepped away.

"Bonsoir, Mademoiselle O'Brien, welcome to the Metropole Hotel. I am Philippe, votre concierge." He beckoned to a bellhop. "Baron Vasilievich has arranged for all your needs while you are here."

"Merci, Philippe. This is Nikki Suassuna, my assistant. I requested an adjacent room for her. Has that been arranged?" Micaela had convinced Nikki that adjacent provided sufficient protection and adequate privacy.

172

Philippe blinked at Nikki as if one of the hotel wraiths had materialized.

"Ah oui, your assistant. All has been arranged as you requested, Mademoiselle. I will not disappoint you or Monsieur Le Baron."

To Philippe's chagrin and her amusement, Nikki carried her own luggage. Micaela was sure that the arsenal in Nikki's bags would have disturbed Philippe more than any breach in protocol. Micaela wondered how he would react to the silver and titanium machete tucked away in the bag.

The elevator opened on a semi-private hallway with only two doors and a fire exit. Philippe gestured to a plain white wooden entry across the hall. "Your assistant's quarters, Mademoiselle."

Nikki positioned herself beside Micaela by the massive oak door to the other suite. Philippe's disapproval was a not so quiet harrumph. Nikki gave him the cop face and made no move toward her own room. He opened the door to Micaela's suite.

"The Maurice Bejart Suite, my personal favorite."

Ivory and mauve colored furniture was arrayed under a cathedral ceiling that sheltered a lofted bedroom. A private balcony overlooked the heart of Brussels. Vase after vase of lilies, gardenias, and roses of various colors turned the living room into a conservatory. A Queen Anne table draped in Belgium lace held a tray of grapes, apples, and Brie and Roquefort cheeses. Beside it, a bottle of Cristal chilled in a gold pedestal bucket.

This wasn't the Spartan business suite she had booked. Ivan had gone over the top. While it was not professionally appropriate, it was sweet and romantic. She would have to think of a way to make it up to him. The idea brought a warmth to her face and a chill to her spine. She massaged her neck. Her nap on the flight over had made it stiff again. Next time she was at the airport, she would have to buy one of those neck pillows.

"Compliments of Baron Vasilievich and the Metropole Hotel." Philippe handed a delicate cut crystal flute to Micaela.

She wandered through the suite and caressed the soft petals, swam in the sweet scents and sipped the champagne. Her gaze drifted to the loft bedroom where the bellhop unpacked her bags. It, too, was filled with flowers. Ivan was near. She had to speak to him, touch him. The thought was over ridden by the image of a raven hovering over her head. It was so real Micaela had to fight the urge to fling her arms up and cover her head.

Fortunately Nikki's attention was elsewhere. She prowled the suite, not with a champagne glass, but with a small electronic device tucked in the palm of her hand. Her nostrils flared as she scanned the windows, second exit and patio door locks, even the closets.

Philippe tugged his cuffs. "If there is anything else, Mademoiselle, please do not hesitate to call on me. I have pledged to make your comfort my personal mission." The door clicked shut behind Philippe and the bellhop.

"The Baron is quite an admirer." Nikki passed the electronic device over the phone and internet connection wall jack.

"He does have a flair for the dramatic." Micaela could still feel his arms around her on her sofa, his lips. The memory ended there.

Nikki slipped the device into her purse. "The room is clean, no bugs. I'll recheck anytime housekeeping has been here. I'm not crazy about the patio door. The lock isn't the best."

Micaela stepped onto the patio and leaned over the railing. "We are on the thirtieth floor and the nearest patios are twenty feet away with smooth concrete in between. Someone would have to be a very determined daredevil, or fly to get here."

Nikki frowned. "Still, I'll take some additional precautions. I have a door alarm and motion detector in my bag."

"This high?"

"We need to consider every possibility." Nikki punched a code into the pad; a small light on the lock flashed green. She stood a moment longer, her lips moving in a silent chant. Her hands moved

174

across the seam of the sliding doors. Micaela didn't need to hear the words to know the meaning. Nikki was placing a ward on the door.

"What's the code?"

"No one is to know but me. I can shield myself, I'm not certain of everyone else."

"I guess I see your point. Is shielding a specific gift or can it be learned?" Was that what she had done on the plane?

"Most gifted people have the raw ability. I can work with you, or we can find someone."

"I'll take any help I can get." Micaela added it to her list of things to talk about with Una.

Nikki pulled her phone out. "Liam just texted. He'll meet us in the lobby in an hour. You shower. I'll finish here and then freshen up in the servant's quarters across the hall."

Dinner tomorrow night would be European haute cuisine. Balance was required, so the three of them had a relaxed dinner of burgers, fries, and diet cokes at a local American bistro.

Afterwards, they returned to the hotel's bar. An intense young man in a tuxedo sat at a grand piano lost in his own admiration of his talent. The wraiths in the lobby lingered beside the piano and sipped vaporous brandy. Some seemed to snicker and mock the poor pianist. Thankfully none of the auras of the living were visible. She splurged and nursed an Armagnac.

Liam rested his whiskey on the table. He had taken his hair out of the tail and it cascaded over his shoulders. "The meeting will go fine tomorrow, 'Caela."

"How did you know that's what I was thinking?"

Nikki shook her head. "It's easy. All you think about is work."

"This financing is more involved than anything I've done. On top of it, I'm not dealing with the principals and only some of them will be at the dinner. It makes it hard to get a read on the players."

"Each representative is well attuned to the wishes of their… employers," he said.

"Micaela, it's just the first read through of the documents. How many times have you done this before? " Nikki asked. "And afterwards, you get to play hostess and wine and dine everyone at Villa Lorraine."

"Sounds like more fun than I should be allowed to have." Micaela's smile faded when over Liam's shoulder, she watched Kat walk in on Sergei's arm. She wore a metallic gold satin dress with a deep neckline. Her black hair was in a tight French braid that highlighted the neckline. They chose a small nearby table. Sergei's fingers trailed down Kat's arms.

Liam shifted position so he had a better view. "It appears Sergei has taken on some additional duties."

If Kat was here, maybe Ivan was nearby. She stifled a yawn and stood. "I think I'll call it a night."

Liam rose. "Rebecca's people invited us to join them at a jazz bar. You could use a little real fun. Won't you come?"

"Go on without me. I'm going upstairs and ordering some strong coffee. I want to go over the documents one more time before tomorrow."

Nikki moved closer to Micaela and whispered, "Are you sure? I can stay here with you."

"I'll be fine. You checked everything, twice, and I promise I'll be a good girl and lock the door. Go have some fun."

As they passed Kat, she smiled up at them. The room temperature dropped ten degrees.

"I do hope you will enjoy your brief stay in Brussels, Ms. O'Brien. You should get out while you're here, the night life is amazing."

"Perhaps after our work is done," she said.

Kat's gaze slid over Liam, lingering on his crotch. "We haven't had a chance to speak privately, Liam. Do you still serve Lord Connor as thoroughly?"

Micaela felt the heat explode off Liam. She stole a glance at his face. His eyes were goldenrod yellow. Out of some instinct, she angled her body a little toward him, fitting the curve of her hip to his side. She laid her hand over his hand and began to stroke his palm with her thumb. She felt his temperature drop as he regained control.

He smiled at Kat, matching ice for ice. "Not as completely as you serve Baron Ivan."

So, Kat slept with Ivan. Micaela's stomach clenched. "Shall I see you tomorrow Kat, or will the Baron be attending?"

"The Baron? I was under the impression that you were on more familiar terms. No, he will not be there. He is detained by other matters."

"Give him my regards. Tell him I would be pleased to review the results of the meeting with him later." She relaxed her guard and opened the door a little to see if she could read Kat.

Kat's composure had cracked and her aura shivered. It was a flash of lemons, bright yellow and sour in a deep green whirlpool. Interesting, thought Micaela.

"I shall brief him thoroughly after the meeting," she purred.

"I'm sure you will." Micaela smiled, although she knew it didn't reach her eyes. "Kat, Sergei, I hope you have a lovely evening."

As they walked out she whispered to Liam, "Charming, isn't she?"

"Oh, you'll get used to her." His eyes sparkled grass green. He still had her hand. "Are you sure, you don't want to join us for some of that amazing nightlife? You know, all work and no play."

"As tempting as it is, I don't think I'd be much fun, too much to do before tomorrow."

"If you change your mind, one of us will come for you." He let go of her hand. She could still feel its warmth as he and Nikki walked across the lobby. A female ghost dressed in hundred-year-old evening attire, her face clearly puzzled, looked from Liam to Micaela.

177

Micaela glanced back as she headed for the elevators. As much as she would like, she couldn't go out tonight; she needed to be ready for tomorrow.

28

Philippe poured coffee into a delicate porcelain cup. "Your café, Mademoiselle. I have taken the liberty of including a selection of our finest pastries." Micaela had waved off the creamer, no need to blunt the caffeine.

She started in the chair by the fire but found it difficult to concentrate, so she shifted to the desk, with even less success. She stretched out on the sofa but the restlessness won out and she paced the room, document in hand. The evening had gone fine until Kat had arrived. Liam had never talked about women, not that it was any of her business. Liam was a good man; Kat was a bitch. But the last Micaela had checked that wasn't lethal or an impediment to sexual attraction. She'd made her share of bad choices. The thought of Kat in both Liam and Ivan's beds chilled her. She pushed the éclair aside.

Two cups of coffee later, Micaela had jotted notes in the margin of the Articles of Incorporation and moved onto the Private Placement Memorandum. A pulse of electricity travelled down her spine; she felt like she was being watched. She roamed the suite, even looking in the closets. Nothing. She had no idea how to disarm the alarm or counteract the ward to check the balcony. She sent Nikki a text that the suite was stuffy and asking her how to open the damn door. She shielded her eyes and peered out onto the patio. A shadow vanished over the railing. *This is nuts, next I'll be checking under the bed for the boogie man.*

Micaela packed up for the night and placed her cell phone on the night table in case Ivan called. She slipped out of her clothes and crawled into the king size bed. The cerulean silk sheets brushed against her skin, like the light caress of a lover. She extended her body diagonally to fill the empty space.

She didn't know how long she had been asleep when a voice woke her. At least she felt awake. The bedside alarm clock said it was two A.M. Micaela heard the voice again, rose and pulled on her black silk wrap. She peeked over the loft railings; the living room was empty. But he was here somewhere, she could feel him.

"Ivan? Is that you? What are you doing here? Did Philippe let you in?" Her eyes were drawn toward the patio. He waited on the other side of the open doors. This must be a dream, she thought, but it feels real enough. Ivan smiled at her; his blue eyes glowed and sparked with the Northern Lights. He held his hand out to her.

"You are a difficult one to reach, Mischa, but I enjoy a challenge. What did you think of the flowers?"

"They are beautiful." She felt light, floating outside herself. A warm breeze, more June than early March, fluttered the edges of her robe.

Ivan took her hand, his smile widened. She moved closer. She ached to be in his arms. He understood her, respected her, and desired her. There was no point in denying it, she was attracted to him. To hell with professional rules. His hand cupped her face. She closed her eyes. His lips brushed hers and moved on to her cheek and her neck. She reached up and tangled her fingers in his hair, a sigh whispered from her lips. He wore nothing under his jacket. She slid one hand onto his pale perfect chest. Her pulse raced as he loosened the tie of her silk wrap and trailed one hand down her ribs to her hip. His other hand pushed the robe off her shoulder and traced a line around the curve of her breast. His thumb brushed her already hard nipple. Her heart pounded. She gasped and sucked in the warm night air.

Something was wrong. It was a warm night. She knew how a man's touch should feel. And this was not it. She released his hair and coiled her hand around his neck. His skin was cold. Her other hand was at the center of his chest. It was still and silent where there should have been the matched drumming of his heart. His teeth grazed the skin on her neck. A memory from that evening on her couch surfaced. Seduction became a threat.

When she was young and lay in her bed terrified by the visions, she had found a way to protect herself. Now, she called up that same imaginary castle with its round gray towers and high stone walls. She ran across that same drawbridge over the moat. Her guardian was still there. He closed the gates behind her and signaled the archers. Ivan was close behind.

"No, I won't." She pushed Ivan away. "You can't."

"I have had you before and I will again." Ivan's smile became a snarl. "You must understand. Our powers… we are destined to be together. My Elena, you have come back to me."

"I am not your Elena. Not now, not ever."

A bell reverberated in the distance.

"You will change your mind. Until then, Mischa." He vanished over the side of the castle wall. She ran to the edge expecting to see him sprawled on the ground below, but he was gone.

Micaela heard the ringing again and struggled to understand the sound. She blinked, awakening from a dream. She stood on the balcony of a hotel, not a castle, and the ringing she heard was the phone. She ran to answer it.

"Are you okay?" Nikki's voice sounded so far away.

"I'm fine." She struggled to steady her voice.

"You don't sound fine, we'll be right there."

"Who's we?" She tried to clear her head.

181

"Me and Liam." Nikki's voice became muffled; she must have covered the speaker on the phone. Micaela could hear her whisper to someone, "The ward's been breached."

"Nikki, you don't need to come over. I'm fine." Micaela said. But there was silence on the other end of the line. She returned the receiver to its cradle, and then ran her fingers through her hair. She had to find her crane bag before Nikki and Liam arrived. It would chase away the fog in her head.

On the floor by the phone was her briefcase; she rummaged through it looking for her crane bag. It wasn't in there. She searched the suite until she spotted her makeup kit on the bathroom vanity. She pulled the velvet pouch out of the kit and draped the crane bag around her neck. While the panic did not disappear, it eased. She stared out at the empty balcony and re-tied her robe.

Pounding on the door. Micaela took a deep breath and opened it. She put on her brightest smile and tucked her still trembling hands into the pockets of her robe.

"So what brings you here at…" she looked at the clock on the mantel, "three in the morning?"

"When I saw your text about unlocking the patio door, I called. You sounded strange." Nikki headed straight for the open patio door and looked over the balcony edge.

Liam twisted Micaela's head in his hands. This was bad. He hadn't noticed that all she wore was a half-closed robe.

"I told you, I'm fine." She pulled away. His hands felt hot. "What is your problem?"

"Rebecca said you were in danger. We came back as fast as we could." The muscles in his face seemed to flow over the bones, his black pupils imbedded in amber irises. He moved through the suite, tense and alert. His eyes seemed to search for anything he could tear apart.

Nikki stood in the open patio door. "How did you get this open? How did you get past the ward?"

"It was open when I got up. Maybe it malfunctioned."

182

"Bullshit, I checked the lock three times, and wards don't malfunction."

"I'm fine, you're both overreacting. Now if you don't mind I have a meeting starting in five hours and sleep would be useful right now."

Liam yanked a lily from a vase. "Who sent these?"

"Baron Vasilievich." Micaela saw the flowers for what they were. "A little funereal, huh?"

A low rumble came from Liam's throat. "We're not leaving you alone."

"He's right. I shouldn't have left you alone in the first place." Nikki pulled her Glock out of her shoulder holster; a machete appeared from her duffel bag.

How did Micaela explain what she had experienced? It had to be a vision. Ivan had been so cold and lifeless, a dead man. Perhaps it was meant to tell her that he was in danger, the target of whoever had killed François. Yet, she was the one who had felt threatened by Ivan. Then again, if it had been a vision, why had Nikki looked over the balcony? Nothing made sense.

Liam pulled the chair in front of the patio door and sat in it. Nikki held the Glock at her side as she climbed the stairs to the loft. The machete was in a sheath on the outside of her left boot.

"I'm bunking with you. Think of it as one of those pajama parties in high school."

Micaela drew her wrap tighter. Silk wasn't very warm but even flannel wouldn't rid her of the chill that settled in her bones. Pajama parties in the Ashwood Preparatory School for Girls were never like this.

29

"Before we adjourn for the day, I think we should address the issue of reallocation of shareholder interest should someone resign." This came from Erik VanHouten, representative for the South African member, Thulamela Corp. Micaela had to look down the table to be sure he had spoken or that he was still there. He hadn't spoken all day.

"And what is your concern?" she asked.

"The documents as currently written require that shares be made available first to new members. That would usurp the rights and priorities of the current member. We believe that they should be offered to existing members before we even consider who might make an acceptable new member."

Micaela watched the faces of the other nine people at the table, especially Connie, representing the newest member, First Colony. Good thing Ethan got in when he did. These ten were the representatives of the principal investors, authorized to act in their employers' interests. A simple majority would bind the group. She tried to gauge their reaction to what to all outward appearance was a power play. The only reaction was a slight lift of an eyebrow by Liam.

Kat leaned forward, her French manicured nails laced before her on the oak conference table. "That is an interesting and important issue, Erik. Does Heitsi-eibib, your employer, have a proposal that he wishes you to submit?"

Erik circled the table and handed out copies of a six-page memo delineating changes to the basic document. Micaela reached for the crystal pitcher and refilled her water glass. She sipped water as she scanned through the suggested revision. *Fascinating*. Buried in all the legalese was the auction of shares to existing owners; winner take all. There was no mention of distribution among multiple owners or new members, solicited or unsolicited.

She set her water down and closed the folder. "Quite detailed. I'm certain everyone will need time to study it. I suggest we put this at the top of the next agenda." Micaela flipped her planner open. "The revised schedule calls for a meeting in one month in Ottawa to be hosted by Tsonoqua of the Glenrose Company. Does that date still work for everyone?"

Heads nodded.

"My office will have the revised documents to you in the next week, excluding the Thulamela Corp. proposal, which will require separate discussion. I want to thank everyone for their cooperation today. We have accomplished a lot. That said, I shall see everyone at dinner."

She walked from the building, Nikki at her side. She could feel Liam behind her. She had asked them to be discrete and they were trying. Sort of. Connie caught up with her in the lobby.

"Well that was fascinating. I shall brief Mr. Lowell. Do you think that this idea originated with Thulamela? A power grab doesn't seem to be their style."

"I don't know them well enough to judge." What she had seen was Kat lay her hand over Erik's as he placed the memo in front of her. Was Erik yet another of Kat's conquests?

"We have two weeks to prepare a response." Connie shook her hand. "It's so nice to see you again, Ms. O'Brien. Mr. Lowell and

I shall see you at dinner. I must say, you made quite an impression on him."

"Really?"

"Mr. Lowell can be stoic. I hope you visit again… without your police escort, of course." Connie slid into a waiting limousine. "May I offer you a ride?"

Micaela glanced at Liam and Nikki. "Thank you, but I think we'll walk."

The normal work day in Brussels had not ended, and the crisp March air had deterred all but the hardy, so few others were on the street with them. The meeting had ended earlier than normal. She had tonight's dinner to dress for and the events of the day to digest before seeing the group again. Ivan would be there. Her dream or vision, whatever it was, nagged at her. Liam and Nikki's responses were equally troubling. She hadn't told them any details about Ivan on the balcony, but they had reacted as if they had witnessed the event. Nikki had sat outside the conference room door all day, while Liam had sat at the far corner of the table. He'd spent the meeting twirling his pen, eyes watchful above shoulders tensed and ready to move. Her crane bag was still looped around her neck. She had tucked it between her cleavage and snug against the underwire. Just in case, she had decided she would add the lunula and disc earrings for insurance before leaving for the restaurant.

The private dining room of white and gold at Villa Lorraine glowed in the flicker of dozens of candles. In black satin slacks, a pale gray silk blouse and a smoke gray short-waist jacket with black bead trim on the lapels and cuffs, she was one of two women, the other being Nikki, not in a full length gown with a plunging neckline. But then, perception was critical. Tonight she was all business. As she mingled, she overheard bits of remembrances and stories that

186

sounded more like the chatter of a family reunion than a professional gathering.

The nine investors came from every part of the globe and represented some of the oldest bloodlines of their countries. Most of the investors were present, except for Byrne Connor and Liao Sungling of Japan, who was prevented from attending by injuries incurred in the crash of her helicopter.

Ethan appeared beside Micaela. "I want to thank you, Micaela. If it wasn't for you, I might have sat this one out."

"It is off to an interesting start." Right now, she wouldn't mind sitting this one out, preferably on a warm Caribbean beach.

"When you put such a collection of egos in one room things can get interesting. Myself excluded, of course."

"Everyone seems to be playing nice."

"They've had years of practice, but you're smarter than that. Look deeper." Ethan passed her a mineral water, and then wandered over to Henri Montbelliard and his new assistant, Monica LaPrete.

She remembered François' reaction at the Met when he had felt her accidental touch. She didn't dare reach out now to explore the auras in the room. She wasn't sure she had enough control to sort one from the other, anyway. So she watched, just like every other normal person. *Ha!*

Ethan was right. She hadn't been paying attention. The cordiality that marked the evening was part of a dance. Ethan and Liam strolled between clusters of guests. They spoke to Montbelliard, who was polite and formal. Ivan moved from one group to the other, but his body language changed with each encounter. It became very clear who his allies were, and that included Heitsi-eibib from Thulamela Corp.

Her breath caught in her throat. Framed in the open patio door and the moonlight beyond, Ivan looked more handsome than usual. He wore his hair loose in a white gold sheet down the back of his brown frock coat. A cream colored silk shirt with a high collar framed his jaw. He hadn't had any shirt on last night. His chest made been muscled and marble smooth under her hands. She knew she shouldn't be alone with him, but the memory of the brush of his lips on hers pulled at things lower in her body. Maybe just a minute on the patio. The crane bag vibrated on her chest. That other memory, the one that had sent her fleeing into her psychic castle, floated before her eyes unseen by anyone else, but through it she could still see his broad shoulders and narrow waist. The waist with the thin line of downy hair that led lower. A trail to be followed.

"Micaela, it's not polite to stare." Nikki touched her elbow.

"Was I?" Ivan looked over at her.

Micaela yanked her gaze away.

Across the room, Sergei whispered in Kat's ear. Sergei's smirk and the press of Kat's hip against his groin broadcast their plans. She slipped him a key. He kissed her on the cheek; his hand brushed her breast as he turned to leave. He would not be staying for dinner, but dessert seemed to be on his menu.

The conversation continued over dinner; each representative sat beside their employer, if they were available. The rest of the guests were arrayed in a single rectangle that mirrored the earlier conference table, with one exception. Ivan sat to Micaela's right, although that was not the arrangement she had given to the banquet manager. Kat sat on his right, laying her hand on his arm at every occasion. You could draw alliances by looking at a seating chart.

Micaela ended the evening with the usual thank you speech and toasts. In the crush of goodnights, she felt his presence before she saw him. *Ivan.*

"You are not your energetic self tonight, Mischa." He had slipped his hand under the back of her jacket. His hand was hot, his voice a warm current flowing over her.

"I'm fine."

"When is the last time you took a vacation?"

Did a week hiding at her grandmother's count? She didn't think so. "Maybe after AGF is done."

"I have a villa on the Black Sea. It is not the Caribbean, but I would be honored if you would be my guest. The beach is lovely, my staff the best, and your privacy guaranteed, no intrusive phone calls. I can even turn off internet access. We could sit at the edge of the sea and count stars." His fingers played at the base of her spine beneath her silk blouse and out of view.

"I'll keep it in mind, thank you." She fought off the shiver that ran through her body.

He would be there. Did she want him to be? His breath whispered across her neck. She'd had a vision of him last night as something cold and lifeless, yet here he was very vital, very alive. Her pulse accelerated as her hand slid back to brush his thigh. The lunula began to heat up.

Ethan burst through the crowd and threw his arm across Ivan's shoulder like a long lost fraternity brother. Kat's look of horror was priceless. Rebecca Black Owl tapped Liam on the arm. A crooked smirk formed on his face. It was a shame cameras were prohibited under the rules set by the investors.

Ethan slapped Ivan on the back. "Baron Vasilievich, I haven't had the chance to speak to you tonight. I'd like to hear about your Black Sea development project, First Colony is considering a similar project near Bangor. I'm thinking it has timeshare potential." Ethan steered Ivan toward the veranda.

After a nightcap, a double espresso, Micaela stood at the edge of the Sonian Forest with Liam, Nikki, and Connie, and savored the fresh air and open space. "It's such a nice evening, can we walk to the hotel?"

"I could use the exercise." Liam fell in alongside her while Nikki and Connie walked ahead. Micaela knew Nikki would use the time to learn more about Ethan.

The Sonian was more primitive than Central Park. In times past, wild predators had roamed the forest. The bears and wolves had been hunted to extinction at the beginning of the nineteenth century, but others creatures still called it home. They followed the path into the forest; the only light was the crescent moon and the occasional low voltage path light. Micaela smelled the spring earth, that combination of last fall's decay and the fresh new growth pushing through the soft soil. Far from the streets that flanked the forest, she could hear the night sounds, the rub of branches in the breeze, the scratching of small rodents, the soft hoot of an owl. She allowed her senses to spread out. She found the soft footfall of the deer and wild boar that still wandered beneath the old growth beeches and oaks.

The path turned and the wind now blew in her face. She caught a whiff of a musky animal scent nearby. The modern part of her mind didn't recognize it, but from somewhere deep inside came the answer: large cat and wild canine. She shook it off. The city of Brussels would not allow large predators to roam in a public park. Distracted by the scents and sounds in the darkness, Micaela didn't see the tree root. Liam grabbed her arm before she embarrassed herself and ruined the silk.

"Be careful, 'Caela. Not much light on the path." His eyes glowed amber and she could feel the tension and flow of muscle under his jacket.

They entered a small clearing ringed by a low stone wall that was topped by an ornate cast iron rail. Scattered benches hewn from oaks provided a resting spot. She sat down and stared up at the night sky. A moment of peace.

A twig snapped to her right. A prickle of energy ran over her skin, someone's aura. They were being watched, followed. She didn't dare turn in the direction of the sound, but she could search with other senses. She rose as if to leave, but positioned herself in the direction of the noise. She closed her eyes, relaxed and reached out with her mind. Living fur, not clothing. Perfume. A familiar scent.

190

A snarling shadow leapt through the air. Liam shoved her to ground. She struggled to her feet. More dark figures vaulted over the stone wall. One grabbed her around the waist. She looked down. A clawed limb lifted her off her feet. An upright animal, it carried her toward the forest.

"Liam!" Her scream was silenced by a claw clamped across her face. She felt this before on the mountain with Reece.

Liam danced around the beast, a crouching hunter. Low sounds rolled from his throat. The beast mirrored his movements as its grip tightened on Micaela, crushing her ribs. When Liam lunged, it tossed her away like an old toy. Pain jolted through her back as she hit the metal railing and tumbled over the fence. Face down on the ground, she struggled to get up on all fours. Her chest burned and drawing breath made it worse. She had to stand and climb over the wall. Ahead of her, two figures wrestled on the ground.

Her vision was blurred and the light was dim, but she could make out the silhouettes of Nikki and Connie. One of Nikki's arms was extended, a pistol gripped in her hands. *There didn't seem to be enough light get a shot off.* The other arm rested on Connie, who was crouched low. She would not hide while her friends fought.

A figure moved through the darkness that for a moment she thought was Kat. Was she here to help? Was Ivan with her? In the halo of a lantern, she saw Liam underneath a wolf-like figure. The wolf raised its head, teeth bared, poised to go for Liam's throat.

Fury gripped her. She grabbed a broken piece of the metal railing and swung, her own injury forgotten in the moment. It smashed into the back of the wolf's head. Stunned, it faltered. Liam pivoted, rolled over the beast, and pinned it to the ground.

Another wolf slammed into her. Micaela saw red eyes and then stars. She dragged herself to her feet. The right side of her head throbbed. She tried to look around but it hurt to move her head. They needed help. The street couldn't be too far, the problem was… which direction? She wiped the blood out of her eyes with her sleeve.

Micaela saw Connie explode from her crouch into the darkness of the forest. Snarls and growls filled the air, the yelp of an injured animal. Where had they come from? The shadow of a large beast raced toward her. Whether it was the same one didn't matter. She needed a weapon. She'd left her H&K behind, concerned what her dinner guests would think. *Dumb idea.*

She stumbled back into a tree trunk. She ran her hand over the bark. It was an oak. Not a weapon, but at least a barrier. It would have to do. She put the ancient tree between her and the wolf. It helped her stay on her feet and plan her next move.

She probed the gash in head and could swear she felt bone. Nausea threatened to overtake her as she slid to her knees. Liam, Nikki, and Connie were out there fighting for their lives. She couldn't abandon them, she had to do something. She was the daughter of Donnachadh and Maura O'Brien. She had her voice, damn it, she had her powers. She couldn't die, not now, not like this.

"Please, help. Ma, Da, Grandma. Oh Goddess, someone help us. " She reached into her torn blouse and grabbed hold of her crane bag. She tried to yell but could manage only a whisper into the bark. She braced for the attack. It would be over soon.

The lunula still safe around her neck grew hot, hotter than that night after the Kirov. A loud crack from above, then a soft wet sound and a whine. Micaela waited for the teeth and claws of the beast. Nothing happened.

She could hear the battle beyond her, on the other side of the tree. Seconds passed like an eternity until she crawled toward the base of the tree, knowing but not believing what she would find. Her hand found fur, warm and wet. She raised her hand to her nose. The metallic odor, the slick ooze… she remembered François' suite, his body. Blood. She continued to search in the darkness until she found what she had heard. A large limb had split in two and fallen. Part of it had crushed the beast's skull; the other had impaled it. It was no longer a threat.

"Thank you," she whispered to the air.

192

She pulled herself up with the fallen branch for support. It sank further into the body of the beast. The soft squishing made the dizziness worse and her stomach churn. Nausea and blinding pain followed. Her ribs ached, breathing was hard. She reached for the tree trunk, but instead she stumbled over the limp body below. Her leg twisted at an impossible angle. Pain shot into her hip and back, shocking her mind into focus. She slipped; her hands fell onto the beast. The fur was gone. Oh Goddess, it was flesh. It was human.

A shot rang out. Nikki called Liam's name. Again, Micaela found herself on the ground, Liam arched over her, shielding her body. At least she thought it was him. He seemed bigger, he smelled different. She must be in bad shape; she couldn't make out his arms or legs. Fear knotted her stomach. What if it was one of the beasts above her? She kicked at the figure above her with her good leg and tried to crawl away. She scrambled on all fours a few feet until her leg collapsed out from under her.

As the darkness enveloped her, she heard Liam tell Nikki to carry Connie, he would carry Micaela. How would she explain to Ethan that she had gotten Connie hurt?

She drifted in and out, waking once to the rumbling of a familiar engine. *Da? Where am I? It's so dark on the plane. I can't see.* She dreamed of the red and black rain again. Her eyes opened to green and yellow eyes.

"Grady? What are you doing here?"

"'Caela, hang on. Please don't leave."

"Da, but you said I should go with him. Why can't you and Ma come?" A hand in hers, warm, filled with light. She struggled to the surface. The eyes above her were her life raft.

"Do not come for her, Dagda. I have served you well. My family has served you well. Do not punish her. It was I who did not protect. My failings."

193

The darkness came again. From the depths of it, she could hear her mother.

"Micaela, my daughter." Maura stood before her, her red hair just as Micaela remembered.

"Mother, I have missed you." She embraced her.

"You cannot stay." Her mother's voice was firm.

"But it hurts so much. I don't want to go back." If she could just walk down that road with her mother, it would be easier, better. Over the greenest ridge she had ever seen peeked the towers of her castle. She would be safe there.

"You must return. You have much to do."

"Why me?"

"It has been our place since the beginning of time to follow the path. An now is more urgent. The time approaches."

Behind her mother, Micaela saw the shimmer of those who had come before. She was them and they were her, if only she said yes.

A loud scream pulled her back. She opened her eyes a slit. Liam, that was who it was, had his lips pressed to hers. What a strange time to kiss her. She choked and tried to push him off.

"You're breathing. Thank the gods. 'Caela, I thought you'd gone on." He was crying.   "What's that noise?" It sounded like the whine of a dying animal.

"The plane is landing on Byrne's airstrip. We're in Ireland. Med techs are waiting. Just hold on."

Why did he say they were in Ireland? She was still at dinner, standing on the veranda of the restaurant. The waiter brought foie gras. The plate was a pool of blood. Ivan offered her a glass of red liquid. She started to raise it to her lips. It smelled like Francois' hotel suite. The chalice crashed to the floor.

She opened her eyes again and inched her gaze to the side. Nikki sat beside her and gripped the hand that Liam did not hold. Long bloody stripes ran down her face. She had been clawed by something. The room jolted and Micaela's body screamed in rebellion. She was on a plane, she remembered now. Micaela squeezed Liam's hand. Not again.

She screamed. "It's going to blow up. We have to get everyone off. I won't leave without everyone this time."

30

Murmurs carried on the wind from far away. One voice, Liam's, made its way to Micaela, an anchor to the now. Every lurch and twitch brought nausea that swirled through her. Pain tore from her shoulder to her mouth where it exited as a moan. He had begged her not to leave and she couldn't let him down. When she dared crack a slit in her eyelids her only view was a vaulted stone ceiling where flickering candles and shadows danced. A pinch in her left arm and then no pain.

"Am I dead?" she croaked out the words. Could anyone hear her?

"No, and I won't allow that to happen." A face appeared over her, long black hair loose and wavy and storm gray eyes.

She'd seen that face before. "Where?"

"Knowth Manor. I'm Byrne Connor. Your injuries were severe. We've given you morphine for the pain. We are going to have you stitched up. What you need to do now is rest."

"Liam?" She couldn't turn her head.

"I'm right here."

"Is everyone else all right?"

"Everyone's fine. Sleep now." He held her hand as they wheeled her through a door. The vaulted ceiling was replaced by fluorescent lights and stainless steel. The last words she heard were, "She's lost a lot of blood."

She didn't know how long she faded in and out. In her dreams, she wandered over green fields, sailed tall masted ships on the Irish Sea, and drank mead and sang with men and women in leather breeches. Ivan appeared in her dreams, but he was so far away. Every time she opened her eyes, either Liam or the man with the gray eyes sat by her bed. Sometimes an older woman hummed as she painted her shoulder and wrapped it in canvas. Eventually she remembered the other man was Byrne. Liam worked for him. She kept thinking she had met him before. Must be the drugs.

She woke to find Liam sitting in his usual place, dozing. Her stomach growled.

"Got anything to eat around here?" She was rewarded with a blinding grin.

"Absolutely." He reached up and actually pulled one of those cords you see in the movies. Moments later, a round face crowned by snow white curls with a smile almost as wide as Liam's came in. It was the humming painter.

"Fae, Ms. O'Brien is hungry."

"I'll fetch some broth. Then I'll change the poultice on your shoulder, Miss."

Micaela tried to sit up. "Fae, if it's no trouble, could you include something that requires chewing? I want to feel like I've eaten."

Fae curtsied and dashed from the room.

"How do you feel, 'Caela?" he asked.

"All things considered… I'm alive." She made another attempt to sit up.

"Grab my elbow and I'll lift you." He leaned over her, his lips brushed her forehead as he pulled the pillows into place.

She wanted to hug him, thank him, and hold him. She would as soon as she didn't feel like she'd been trampled by a herd of elephants. She finished the scone and half the broth that Fae had

197

brought. It was amazing the difference a little bit of real food made. Liam beamed with pride at every bite Micaela took.

"How long have I been out?" she asked.

"A little over three days."

"Does my grandmother know?"

"Byrne spoke to her that first night. We keep her updated."

"I want to call her." She looked at the clock. Nine A.M. It would be four in the morning in Bridewell. She would call later.

"I sent word to the deal team. I also called your office. Your assistant, Judy, is a tough one. She was ready to jump on the next plane. It took some work to convince her to stay put." He rolled his shoulders and the crack was audible. Micaela wondered how long he had been sitting in that chair.

"Judy worries too much. How's Connie? I remember seeing her, she looked pretty bad. I think I saw Nikki, too." She rubbed her temple as if the massage would break the mental logjam. "So much is lost."

"Connie's fine. Ethan is taking care of her. They're back at Lowell Manor. She's bugging him to let her go back to work. Renee is with her."

"Renee?"

"Her partner." He started to draw the heavy window drapes.

She waved him off. "Leave them open. It's nice to be able to see the sky."

Liam pushed them all the way back. He squeezed her hand and took the tray of near empty dishes.

"Before you go." She felt foolish asking. "That night in Brussels, I had some jewelry and…."

"Your crane bag, lunula and earrings. Fae has them. She got as much of the blood out of the crane bag as possible. I'll have her bring them to you." He pulled the door closed behind him.

Micaela looked around the room. It was a page from history. The furniture was large and oak. The bed was a four-poster with a square framed canopy. At first, she thought it was Elizabethan, but it was much older. The drapes were deep green velvet. Oriental carpets covered the floors. She peered over the edge at the moveable steps required to get in and out. Not a problem. She wouldn't be jumping up for a midnight snack in the near future.

Fae came in with a gold tray draped with linen. She set it down on the bed and uncovered the bag and the jewelry. Micaela managed to put in the earrings by slowly dipping her head to the side. Her shoulder screamed in pain when she raised the lunula toward her neck.

"Fae, would you help?"

She looped the lunula around Micaela's neck. Micaela handed her the crane bag.

"I am honored, Miss." She gently slipped the cord over Micaela's head. Then she took Micaela's hands and pressed her forehead to them.

"Fae, after all you've done for me."

"Oh no, dear, you're The O'Brien."

Fae busied the staff with acquiring clothes for the unexpected guests. Mid-afternoon, she came in and gently removed the bandages from Micaela's shoulder, cleaned the wound with warm water and spread a paste over the area. Micaela had to sneak a peek. What had reportedly been a serious injury now resembled a jagged red slash on her skin. She asked for a mirror and watched as Fae repeated the process on her scalp.

"What's in your poultice, Fae?" she asked.

"Nothing that your grandmother wouldn't approve of and you haven't heard of." Fae set the bowl containing the mixture on Micaela's lap. She hoped it wasn't a quiz; she didn't want to show her ignorance. She had a lot of catching up to do.

"I smell lavender, verbena, and comfrey." The scents drifted through memory to a little girl in Una's kitchen peering into her mother's bowl. "And rose hip. Is it the moss that makes it so green?"

199

"'Tis. With a healthy dose of ground rowan and willow to help the healing." Fae patted Micaela's hand. "Rest now child, it's still the best medicine."

While Micaela followed orders and rested, Byrne sent someone to Brussels to retrieve their belongings and check them out of the hotel. With each day that passed, she regained her strength. He stopped by every evening to check in and sit with her. They sat and talked about business and world events like two old friends; he never pressed her for details of the attack. She lay awake before dawn of the fourth day when Byrne tapped on her door.

"I saw your light on. Are you all right, Micaela?"

"Bad dream." She sat in the window seat, in borrowed sweatpants and a Galway College sweatshirt. She had pulled her legs to her chest.

"May I join you?"

It was four in the morning and he was dressed in black khakis, loafers and a gray polo shirt the same color as his eyes. Micaela had already figured out this was Byrne's version of comfortable clothes.

"You are a strong, young woman, but you are not invincible. After what you went through, this kind of thing is to be expected."

"It resurrected an old nightmare that I haven't had in years. When I think about it I can see why."

"Want to talk?" His gaze was steady but gentle.

"I don't know how much you know, but when I was thirteen my parents were killed. The private plane they were on exploded over a farm north of Dublin. I was the only survivor."

"I remember. The farm is just twenty kilometers from here. It must have been a terrible time for you."

"In so many ways. I still don't recall details of the accident and right after it. A farmer found me wandering in his fields. The Garda knew it was me because my passport was in the back pocket of my jeans. I hardly spoke for days, except to talk about the gray angel and the red rain."

200

"The human mind has an amazing capacity to protect itself." He stared out the leaded glass window.

"I stopped seeing a counselor who insisted that I could eventually regain the memories. I decided forgetting was a good thing. It took years but that nightmare went away, until now. I think it's because of the attack and the plane ride." And let's not forget, Micaela thought, the conversation with her mother's spirit.

"What happens in the dream?"

"I'm falling and this gray angel, the one I told the counselor about, swoops in and grabs me. It's dark and the air burns my nose. All around me, big raindrops are coming down. I tuck my head into the angel's wings because the rain is red and I don't want to get any on me. I try to see what the angel looks like. That's when I wake up."

"Doesn't sound so terrible… having an angel save you."

"No, but he could only save me." She turned toward the window not wanting Byrne to see the tears that trickled down her cheeks. The seat cushion shifted slightly as he moved closer.

"I know that if it was a choice between saving themselves or you, that's the way they would have wanted it. It's the choice any parent would make." He laid his hand on the side of her head.

The tears flowed faster. "Why couldn't the angel save all of us? Listen to me. I'm talking like this angel was really there."

"Well, if the angel or whatever it was had really been there, he might not have been strong enough to save everyone." Byrne leaned back, his knees up in a mirror image to hers.

"This is just silly talk. I don't know what happened or why I was the Miracle Child of the Moors."

"The moors?"

"Some reporter made it up and the rest jumped on it. Sounded more romantic, more Wuthering Heights, than the Miracle Child of the Cow Pasture."

He laughed; it was a nice laugh.

"Get back to bed and stay there until at least noon." He squinted in an attempt at stern, though the twitch of a grin gave him away.

"All I'm going to do is stare at the ceiling."

"Then stare away, but rest. I'll tell Fae that you are not to be disturbed."

"Byrne, I want to thank you for everything. You have gone above and beyond. You don't know me or Nikki but gave us refuge and care. I don't even know what the right words are."

"You are an O'Brien. I consider it a promise kept, a matter of honor." He closed the door behind him.

That afternoon, showered and dressed, she sat at the cherry Victorian vanity attempting to braid her hair. Her shoulder was still sore so she abandoned the effort. As her arm came down, it knocked a perfume bottle off the table. The vial rolled across the Oriental carpet and under the bed. As she crawled on the floor after it, Micaela remembered another perfume and an image in the darkness of the forest. She knew whose distinctive fragrance it was; she'd smelled it once before in the ladies room at the City Center in New York. That scent had followed after a shape in the forest. A shape that was foe not friend. It had moved like an animal but at the same time Micaela was sure now that it was Kat, a good and loyal employee of Ivan's. If she was involved, it was because Ivan stood to gain.

31

She wasn't going to get any answers sitting around, so Micaela made her way to the terrace with its view of the green countryside. It was a good place to think, serene with brilliant green hills rising in the distance and fields dotted with cattle. She sipped Fae's magic herb tea. Between the tea and the poultice, Micaela felt better than she should feel after a week. The stitches were already out and, other than a few twinges and stiffness, it was almost as if nothing happened.

She closed her eyes and replayed the entire trip to Brussels in her mind. The more she thought about it, the more certain she was that Kat was behind the attack. She heard the scrape of a chair. Nikki gave her a quick squeeze of the arm and sat down in the chair beside her.

Micaela searched Nikki's face. "You look great. I remember scratches on your face, but they're gone."

"Chasing bad guys through the woods. No big deal. You're not doing so bad yourself. Though I heard there was no lack of TLC in your room. Liam and Byrne practically moved in and Fae has decided that you are The O'Brien and, therefore, queen of the manor."

"The O'Briens haven't been royalty for centuries. What happened that night? What do you remember?"

"We were ambushed. You and Connie got pretty banged up. Ethan met us at the Brussels airport and took charge of Connie. Liam loaded us onto the Knowth plane and brought us back here. The rest is history."

"I remember things... before you say anything, it's not the knock on the head. The more I think, the more certain I am that what attacked us wasn't human."

"Animals released by the attackers. Dogs, maybe." Nikki turned toward the fields.

"No, Nikki, not animals, not really." She wasn't ready to share her theory about Kat just yet. She wanted to be sure, think it through first.

"I don't know what to tell you. Maybe you should talk to Liam or Byrne." Nikki's eyes tracked a herd of cattle as they made slow progress down the hill.

They sat in silence until Nikki went into the house, murmuring about calling New York to extend her supposed vacation. Nikki knew something. For the rest of the day, Micaela tried to get Liam alone to ask him what had happened.

Day eight post-attack was looking up. Micaela woke, took her shower, dressed, and went down for breakfast without any assistance. She was determined to speed her recovery with as much activity as possible. If Ivan was involved, she needed to get healthy and get back in the game.

Liam was locked away in the office he kept at the Manor, so she stuck her head into the study. Nikki was curled up on a leather sofa. Micaela cleared her throat.

"I'm going for a walk. I should be back by lunch."

Nikki looked up from the screen. "Not alone, you aren't." She tucked her Glock in her belt and covered it with her leather jacket.

Micaela stood for a moment on the veranda.

"So, which way?" Nikki asked.

She followed her gut and headed toward the hills north of the Manor. "Ivan hasn't called my cell. Has he called the house line?"

"Did you think he would?" Nikki's tone sounded cautious.

"No, but I guess I hoped I was wrong."

"Wrong about what?"

"Just a feeling I have."

They walked along, Micaela lost in her thoughts as she wondered why he would have François killed, send people after her, and attack her and her friends, nearly killing them. At the same time, he had been sweet, romantic, and, she had to admit, very sensual. Then, the episode on the balcony. It had to have something to do with AGF. A power grab fit with what happened to François and the *unfortunate* accidents that had befallen some of the others. But, the attack in Brussels had been aimed at her, she was sure of that. She was just the banker, not an investor. Once the deal was consummated, she would have little or no involvement with AGF and its future. Why did he want her dead? It didn't make sense. She needed to go back to New York and start at the beginning. To do that, she needed to get well and strong.

She pushed the thoughts aside and turned her attention to her walk. The scenery was postcard beautiful, with an azure sky and brilliant green landscape. Distraction was easy.

They had walked a short way when Micaela spotted the ruins. She grabbed Nikki's arm and dragged her over scattered stones and mounds.

"I know this place, Nikki. I've been here."

"When you were a little girl?"

"Maybe, but it's whole when I see it. It's my castle. The refuge." She wandered along the mounds and scattered stones. "There is… was a tower here and one just like it over there, there, and there. The four corners." She ran down an incline, Nikki close on her heels. "This was the moat and the drawbridge was here."

205

"How do you know all this?"

"I see it. Whenever I felt threatened, like at the hotel." *Shit.*
She hadn't meant for that to slip out. "Ever since I was little, when I
was being bothered by visions or spirits, I would run across the
drawbridge. The guardian would close the gate and there were
archers everywhere. My room was here and my bed…"

"What about your bed?"

"It's in my room at the Manor." A wave of dizziness washed
over her.

Nikki eased her onto a large stone. "Micaela, you're
overdoing it. You've been through a lot."

"I'm not crazy. I thought I was at one point, but this all feels
right." She looked down at the stone under her. With her finger, she
traced the faded outline of a triskele. It had once been painted ochre
and blue, she was certain.

"Listen, we've talked before. I understand your talents, your
gifts. I don't think you're crazy at all. Just take it slow. Too much,
too soon and you'll end up flat on your ass again."

"I've never felt better. For the first time in years, I don't feel
like a misfit. I have to call Una and tell her." She pulled out her
phone, no signal. She started sprinting for the house to call Una and
touch the bed of her castle.

Micaela threw herself on the mattress and stretched out. This
was her bed, the bed of her childhood castle. The only difference was
the pillows and linens. Now she was swallowed up in mounds of
down filled pillows and silk sheets; in her imagination, the pillows
were fewer and the linens, though the finest weave of the time, did
not compare. The castle that had protected her from Ivan that night
on the balcony had been real. It was not the creation of a little girl's
fear. Her gifts and visions were real. It was time to stop running.

She picked up the phone and called her grandmother. The words rushed out about the ruins and the bed. She told Una she would be home in two or three days. Una made her promise to tell Byrne and Liam. Liam was not at dinner that night, some business matter was all Fae would say. After dinner, Micaela met Byrne in his private study. A fire crackled in the grate. He poured a coffee for her and a deep red wine for himself.

She told him about her trip to the ruins and her call to her grandmother.

"I need to know, when was the castle destroyed?"

"Under Cromwell, the Puritan. He and his followers thought the family harbored royalist Catholic sentiments. We had friends who gave us enough of a warning that all the occupants and much of the important things, including the bed, were removed to a safe location." He stared into his goblet. "They used cannons to bring the towers down, and set fire to the interior."

"It must have been terrible."

"We could not have cared less who sat on the English throne and have never been fervent Catholics. As usual, it was just a land grab."

"Not a very successful one, I gather." After her walk today she doubted the boundaries had shrunk in the last six hundred years.

"The invaders were dealt with."

"I feel like I'm on the edge of something. The ruins, my castle, my bed. I belong."

"I'm glad. The O'Briens have had ties to this land for centuries. I hope you will make Knowth your other home. We have much to offer to you. There is also a good deal to talk about and for you to see. To a renewal of family ties." He touched her coffee mug with his wine glass. "There are other items that were saved, other places you need to see. Perhaps tomorrow evening."

32

Micaela tiptoed down the wide stairs and into the dining room. She wasn't sure why she was trying to be quiet; it sounded like she was the only one in the house. The midday sun streamed through the floor to ceiling arched windows. Brunch was laid out on the massive oak buffet in the dining room. The food was hot, even though it was almost one in the afternoon, and smelled wonderful. She piled her plate with scrambled eggs, Irish bacon and two biscuits. A second plate was needed for the mixture of berries and apples and the dollops of fresh butter and marmalade for the biscuits. She made a second trip for coffee and juice.

She'd put a major dent in the eggs when Liam's arm came around her with the coffeepot. He smelled like sweet hay and the earth.

"More coffee?" he asked.

"Of course. How long have you been up?"

"Since about five. I worked for a while and then went out to the stables to check on the horses."

"Is everyone else still asleep?" She pushed the remains of eggs and bacon away and started on the fruit.

"Byrne is unavailable and Nikki's napping on the couch in the study. Byrne filled me in on your trip to the castle ruins. I'm glad for you. No one should feel apart from the world."

"It is such a mental weight off me." She patted her now full stomach. "I was going to go for a run to the ruins before it gets dark to deal with the other weight."

"There are some nice trails to the west if you like hills." He paused. "Or perhaps, you would prefer to ride with me instead?"

"I haven't ridden in years. I'll slow you down, but if you're game, I'm in. Can we go past the old castle ruins?"

"I have something else you might find interesting." Liam plucked a raspberry off her plate and popped it in his mouth. "I'll get you riding gear to wear from Aislin."

"Aislin?"

"She's Byrne's personal assistant. You wore her sweats and t-shirt right after you got here. She's about your size, just smaller on top." His eyes drifted from her face.

"I'd like to thank her." She felt the blush rise at his appreciative look. "Do I have time for a quick shower?"

"Sure." He picked up another raspberry and held it up to Micaela's lips. "One for the road. You'll need your strength to keep up.

She peeked around the bathroom door to be sure the coast was clear before she stepped out wearing only a towel. Someone had been in the room and laid jeans, a long sleeve t-shirt, socks, and a magnificent Irish knit sweater on the now-made bed. Hopefully, it had been Fae and not Liam that had been in her bedroom. She pictured him smoothing the covers to lay out the clothes. She remembered the taste of his kiss that night in Bridewell.

Micaela followed Liam to a tack room filled with riding boots of various sizes. She pulled on a pair of buttery soft leather boots that came to just below her knees. They felt like they had been waiting for her.

209

She sat on a hay bale outside the barn and waited. The earth scents brought memories of riding with her parents and racing her horse in high school. The muffled clopping brought her back to the present where a groom held the reins of two beautiful animals. A magnificent pure white stallion with a broad chest and a gleaming coat danced when he heard Liam's voice. She fell in love with the mare at first sight. Her coat was a glistening auburn. Her coppery mane was braided with green and black ribbons.

Liam handed her the reins of the mare. "Her name is Banríon. The two of you are a matched pair." He snuck an apple into Micaela's hand.

"Queen." Micaela approached the mare slowly, speaking softly. "Well hello, Banríon. I hope you're patient. I haven't done this in a while."

The mare seemed to nod and nuzzled Micaela.

"Oh, you know what I have behind my back, do you?" She smiled and fed the apple to the mare. Micaela rested her cheek against the horse's face and lost herself for a moment in the scent and warmth of this queen. "What's your stallion's name?"

"Embarr." *The warrior.*

They rode west for an hour, varying the pace from a walk to a glorious full gallop across an open field of clover. The sun was already low in the March sky when Liam turned onto a trail that led into an old growth forest of oak and rowan.

"I want to show you one of the treasures of Knowth."

Micaela bent close to Banríon's neck to avoid the limbs of the ancient oaks. Darkness came early in these old forests. They had ridden about a quarter mile when the trees opened onto a clearing the size of two football fields. Scattered around the field were large stones similar to ones she had seen in pictures of Stonehenge and Newgrange. Some had toppled, but the ones on the east and west ends were intact and upright. In the center sat a large stone that had been an altar or gathering place. A near-full moon peeked over the eastern stone, a pale disc in the still blue evening sky. They left the horses to graze and Liam led her to the monuments.

"Byrne doesn't like word of this to get out. Attracts the wrong kind of tourist. It's been in the Connor *clann* for as long as anyone can remember."

"It's magnificent." Micaela walked toward the center. The ground thrummed under her feet, but this time, she didn't fight or run. She belonged now.

He circled to the other end of the large stone altar, his back to the west gate. Micaela faced him from the east end. The long waist-high stone stretched between them.

"The Connors and Farrells have gathered here for several millennia." Liam placed his hands on the edge of the altar. "It is said that Brian Boru, himself, consulted the Druids here. Perhaps your people were here, too."

The stone was warm and alive. She felt Liam's energy on the other side and she reached her hand out to him. The sun moved behind the west gate. The alignment wouldn't be perfect until the solstice, but still the gate glowed blue. The thrumming grew louder. Time shifted.

She still stood by the altar, but she wasn't Micaela; she was Brigid and she belonged here. Her long green robe was embroidered with Ogham. Liam faced her in a similar robe. An acolyte stood to either side of them. Brigid reached up and undid the gold brooch that held the robe closed. Liam mirrored her movements. They handed the brooches to their acolytes and slipped off their robes. All she wore was the lunula and earrings; the same ones she had received from Una. Two spiral gold arm bands, torcs, twisted around Liam's incised biceps. His bronze hair cascaded over his shoulders. He was breathtaking. They moved to the front of the altar. His carved abs bunched as he lifted her onto it.

In the background, their people, hers and Liam's, the people of Dana, began the incantation to the Medb and the Dagda. They invoked the Great Marriage and asked that it bring fertility to the land and protection to the *clann* and glory to their new King, The Connor, as he faced the Eastern invaders. She and Liam would use their power to bring these blessings of the goddess and god.

She and Liam knelt at the center of the altar; the sun framed his muscled torso. He had the spiraled triskele tattooed above his heart. She traced it with her finger. He reached out and touched the vine tattoo that wove around her upper arm, Brigid's upper arm. Micaela tried to remember that she didn't have any tattoos. She couldn't keep it straight in her head.

Liam's hand moved up her arm to cradle her face. His eyes betrayed him. This was more than a ritual. His lips met hers. She opened herself to him. Her tongue traced his lips and probed further. He tasted like honey wine, the mead. She felt the world shimmer around her. The voices went silent.

She was just Micaela again on the altar in his arms. They were shirtless; her hands on his back, his hands twined in her hair. She could feel his muscles flex and pulse under her touch. The movement became fluid and violent. Liam made a sound somewhere between a moan and a growl. He pushed himself away.

"No, not now. Please." His face contorted with pain. "Micaela, go home. In the name of the goddess leave. Banríon will get you home." He crouched and sprung off the altar. Micaela watched as he raced off through the west gate. He never stood straight up.

It was full dark; the trees were a mass of black, the path lost. Maybe she should stay here until dawn or someone came for her. Then again, she should go after Liam. His voice echoed in her head, his urgent plea became a command. He had promised the mare would get her to the Manor. She groped around until she found her shirt and sweater and put them on. She found Liam's shirt where he had dropped it.

"Banríon, where are you girl? Embarr?" She had no idea where either horse was. Had they bolted and left her alone in the circle? She called out to Liam. Nothing but the howl of a dog in the

212

distance and the constant vibration of the stones. She couldn't stay here alone with the stones; she didn't know how to control the magic. She hugged Liam's sweater to her; his scent was a comfort.

Maybe the Irish would work better. "*Tar, le do thoil.* Come, please." She remembered the words from her childhood when her father would call her to dinner. She choked back a sob of relief as she felt Banríon's warm muzzle on her neck.

She climbed into the saddle and leaned over to whisper in the mare's ear. "I hope you understand some English. I don't know where Liam is, so it's up to you, girl. Get me and Embarr home. *Téigh abhaile.*"

The mare whinnied and Micaela heard the stallion come up alongside. She held Embarr's reins loosely as Banríon brought them to the main trail and turned for home. Branches lashed Micaela's face. It was deserved punishment from the oaks. She had done something terribly wrong, though she didn't know what, to cause Liam to run off into the night. How would she face him?

The ride back felt three times longer than the ride to the stones. The stable boy took the horses without a word about Liam's absence. She walked into the house to see Byrne Connor coming down the stairs followed by a young woman and man.

Byrne came to her, but her eyes locked on the two people behind him. "Micaela, are you all right?" Byrne asked.

She looked at the woman. "Who are you?"

"I'm sorry we haven't had a chance to meet. I'm Aislin and this is Diarmid."

"I saw you, both of you. You were in the clearing, at the altar. Tell me what happened. Where did Liam go?"

Aislin eyes darted to Byrne. Diarmid answered. His voice was cool and professional. His tie carried the crest of Trinity College. "I'm not sure I know. We've been here in a meeting with Mr. Connor into the evening."

Micaela wheeled around to Byrne. "What is going on here?"

213

"Liam will return. He has commitments that will require his attention most of tomorrow. I wouldn't worry, he'll be fine."

"Easy for you to say." Micaela raced up the stairs two at a time. She peeled the sweater and t-shirt off. In the bathroom she flipped on the light and turned on the shower. She looked at her reflection. Her eyes were drawn to her right arm. There it was the vine tattoo she had seen in the vision. She clamped her hands over her mouth and stumbled to the bed. She was barely aware of the pounding on her bedroom door.

"Micaela, it's Nikki. I'm coming in."

Micaela opened the door and held out her arm.

Aislin stood behind Nikki. She stared at Micaela's arm. "I should advise The Connor."

"No, don't tell Byrne, not yet. I'll be fine. I want to know where Liam is."

"He'll be back in due time." Aislin handed her a clean t-shirt.

Micaela grabbed Nikki's arm. "Nikki, you and I have worked out together for more than a year and you know I don't have a tattoo."

"It seems you do now. We'll figure it out in the morning. Try to rest, there's nothing more we can do tonight." The bedroom door clicked shut behind them.

Micaela stared upward. Damn, she was sick of that ceiling. Her hand went to her arm and then to her lips. She could still taste Liam on her lips. *Oh, Goddess, what am I going to do?*

One thing was sure as she tossed and turned, sleep was not on her to-do list. She flipped through *The Economist*. The ongoing debate of the euro versus the dollar would not distract her from the fact that Liam had not returned.

When she was sure the house was quiet, she tiptoed downstairs and rummaged through the library shelves. She sat on the bottom step and tried to lose herself in *The Turn of the Screw*. Around page one hundred, her eyelids drooped. She turned to go up the stairs. Behind her the front door latch clicked open.

Liam closed the door, unaware of her presence. His pants and chest were caked with mud and who knew what else. His face glistened with sweat. He slumped against the door.

She whispered his name, not wanting to startle him or attract the attention of the others.

"Micaela, what are you doing up?" His voice was a rasp.

"I was worried." She took a small step toward him.

"As you can see, I'm fine." He made it three feet before his knees buckled. She caught him around the waist and tucked her shoulders under his arm. He didn't smell of alcohol. She looked at his face; his eyes looked tired but focused.

"Yeah, you look fine. Now let's get you upstairs." He outweighed her by half, but she had stubbornness on her side.

He stopped at his bedroom door. "I can take it from here."

"Would you please let me take care of you for once?"

He released his iron grip on the door frame and leaned on her. "Okay, but just this once."

She sat him in a chair outside his bathroom and went to turn on the shower. This was awkward, but he needed to shower and she was afraid he'd collapse and hit his head. She began to unzip his jeans. He gave her a weak attempt at a smile and took her hand away.

"I'd hoped we'd at least go to a movie first."

"Very funny. You'll feel better if we clean you up."

"I usually sleep first."

"Well, I won't answer to Fae when she sees the mud and whatever else all over her clean linens."

"She's used to it."

"Humor me." Micaela had managed to work his jeans off. She tossed them into a corner. It would be easier for Fae to buy new ones than clean these.

She didn't have to worry about whether it was boxers or briefs, apparently the answer was commando. Her breath caught. She tore her eyes away and looked up into his face. Bad idea, he was staring back.

"Can you get up… I mean stand?"

"I'll try for you, 'Caela."

She studied the cream colored marble floor tile as she helped him into the shower. Next to the shower was a magnificent deep green marble tub with a high brass faucet and whirlpool jets. She pictured him stretched out in the tub, the water swirling around his chest, his hips.

If that was what he looked like soft. She adjusted the water temperature. The memory and desires of the vision in the circle surged through her body.

Liam leaned his forehead against the tile. She reached to grab the soap and was doused with water. She would end up almost as wet as he was.

"Can you stand for a minute?"

His head slid across the tiles in a slow nod. She peeled off the Trinity College t-shirt and jeans and pushed them a safe distance away.

She scrubbed the mud off his back and helped him shampoo his hair. He was covered in small scratches. He lathered his abdomen and crotch; she looked away, trying to erase the images in her mind. She turned her eyes to the walls and the small diamond-shaped green tiles interspersed between the cream tiles. The green matched his eyes. They even had the same flecks of amber in them. He groped behind his back to turn off the water. Micaela handed him a towel, which he tied around his waist.

"Thanks for insisting on the shower." He leaned on her as they left the bathroom. She wasn't so sure he needed the help anymore. But, best not take chances.

She was tucking him when she spotted it. There on his chest, where it should be, was the tattoo of the triskele. Had he had it before today? She stood to leave.

216

He grabbed her hand. *"Anam cara,* stay," he whispered.

She should go, but he looked so helpless with his wet hair spread across the pillow and his eyes closed. She sat on the edge of the bed as he held onto her left hand. His hands were so hot that he felt feverish. She touched her free hand to his forehead. He was warm but his cheeks and lips were not flushed. He pulled her hand to his lips. After what happened in the stones, the need to touch him was overwhelming. She stretched out on top of the covers, next to him.

33

Aislin was adjusting the drapes when Micaela opened her
eyes. She was alone in the bed, not sure if that was a good thing or a
bad thing.

"Aislin, I'm sorry I snapped at you last night."

"Don't let it trouble you, Miss. You were just fretting about
Mr. Farrell. I saw him earlier and he looked himself."

"After my near breakdown last night, I think we can dispense
with the formality. If I can call you Aislin, you can call me Micaela."
She swung her legs over the edge of the bed. "What time is it
anyway?"

"It's half past three, 'tis near dark. Supper will be ready soon,
if you've a mind to eat. I could bring a plate to you, if you prefer."

She'd slept most the day away. "I'll go downstairs."

"Diarmid and I picked up some more clothes for you today in
Dublin. Not only for dinner tonight but for hiking and such. If
they're not to your liking, we can exchange them."

"I'm sure your choices will be perfect, Aislin." Micaela
strode down the hall to her own room. At this point in the day,
everyone must know where she had been. Hopefully, they knew
which side of the sheets she'd slept on.

The closet had been filled with enough clothes for a month-
long stay. She pulled out a turquoise turtleneck and black skirt. By

the time she had turned around, Aislin had laid out thigh-high stockings next to a bra and panties the same color as the turtleneck. Four-inch black heels with a line of turquoise between the heel and the shoe peeked out from under the bed.

"You really don't need to fuss, Aislin."

"It's no mind."

So odd, she and Aislin were about the same age. Aislin was Byrne's assistant and so Micaela assumed highly competent. But here she acted like a maid or a lady-in-waiting, the young acolyte in her vision.

"Where's Liam?"

"He's with The Connor. Please don't tell Mr. Farrell I woke you. He gave strict instructions."

"He won't hear it from me. Besides, you didn't wake me, it was time." Micaela put the final touches on her makeup. "It's a nice evening, maybe I'll sit on the veranda until dinner. Would you like to join me?"

"I have some work to finish, but if you need anything, please send for me."

Micaela raided the refrigerator for a diet soda and headed for the terrace. It was another clear night and somewhere beyond the tree line were the standing stones of Knowth Manor. Something had happened out there, beyond the appearance of the tattoo. She felt different, healthier. She had been healing quickly before today, but now she was ready to run a marathon. She shrugged it off as the lingering effect of the stones. It would pass.

She watched the moon rise over the slate roof of the Manor. Lights began to flicker on behind the leaded glass windows. In the dining room, she saw Fae scurrying back and forth, setting out china and crystal, directing the staff. Through the parlor window, Nikki chatted with Diarmid in front of the fire.

On the second floor, a single window glowed with a soft light. Silhouetted against the glass, she recognized Liam's broad shoulders, and narrow waist that led to all the things seen in the

219

shower. A male figure approached him. It was Byrne. Liam's left arm reached behind his own head and pulled his hair back. He tilted his head to the left as Byrne drew close. He wrapped his arms around Liam and leaned in. The shadows of their heads merged into one.

Fool. She knew she had been getting mixed signals from Liam, she had chosen to misread them. Why didn't he just say something? So he was gay and she was an ass. She had fallen for meaningless banter; wanting him when she wasn't his type. Did he enjoy watching her admire his body when he didn't return the interest? Was last night merely comfort in sisterly arms?

A mixture of humiliation and rage filled her. She tore her gaze from the window as the men separated. She remembered the bottle of whiskey on the table inside the patio door. To hell with what alcohol might unleash, it had to be better than her reality. She poured a healthy shot and returned to stare out at the fields. The man in the moon's smile mocked her. She had two sips of her drink when Aislin stuck her head into the parlor.

"Dinner is ready, Miss O'Brien."

Micaela drained the glass and marched into the dining room. Byrne stood by the fire inches from Liam. Diarmid and Aislin moved through the buffet. Nikki had filled a plate at the table. Micaela made a small plate of grilled lamb, potatoes, and vegetables. At least she could focus on the food instead of Liam. Byrne pulled out the chair to the left of his chair at the head of the table. Liam sat to Byrne's right. Micaela stood motionless as Byrne's gesture sank in. He expected her to sit across from Liam. Maybe she should excuse herself and eat in her room. No, she wouldn't cave. Liam and Byrne chatted away about the stock market and Manor issues, seemingly oblivious to her fury.

Nikki leaned over and whispered. "Sleep well?"

"Just great." Micaela squared her shoulders and looked across the table right into Liam's eyes. Rules of negotiation say that the first one to speak has already lost. She had nothing to say to him.

He said nothing. His face was a blank.

220

She turned to Byrne. "I want to thank you for all you've done for us. I don't know how I can ever repay such kindness."

"You have Liam to thank." He laid a hand on Liam's arm.

She flashed a smile at Liam and turned back to Byrne. "I wouldn't know where to begin."

34

The morning sky was still deep red when she arrived at the gym to meet Nikki. Nikki had started teaching her martial arts in New York, but, in light of recent events, Micaela needed more. In the far corner of the converted barn, Liam pummeled the heavy bag.

"You can stop now, Liam. It's dead."

He turned around. Beads of sweat made tracks down his face. The drenched parts of his shirt were three shades darker than the one or two dry spots. It clung to every muscle of his chest.

"I'm done." He grabbed a towel from a nearby bench and mopped his face.

"You were here first. Don't run off on my account." Sarcasm was safer than rage.

"Micaela, I… the other night…" He shook his head. "Never mind." He headed for the men's locker room.

"Never mind. Never mind about what?" She grabbed his arm and wheeled him around. "Never mind that you ran off and left me in the pitch dark, or never mind that all kinds of crazy shit is going on and no one can give me an explanation, or never mind that I get nothing but lies. Which one is it?"

Liam stared down at her hand on his arm. She was leaving marks.

"I'm sorry about taking off the way I did. I wish I could explain." His eyes travelled from the tattoo on her arm to her hand. "Can you let go before you draw blood?"

She enjoyed seeing her handprint on his arm, a small dose of the pain he had caused.

"I wouldn't want to mark you. Byrne might not think you so pretty."

Liam reached toward her. "What are you talking about?"

She flinched. "Why didn't you just tell me? I wouldn't have outed you. I thought it was me. It would have been easier if I'd known."

His fingers brushed her tattoo like feathers. It sent a shiver down her spine. *Damn him.*

Her other arm recoiled and she swung at his jaw. He was on his back and she stood over him. On second thought, rage was better.

Nikki stood in the gym door. "Sorry, am I interrupting you two lovebirds?"

Micaela hissed at him. "Listen, we have to work together. That's it. As soon as this ordeal is over, I will see that you don't have to deal with me. Ever. I prefer not to work with people who can't be honest with me."

She turned her back to him. "Nikki, I think you and I had planned a workout. Let's get to it."

Out of the corner of her eye, Micaela could see him rise from the floor. He rubbed his chin and watched her for a moment before disappearing into the men's showers.

Nikki started off slow, as usual. Basic moves, master the fundamentals. After the first hour, Micaela pushed up the tempo. She wanted more. She needed to unleash her anger. Nikki obliged. By the third hour, Micaela had learned to fight with the Bo staff and the Shinai sword.

"Micaela, it's after twelve. Why don't we grab some lunch?"

She had worked up an appetite. "Thanks for the workout, but I'm going to eat in my room. I'll shower here and head up to the house." Liam was long gone.

Nikki took a swig of her water bottle. "Where did that come from? You've taken some quantum leap physically. You're tough."

Not tough enough, Micaela thought, but she'd get there.

Back in her room, Micaela sat on the red velvet cushions of the window seat, watching the shepherds, probably tenants of Knowth, move their fleeced charges between pastures. Beyond a stand of ash to the east, she could see a barn and the pens the wooly ones called home. Soon, it would be time for the lambing and then the spring shearing. Just like at Bridewell... She took her lunch tray and headed downstairs. It was time to go home.

Fae met her midway down the stairs. "Miss O'Brien, I would have come to fetch your tray. No need to bring it."

"It's no trouble. Is Mr. Connor available?"

"No. Is there something Mr. Farrell, or maybe Aislin or Diarmid can help you with?"

"Would you tell Mr. Connor when he's free that I would like to speak with him." Micaela paused. "On second thought, don't bother. Ask Diarmid to stop by."

Fae took the tray and curtsied before heading for the kitchen. Micaela heard Liam's agitated voice followed by Nikki's calmer tone through the closed doors of the study. Micaela knocked on the door. Nikki opened it.

"Nikki, is everything okay in there?"

"Just a difference of opinion." Nikki glanced into the study, Liam faced the windows.

Son of a bitch wouldn't even turn around. "You have my blessing to beat the crap out of him."

Nikki stepped into the foyer and shut the door behind her. "I think you've already tried that. Want to tell me why?"

"I hate liars."

Nikki spread her hands and raised her eyebrows, a request for details.

Micaela led her across the hall to the library and shut the door. "I saw him with Byrne. Why couldn't he just tell me they were lovers? Why play with me, pretending he was attracted to me?"

"Tell me what you think you saw."

Micaela bit her lip. Even now she wasn't sure she could put it into words.

"I was on the terrace, I looked up and Liam... he was standing there and Byrne came up and kissed him."

"You're sure?"

"Nikki, we live in New York, it's not like I haven't seen men kiss before. Why pretend to be something he isn't with me? I could understand the need to maintain a fiction for others, we all have our secrets, but I guess I thought we were, at least, friends. Lately, I'd thought maybe more than friends."

"I'm sure he has his reasons."

"To lie to me. It had better be a damn good reason. Actually, I don't want to hear it. There is no excuse."

"Let me talk to him."

"Knock yourself out."

After Nikki left, Micaela sat at the library computer and began searching flights to New York. There was one leaving Dublin at midnight tonight. If she packed quickly she would make it.

Diarmid knocked at the door. "Fae said you wished to see me?"

"Come in. I hear tell that some of you think I am The O'Brien."

"Yes ma'am." He shifted from foot to foot, looking across the hall at the closed study doors.

225

"Close the door, Diarmid." He obeyed but looked more anxious. "I don't bite."

"No Miss, I know you don't."

"As The O'Brien, if I swore you to secrecy, you would have to honor that, wouldn't you?

"Ta." He had lapsed into Irish.

"Then Diarmid, in one hour you will drive me to Dublin Airport. You will tell no one."

"Ta." His eyes darted to the closed door as if he expected someone to burst through at any moment.

"Good. I'll meet you in an hour in the garage."

Diarmid bolted out of the room. Maybe he really thought she would bite.

She packed only those things that had been recovered from Brussels. She could keep herself safe from Ivan. She needed to consider whether to go to Detective Hendricks. It stuck in her throat to think about admitting he was right, even if he had the wrong suspect.

She had no interest in talking to Liam and she would explain to Nikki later. Her last task was to write Byrne a thank you note. She had no idea if he knew that Liam had kept the truth from her. She owed Byrne the courtesy of a farewell; he had cared for them, opened his house to them. She needed to hide the note where it would take at least twenty-four hours to find. She scanned the room. Leaving it on the pillow was too obvious. In the headboard, her headboard, where she knew it would be, was a carved book. To the normal eye, it was a bible, proper for the bed of a good Christian. To the initiated, the swirls and deliberate bars of the Ogham directed the eye to the finger length lever. She tipped it forward and the compartment swung open. She tucked the note inside and closed the book. Somehow she knew Byrne would find it, but not in time.

She crossed the kitchen as one of the maids came down the back stairs into the pantry. Her mouth formed a perfect circle. "Ooh,

Miss O'Brien, you needn't trouble yourself, we can get you anything you want."

Micaela smiled her sweetest and hoped the maid didn't notice the duffel bag and laptop. "I think Fae was looking for you in the dining room."

The maid scurried through the door to the main house as Micaela ducked out the delivery entrance, across the drive and into the garage. She slipped into the passenger seat of a Benz. When Diarmid started to speak, she put the earbuds of her MP3 player in her ears. He took the hint. At the airport, she started to shake his hand, but at the last minute she drew him into a hug.

The boarding was delayed for two tense hours due to weather over central Europe where the flight originated. Micaela spent the time in the most remote portion of the nearly empty terminal watching for any familiar, unwelcome faces. She finally settled into the first class seat and breathed a sigh of relief as the door closed and the plane pushed away from the jetway. Once airborne, she surfed the movie guide and decided on escapism. It was either the latest teenage vampires and werewolf movie or a romantic comedy: girl meets jerk, jerk redeems himself and shows he is a real man. Total fantasy. If this was the selection in first class, she pitied coach. She clicked over to the teen B movie.

She hadn't watched a good horror flick in years, and based on the first half hour, she still hadn't. It was the standard issue, college students on camping trip with a guide who is really a werewolf. They stumble on a mysterious ranch with an owner never seen during the day. But mindless was what she wanted and the Arizona scenery was almost as gorgeous as the werewolf guide.

The flight attendant brought a pâté and cheese platter just as the vampire-rancher was seducing one of the male college students away from the edge of the campfire for the attack. In the foreground, a male and female student were locked in a similar but less bloody

227

embrace. Clichéd. Micaela gave up on the movie, ordered coffee, and stared out the window. Her row mate, an older gentleman in a Savile Row suit, tapped her on the shoulder.

"Please pardon my intrusion, my dear, but may a take I peek out your window? I have flown this route for decades. It still amazes me that we will land in Boston at what appears to be only an hour after we left Dublin. It's as if the sun stands still. Of course at my age, my body reminds me that it is nearly breakfast in Dublin and I have been up all night. Ah, but you're young, four in the morning or ten at night, there's probably a night on the town ahead of you."

"No, only a hot shower and a good night's sleep."

They chatted amiably until the plane landed, after another delay circling Logan, at three-thirty in the morning. As she exited customs, her row mate fell in beside her. Micaela looked around for the taxi station and spotted Ethan headed toward her like a guided missile.

The elderly gentleman squeezed her elbow and pointed toward Ethan. "It would seem the remains of your evening are looking up."

"Up is not the word I would use." She should have realized Ethan would be the first person they would call.

"Shall I defend your honor, my dear? Lieutenant Colonel Anderson, formerly of the RAF at your service." He squinted at Ethan in mock fierceness.

"Thank you, but he's harmless."

"You are a most impressive young lady if that is harmless." Lt. Col Anderson headed toward his waiting driver with a final remark about youth being wasted on the young.

Ethan grabbed her arm and steered her toward an exit. "You mind telling me what you were thinking, taking off like that?"

"Last I looked you weren't my keeper."

"A frantic call from Knowth makes me your keeper on this side of the Atlantic, at least until the jet lands tomorrow evening."

Connie stood by the waiting car ignored by the transit police, who were hustling every other vehicle from the curb along the arrivals area. She loaded the luggage into the trunk then got behind the wheel. The soundproof barrier slid shut. The blue flash of her hands-free earpiece blinked beyond the smoked glass.

Micaela moved to the furthest end of the backseat. "You can have Connie drop me off at Moran & Boru's townhouse in Beacon Hill."

"Not likely." Ethan sat in the opposite corner, his long legs stretched to within inches of her feet. "You are coming back to my place where there is proper security."

"I can take care of myself." She uncrossed her arms and tried not to look so defensive.

"You have no idea what you are up against."

"I got a quick education in Brussels and a few more extra credit classes in Ireland." Broken body, broken heart, the end result was the same.

35

Micaela managed to keep silent until they pulled through the gates of Lowell Manor. That was a big improvement. Lately she'd lost the filter between her mind and mouth. Perhaps, her better self had finally resurfaced. She could only hope.

A tall man with a close-cut military haircut held the car door for her. His leather thigh- length coat stretched across his broad shoulder. It hung loose over a black t-shirt. She saw several other silhouettes at the edges of the driveway beyond the lights.

"Diarmid's okay, right? And the maid in the kitchen? I sort of pulled rank," she said to Ethan.

His frown was visible in the dim lights of the lanterns on either side of the heavy oak front entrance. She doubted it would help if she told him that she really did feel bad.

The tall man and one of his colleagues had taken up position on either side of the entry. Ethan gripped her elbow as they climbed the steps.

"Liam knows you well enough and Byrne is figuring you out fast. Diarmid and Mary, that would be the maid you snuck past, are fine. As soon as he returned from the airport, Diarmid was guilt ridden and told Liam. Apparently he was worried something would happen to The O'Brien."

"They know I'm here." There was no way to explain why she had run without sounding as foolish as she felt.

"Connie was instructed to call Knowth as soon as we were clear of the airport. When I spoke to Liam earlier, he anticipated arriving around eight tomorrow night. Byrne will be with him."

Once inside the Manor, Ethan marched Micaela to the study. He stood in the doorway and spoke softly to Connie. She excused herself to attend to other matters. Micaela stared into the fire, she could feel his eyes burn into her back. The double maple pocket doors clicked shut. They were alone.

"The night grows short and I will be unavailable during the day. Please remain on the grounds and make no phone calls. No side trips." He stood behind a massive Georgian-style desk, his hands clasped behind him.

Micaela flashed to the headmaster's office at Ashwood Hall Prep School after she and her roommates had snuck off to the rodeo. For a moment she had the same knot in her stomach, until she reminded herself she and Ethan were peers. He couldn't pull that Boston Brahmin crap on her.

"Some keeper. My life is in danger and you take a powder. How can I be sure that you leaving me alone isn't a set up?" She walked to a side table to pour herself a coffee.

"You will be well guarded." Suddenly he was beside her, whirling her around. "If I could be here, I would. This is beyond my control."

"Everyone has their priorities." She spat the words in his face.

"You are my priority." He released her and dropped his clenched fists to his side. "I must go. We will continue this tomorrow evening."

Before she could open her mouth, he was gone. She stood at the window until the sun rose. When the sun was over the trees, Connie returned to showed Micaela to her room.

231

Micaela spent the day sifting through memories of the last few weeks. François' murder, the Seaport, Ivan on her hotel balcony, the attack in the forest, the stones, Liam and Byrne. After a very late lunch, she decided to explore the house. The halls were quiet as she wandered the second floor corridor. Each doorway opened onto rooms that were filled with museum quality furniture of the Georgian and Federal periods, elaborately carved beds and armoires. The walls were decorated with antique pistols and sabers and portraits of Lowells past. The portraits each carried brass plaques with the names and lifespan of the subject. She looked for portraits of some of the prior leaders of First Colony. Perhaps they were at the company's office.

At the end of the second floor hall, she opened a door to a very feminine bedroom. Belgium lace draped the canopy and soft pink velvet covered the chairs. The room looked as if the occupant had stepped out for an afternoon stroll on the lime walk. Over the fireplace hung a portrait Micaela recognized immediately. She had met the subject in the family cemetery on her last visit. Prudence Lowell, mother of the other Ethan.

She had been a beautiful woman: dark blonde hair, startling blue eyes, and a strong up-tilted chin. The artist had captured a quality of her that took arrogance and softened it with fragility and loss in the eyes. Micaela had seen that look on Ethan's face last night.

She headed for the back door to pay another visit to the mausoleum. It was time to try to harness some of her gifts, to direct them to accomplish her own goals. Her first test would be to see if she could set Prudence's mind and spirit to rest.

Micaela followed the same path she had before, but now she knew what lay ahead. After a short walk, she stood before the Lowell Family crypt, slowed her breathing and opened her powers to the energy around her. She touched the edge of Prudence's aura.

"Prudence, are you there?"

She waited and called to her again. "Prudence Lowell. It's Micaela. We talked before. I saw your bedroom and your portrait. They are beautiful."

The voice came like a whisper but grew stronger with each word. "You shouldn't be here."

"I wanted to talk to you. To help you, if I can."

"I am beyond help. Help my Ethan."

"Tell me about your Ethan." Micaela turned in a slow circle as she scanned for Prudence.

"He will rise soon, you should go. He's afraid."

"Afraid, of what? "

"You."

Prudence appeared before the crypt's wrought iron gate, more solid than the vision of François at the Salmon Run.

"Your Ethan is dead." Micaela pointed to the plaque on the mausoleum bearing his name. "How can he be afraid of me?"

"It was so terrible when he first came back to me. I thought he was a ghost." Prudence laughed. "I didn't know what a ghost looked like then. He was confused, without discipline. The hunger was so great. After he hurt Sarah, he ran away. I didn't see him again until after I died."

"Who is Sarah?"

"His betrothed. She is over there now." Prudence pointed to a headstone topped by a graceful marble angel.

Micaela leaned over to read the inscription:

Sarah Stoughton

1758-1779

Beloved.

"She won't speak to you. I think she is jealous. He has not cared for anyone since her."

"Prudence, you keep speaking about Ethan as if he were still alive."

"Not alive, but not dead. That's why he is afraid of you." Prudence's eyes flickered toward the path. "He is afraid you will be hurt. He is afraid he will hurt you. Please go inside before he comes."

Micaela followed Prudence's gaze. Behind them was a long stretch of darkness and, at the end, the lights from the kitchen. "If not one or the other, what is he?"

Prudence was gone, but from behind her came Ethan's strained voice.

"Micaela, who are you talking to?"

She turned to face him. Even in the dim moonlight, he was pale, his face a swirling palette of emotion. Was he really afraid of her? Where was her head? This wasn't Prudence's Ethan.

"I was thinking out loud. I didn't realize the time." The intensity of his stare made her pulse race. He had moved closer. She had seen that look before.

"I frighten you, your heart is racing. I should… you must return to the house." He touched her cheek.

She reached up to take his hand and lead him inside. "Your hand is like ice. Come inside with me. Are you ill?"

"Not ill." He stepped back. "Please, go inside. I will be along soon."

She tried to take his arm, afraid to leave him alone.

"I said go." He dropped to his knees and doubled over.

Micaela squatted beside him and touched his shoulder. He whipped his face toward her. His eyes burned with a blue fire and there in his mouth… fangs. She skittered away in a crab walk, rolled over and launched herself like a sprinter out of the starting block down the path to the house. She ran up to her room, locked the door, and leaned against it. There was no such thing as vampires.

It was time to wake up from this nightmare. She was certain she would find herself tangled in silk sheets in her apartment in New York. Memories of Ivan in her apartment and on the balcony returned. If you accepted the premise that vampires existed and could mind-fuck humans to make them forget, then it all made a twisted

234

sort of sense. Aine had realized what Ivan had done. Her intervention had helped release her. The Knowth stones had finished it. She had not felt a connection with Ivan since.

She pressed her forehead to her knees. This wasn't possible; vampires were things of myth and fiction. She needed to get far away. Shit, she didn't have a car. Would someone go against Ethan's orders that she not leave the property and drive her to the nearest rental location? Not likely, she couldn't pull the same stunt twice. There was a tap on her door.

"It's Connie. The kitchen staff said you were upset."

Micaela laughed. Upset, typical New England understatement. How about terrified? She hesitated, her hand on the knob. Connie couldn't be a vampire; she'd eaten lunch with her today. But she must know, she lived here, took care of his business arrangements. What else did she do for him? She went back and slumped on the bed. Connie knocked again.

"Micaela, talk to me. Let me in."

She knew she wasn't getting away locked in her room. She opened the door and let Connie in.

"I'm sorry Connie. Flashback from Brussels. I guess I shouldn't walk alone in the woods for a while. I'll apologize to the staff."

"Can I get you anything? Mr. Lowell should be here shortly. Should I call a doctor?" Connie moved toward the landline on the nightstand, but didn't reach for it.

"I'm feeling better, really. I'm not sleeping well. Too many strange beds. Perhaps I could go to my Grandmother's. I could call Reece and he could arrange a security detail." Micaela tried for her brightest, healthiest, I'm-not-terrified smile. She hoped Connie bought it.

"I'll take it up with Mr. Lowell. Will you come down for dinner?"

Brave front required. "I'll freshen up and meet you downstairs."

Fifteen minutes later, Micaela sat in the parlor sipping a lovely red wine. Apparently beef was on the menu so a white was out of the question. She stared down at the crimson liquid and shivered. She jumped to her feet when she heard Ethan's footsteps approach.

"Please sit, Micaela, I think we need to talk."

She set the glass down. "I want to leave."

"I'm sure you do, but hear me out first." His voice made her look up. "Please."

The pain in his eyes made her sit down. He looked so like his mother.

"How can I trust anything you say? Things like you are supposed to be able to mess with people's minds."

"I am not a thing. I am still a man and, believe it or not, a gentleman. Yes, I can play mind games with humans, but I would never do that to you. I would never force myself on you." He knelt on the floor in front of her and took her hands. His hands were warm, his face flushed.

"Please don't touch me." She had a pretty good idea where his improved pallor came from.

Ethan stood and folded his arms across his chest. "I can't take back what happened. I can only prove to you that I am not the threat."

"Did you kill to get… warm?"

"No. I have not killed to slack my thirst in over two hundred years." He offered to refill her wine glass. She hadn't realized it was empty. How civilized. Here they were with a very expensive bottle of wine chatting about the dietary needs of a vampire.

"Not since Sarah?" she asked.

"How do you know about her?"

"Your mother told me."

The surprise was clear in his face. "When did the two of you speak?"

"The first time was when I went out the back way to avoid Detective Hendricks. She talked about her Ethan. I assumed she

236

meant the one on the mausoleum plaque. That it was a different Ethan. Silly me. Hendricks was here in the house then. You didn't hurt him, did you?"

"No, but I did, as you say, mess with his mind a little. He was ready to take off out the rear door, certain that would lead him to you. When did you find out about Sarah?"

"I spoke to your mother in the cemetery before you arrived tonight. She didn't give me all the particulars, but the things she did tell me make a lot more sense now." She leaned back in the chair and shook her head. A snort of a laugh escaped before she could stop it.

Ethan had lowered himself to a cross-legged position on the Oriental carpet that covered the floor at her feet. "What's so amusing?"

"Here I sweated about you and the others thinking I was some kind of nut job, if you discovered I spoke to ghosts and did other weird things. I thought you'd call the men in white jackets." She raised her wine glass. "But this is as red as it gets for me."

He took the glass from her hand, sipped at her wine, and returned it. How odd, she thought. Two hours ago, I was terrified, certain I was going to die... or worse. Sitting here talking, she could almost forget he was a vampire.

"Swear to me that you are not messing with my head. Swear on your mother's grave, on Sarah's grave."

His mouth dropped open, but not wide enough to reveal his fangs. He started to reach for her hands and then retreated. "I will swear on my mother's grave, Sarah's grave, my own grave, that I am not playing any mind games with you. Frankly, I'm not sure I could if I wanted to."

"Explain?" She set her wine on a lace doily on the Compass Rose table beside her.

"Well, I haven't tried, so I can't be sure, but I felt your power at the Met. I saw the way Aine treated you at the Salmon Run Inn, and Reece told me about how you found him."

"I'm odd, I'll give you that. But I assume you've got years of practice."

"You're different since Ireland, Micaela. Even more powerful. I can sense it."

Connie appeared in the doorway and announced dinner. He offered Micaela his arm. She declined with a small shake of her head.

As they left the parlor, Ethan spoke to Connie. "She knows."

Connie eyed Micaela. "That explains the mad dash from the cemetery and the half packed luggage."

"I don't think I can stay here right now."

"Connie told me you wanted to go to your grandmother's. Under the circumstances, that is probably best. I cannot protect you, if you are afraid of me." He sounded like his mother.

Part of her was afraid of him; part felt his sadness. She followed them to the dining room.

They tried for small talk at the perfectly set table of gold trimmed china while the staff served a filet mignon dinner. It suddenly looked underdone. Micaela and Connie ate, Ethan didn't even pretend.

As the maid had left the room, Micaela asked, "Earlier, you took a sip of my wine. Can you eat and drink?"

"Clear liquids in small quantities, wine, broth, tea. I confess I took a sip of your wine to try to set your mind at ease. No mind games, just a simple human gesture. It makes socializing easier. If served solid food, I use some of the simplest tricks any child knows. Move it around on your plate." He gave Connie a conspiratorial smile. "Have a dinner companion you can shift food to."

Connie grinned. "I have the finest personal trainers and nutritionists in New England to compensate for my entertaining duties."

Micaela pushed the rarest part of the meat aside. Ivan had eaten only clear broth at Très Couteaux, she thought. When they had finished, Ethan excused himself to arrange for Micaela's transportation to Bridewell.

Connie poured coffee. "He's really not a monster."

"Fangs, blood drinking, undead. It's hard not to think of him as a monster." Micaela skipped the milk. She didn't want to sleep tonight.

"Give it time." Connie snagged a big piece of chocolate cake off the sideboard. "It's not like you're a normal."

"A normal?"

"A human without any metaphysical extras."

"How do you fit in?" Micaela asked.

"I am his daytime representative. It is a convenient relationship for both of us."

"Has he ever… I mean did he…" Micaela's hand reflexively went to her neck. She remembered the hotel balcony and Ivan's touch, the feel of his teeth on her throat. When it had happened it had felt sexual, she had longed for him. Now, it was a frightening distant memory combined with the relief that the tie was broken.

Connie peered at her over her raised coffee cup. "The short answer is yes. I get the impression that you are not ready for me to elaborate."

"I don't think I need to know."

Connie stared at Micaela's face, or was it her neck? Micaela found herself staring back at Connie's neck. Connie wore her brown hair in a loose bun at the nape of her neck. Maybe that made it easier. There were no marks on Connie's throat. Memories of Biology 101 and the vast network of veins and arteries surfaced. There were less visible options.

"I am not his only option and, in case you were curious, we are not lovers. My preferences lie elsewhere," Connie said.

She took a picture frame off the mantel and handed it to Micaela. It was a picture of Connie and a lovely dark-haired woman with pixie-like features on a tropical beach.

"This must be Renee. Liam mentioned her. She's beautiful. It looks like you had a great time."

"I think my being a lesbian works for Ethan. No emotional complications." Connie returned the picture to its place of honor. "I'm easy to get along with."

"As long as you don't get her mad, that is." Ethan's shoulders were squared, his back military straight. "I have made my BMW ready to take you to Bridewell. Garett, my chief of security, will drive you there and return with the car. I took the liberty of calling Reece and alerting him."

"I can be ready in thirty minutes."

Micaela left her bags at the foot of the staircase and made her way down the dark path once more. "Prudence, I'm not sure if you're listening. I'm sorry. I know you tried to warn me. I can't help him. This is more than I can handle. How can I be sure I'm safe?"

She stood in front of the family crypt and traced Ethan's memorial. Of course there had been no body to bury. As she turned and walked to the house she heard the soft sounds of sobbing from behind her.

Ethan walked her to the car. He kept a respectful and silent distance. How do you say thank you to a vampire for not biting you, giving you dinner, and then sending you off to grandma's house? She looked into his solemn face. He looked back, an unspoken question in his sky blue eyes.

"Ethan, I'm not sure where we go from here. This is all too strange. I'm thinking I may resign from the AGF deal."

"I never meant to hurt Sarah. I loved her. I wouldn't let it happen again."

"It's not just you. It's everything, Brussels, Ireland. I need things to go back to the way they were." Micaela drew a deep breath and took his hand. "Don't worry. I won't reveal your secret to anyone. Besides, who would believe me?"

Her driver was the same man who had met them when she'd arrived from the airport. He didn't seem to feel the need to make idle conversation or introduce himself. It was after midnight when they pulled in and it looked like her grandmother was already asleep. Reece stood on the front porch. Ethan had business dealings with the Pokanoket. She would tell Reece. Not tonight; but soon. He should know. She just had no idea how to do it.

36

Liam checked in around nine Boston time. She took the call on computer. He looked anxious. Suddenly him being gay seemed rather tame compared to being the houseguest of a bloodsucker. His hair hung loose around his shoulders and tumbled onto a navy sweater that drew out the green of his eyes. Micaela sighed. She had finally reached the age when it was true that all the good ones were either married, gay or, in her case, undead.

"'Caela, change of flight plans. I know you wanted us to go to Bridewell, but given the make-up of the group and security requirements, we decided that Lowell Manor would be safer."

"Who is we?"

"Byrne, Nikki, and me. We'll land at Logan after eight. Ethan will have cars waiting."

"Why Lowell Manor? You did a good job defending the farm before."

"I'm sure you had your reasons for going to your grandmother's. But Ethan needs to be involved and with Byrne coming... too much has happened."

"What else has happened?" she asked.

Liam glanced off camera and nodded to what she assumed was the unseen Byrne before he turned back to her. "Rebecca Black

Owl's security was breached in Arizona and an attempt was made on her person. The representative of the Australian team is missing."

She rubbed her forehead and shielded her eyes at the same time, so they would not betray her. She had to return to Lowell Manor and face Ethan.

"If you think it's necessary. Should Una come with me?"

"No, this does not involve her. But just to be sure, I'll ask Reece and the Sons of Danu to keep an eye on the house."

"Okay. In the meantime, I'm going to drive down to the city. If I leave now, I should be at Lowell Manor by nine. I need to stop at the office, then pick up a few things from my apartment and check on Grady." Maybe she would talk to Detective Hendricks about her ideas regarding who killed François.

"Who are you taking with you?"

"Reece and Sean Murphy from Danu and possibly a third. Reece is still deciding. It would also help if I knew where Ivan was."

Liam's microphone went mute. He turned his head and talked to someone. The sound returned and Liam made way for Byrne.

"Micaela, it is technically none of my business, but what reason have you to contact Baron Vasilievich?" Byrne's light grey eyes looked almost black and his jaw muscles were clenched.

"I'm not looking to reach him. I'm trying to avoid him." Off camera, Micaela thought she heard a loud exhale. Byrne's shoulders eased down.

"We will attempt to locate Ivan. Do not take any unnecessary risk."

"Define unnecessary."

Liam's growl came from behind Byrne. "Micaela."

In the background, the look on Liam's face tore at her gut. He looked ready to jump through the computer. Just the protective big brother. Anything else she imagined was her mistake.

"I was kidding, Liam. I'll be at Lowell Manor no later than ten."

Byrne waved Liam into silence. "We shall see you then. Give Una my regards."

"Give them to me yourself." Una came in from the kitchen, dishtowel in hand.

Una and Byrne chatted for several more minutes. Micaela hadn't realized that they knew each other that well.

When they had signed off, Una turned her attention to Micaela. "Are you okay with going back to Ethan's?"

"I'm fine, no big deal."

"Come let's have tea and, if you want, you can tell me about it."

Her grandmother was the queen of waiting. They sat at the table, sipped tea and munched on soda bread slathered with fresh butter until Micaela was ready.

"I don't want to be different." She clutched Una's hand.

"If your mother and father had been here, things might have been easier for you. But, perhaps you needed to travel this road." Una pulled a lace handkerchief out of her pocket and dabbed a tear from Micaela's cheek.

"I've seen things, things that aren't supposed to exist."

"There are many things that the rest of the world feels safe in believing to be fiction and fable. They explain them away using logic and science. We who live the Old Way and have touched the Otherworld know differently."

Micaela stared out the kitchen window. Barely six months ago, she had looked through the bare October branches. Now the trees glowed green with the buds of spring leaves. Beyond the trees were the mountains where her nice normal world had begun unraveling. When this was all over, she would tell her grandmother everything.

"I'm going to New York and then to Boston to meet up with Byrne and the rest. Reece and Danny will go with me. The men will continue to watch the house."

"Things have progressed that far." Una slowly stirred her tea.

"Just a precaution..."

Her grandmother drew a chain from inside her dress and pulled it over her head. On the chain was a gold pendant carved with the triskele. At the center was a garnet.

"A stone of magic and protection." Una placed it over Micaela's head so it rested on top of the crane bag. "Just a precaution."

After recent developments, she decided on black pants, white turtleneck and a smoke gray leather jacket. Micaela pulled on her black running shoes, a better choice, she thought, than four inch heels.

We know differently. She had promised Ethan she would keep his secret. What she had told him was true at the time; no one would believe her if she told the truth. It helped to know Una would. Now, Micaela had to come up with a plausible lie, before she got to Boston that would protect the others from Ethan. She grabbed her duffel bag and headed out.

Her three bodyguards waited by the car. They looked more like a recruiting poster for Bad Ass Academy. Reece wore a pirate t-shirt that said 'The beatings will continue until morale improves'. It looked two sizes smaller than it had the last time she'd seen him in it. Sean tried valiantly for tough with a denim jacket and what passed for a five o'clock shadow for the fair skinned red head. Her driver from last night stepped forward. Hair cut high and tight, broad-chested, ex-military type, leather full-length coat with big pockets, unbuttoned, of course. His posture would make a five-star general proud.

His extended hand caught Micaela by surprise; she expected a salute. "We have not been formally introduced. Garett Tyler, Ms. O'Brien. Mr. Lowell sends his regards."

"Garett, if you're going to protect me, I think you should call me Micaela."

"I'll work on that, Ms. O'Brien."

"How did you get back so quickly?"

"I overnighted in Pittsfield. I hadn't gotten far when Connie called to tell me to turn around."

Reece stepped forward with a box wrapped in birthday paper. "I have a present for you from Nikki."

"My birthday is not for weeks." The box was heavy. She had a good idea what was in it.

"You need to open it and try it on before we go."

Micaela opened the box. It was the H&K P30 she had used at the range with Nikki. The consensus had been that it was the best fit for her and the circumstances.

Garett interjected. "It includes specialized ammunition."

"What's so special?"

"Liam and Ethan will explain when we meet them later."

The dealer had taken an impression of her hand, so the grip felt even more comfortable than the practice gun. Reece held out the shoulder holster. She laughed as he tried to figure out how to adjust the fit around her breasts without actually touching her.

"You're married. I'm sure you've seen breasts before."

"Jeez, Micaela, you're like my sister."

"So, let Garett do the adjustment."

"Ethan would hurt me." Garett grimaced.

"Then... Sean."

Reece glanced over at Sean, who'd exchanged his tough-guy face for the deer in headlights look. Reece shook his head. "He'll faint."

"So I guess that leaves you. Just walk me through it. I've touched myself before." Even Garett blushed.

She spent a half hour with Garett practicing with her new toy. They were on the road before ten-thirty. Micaela sped down the

Taconic driving Ethan's BMW. It would be tight but she was making good time.

Reece gripped the oh-shit handle over the passenger door. "Micaela, next time can you arrange for protection for your bodyguards?"

"From what?" She smiled innocently.

"Your driving. I'm going to be a father, you know. Where are we off to in such a hurry?"

"There's a woman I want to speak to. She owns a shop across from the Salmon Run Inn. Then, if time permits, a talk with a certain New York City detective. I have to stop at my apartment to check on my cat and pick up some extra clothes, but that's on the way north."

"The Salmon Run? Do you think we could take turns grabbing a bite? I've heard of the place since I was a boy, but never been." Sean sounded like Micaela had announced they were going to Disney. *Goddess, he was so young. What was he doing here?*

"I'm fine talking to Aine alone. I'd actually prefer it. As far as I'm concerned, you can all go to lunch together."

Reece shook his head. "Sean can pick up take-out from them."

She pulled into a spot on Church Street. The familiar tinkle of the bell greeted Micaela as she pushed the door open. She approached a young woman who was dusting off small Neolithic figures in a glass case.

"You must be Nora. I'm Micaela O'Brien."

Nora set the duster down. "My aunt's talked about you. She's upstairs, I'll get her."

"Don't trouble yourself, I know the way." Micaela headed to the stairs at the rear. She passed the room where Aine had done her reading. Even through the closed door, the energy inside made the small hairs on her arms stand up. She found Aine seated in the parlor, a book open on her lap.

"Micaela, I wondered if I would see you again."

"I wanted to thank you." She struggled to say the truth. "If it wasn't for your cleansing, I don't want to think about where I might be."

"I did not free you completely, did I?" Aine patted a chair beside her.

"I didn't understand any of it at the time. I ended up in Ireland, at a place called Knowth Castle..." Aine's head dipped softly in recognition. Micaela continued. "It was there that I think the break with him was complete. I was in a ring of stones and afterwards I felt different. Lighter, stronger."

"Better than freed. The stones claimed you as their own. So now what?"

"I know who did this. He has killed or tried to hurt others I work with." A cold certainty settled on her; Ivan needed to be stopped.

"When the time comes you will know what to do and the Morrigan will aid you."

Micaela kissed the old woman on the cheek. She said goodbye to Nora. She was a fortunate person, so unaware of the dangerous magic around her. Reece, Sean, and Garett fell in step outside the front door of the Singing Stone. Across the street a man stood in the entrance to the pub; it was Devlin, the bartender. She waved to him. He bowed in return.

Detective Hendricks eased off the hood of the BMW as Micaela approached. The detective's posture was casual alertness, the result of years of experience. Reece and Sean took up positions on either side of her, as Garett drifted off to Hendricks' left side. Micaela realized she could see the detective's service revolver on his right hip. He was a leftie. Garett had noticed, as well, and put himself on the detective's gun-hand side. Did Hendricks notice the H&K under her jacket? She would have to remember to select looser jackets from now on.

A month ago, she would have told anyone that the idea that she would have bodyguards and carry a concealed weapon was insane. One month ago, she would never have considered a New York City detective a risk, now she wasn't sure what the rules were. She shook her head. *Darwin's rules. Adapt or die.*

"You look well, Ms. O'Brien. What brings you here?" Hendricks re-angled his body toward Garett, the nearest threat.

"I could ask you the same question, but I suspect I'm the answer. Gentlemen, this is Detective Hendricks, one of New York's finest. His bark is worse than his bite."

Garett flexed his fingers, Sean rolled his shoulders and Reece's hands dropped to his sides. Hendricks returned to his spot on the BMW hood. She was glad she had forgotten to arm the vehicle alarm.

"Either my reports from Brussels were exaggerated or you have made a remarkable transformation. You've added a security detail, so my information was not totally erroneous."

The Death card. In her heart she knew the transformation had barely begun.

"I'm quite well, as you can see. You actually saved me a stop, Detective Hendricks. We need to talk."

"Shall we go to the station?"

"Actually the coffee place up the street will do. They roast their own beans." Micaela didn't wait for his answer; she needed the caffeine regardless of Hendricks' decision. He squinted at her, apparently deciding his next move. She watched her guards and Hendricks try to wordlessly decide who walked with whom. She settled it by falling into step beside Hendricks.

Inside, she ordered for herself and the boys. The boys? What was she supposed to call three armed men who shadowed her every move? She had a hard time thinking of them as her guards, even if they were; the guys sounded like drinking buddies; her men… too weird. Sean looked so young and she'd known Reece since he was a boy. Garett would just have to live with it.

"Can I get you something, Detective?"

"Large black coffee with two shots and a biscotti, please."

249

The boys sat at an adjacent table piled high with apple fritters, sandwiches, muffins. The food moved with perfect aim to their mouths. A nice trick since the three sets of eyes watched Hendricks and not the plates.

"Detective, you and I got off on the wrong foot. I assume the subsequent reports you received, regardless of the details, convinced you that I am a target of the same people that killed François."

"It would appear so. The question remains, what was your involvement in whatever got him killed?" He dunked the biscotti.

"I still haven't figured that out. I think it has more to do with what someone thinks I know. François wanted to tell me something but didn't get the chance."

"You brought me here to tell me things I already know?" He pushed back from the table.

"Listen, we both want the same thing, to find who killed François Leveque. If you don't find him, it's another cold case." She grabbed his wrist. "If I don't... well, the stakes are a little higher for me."

Hendricks nodded, even as he stared at her hand. She recalled the marks on Liam's arm and released him.

"Detective, I think the person responsible is trying to lead Interpol and NYPD on a wild goose chase."

"And you know this how?"

She flashed back to the forest, the outline that was Kat but not Kat, the scent of perfume that was definitely her, mixed with a muskier scent. Somehow she didn't think Hendricks would buy her description of an attack by wild beasts and subsequent miraculous recovery. She also knew that 'trust me' wouldn't work either.

"Your information that I was assaulted is essentially true. How bad is a discussion for another day. I can tell you that during the attack, it became clear to me that we should be looking abroad for your answer."

"I assume you have a name?"

Her voice dropped to a whisper. Hendricks leaned in, his eyes dropped to her chest. He wasn't ogling her boobs; he was looking at the gun. He met her eyes but had no comment on the weapon.

"Ekaterina Vilkas," she said.

"She works for Baron Vasilievich. I assume she is not entirely independent of her employer. What's the motive?"

"I'm not sure, but I think it's related to the AGF deal that we're involved in. Other participants in the transaction have been attacked, threatened or gone missing."

She looked over at the boys; most of the food had vanished. Garett made eye contact with her. She gave him a quick all-clear nod.

"An interesting hypothesis. You know I will continue to investigate you and your boyfriend, Lowell." Garett coughed while Sean stuffed the remains of a muffin in his mouth. Hendricks continued. "Then again, on the off chance that this is true, I will look into the allegations."

"That's the best I can hope for." She stood to leave. Hendricks and her three shadows followed. "I'll save you the trouble of following me, Detective, although you probably will anyway. I have to stop at my office, then my apartment for some clothes and to check on my cat. From there, back to Boston. Some friends are arriving from Ireland."

"Will you be staying with Lowell again?" Hendricks cocked his head and scrutinized her. He seemed to come to some kind of decision.

"I will be there for a meeting." That was the truth. She hoped she could stay at Moran & Boru's townhouse.

"Is there a number I can reach you at, Ms. O'Brien?"

Micaela scribbled her personal cell number on her business card. "Ethan Lowell is a lot of things, but I am certain that he didn't kill François Leveque."

"You have been fortunate to get this far in one piece. Whoever is behind this is a very dangerous person."

251

Ivan's face on her balcony in Brussels came to mind. After seeing Ethan, she now realized that she had seen Ivan's vampire face. "More dangerous than you realize, Detective."

"Then you had best be careful." He actually shook her hand as they parted.

By six o'clock, Micaela and the boys were northbound toward Boston. Garett insisted on driving. She rode shotgun. They would get in about the same time as the contingent from Knowth. There would be no time alone with Ethan. She hoped.

37

The gates to Lowell Manor were smashed open, one dangled from a single hinge at an unnatural angle. Garett raced the car up the drive, spraying gravel behind it. The entrance was locked, maybe barricaded, perhaps to slow down the entrance of others. Reece crashed through the front door, splintering the frame. Micaela had the H&K in the two hand grip Nikki had taught her, the safety released. Reece and Sean fanned out in the foyer. Lights were on all over the first floor; furniture was upended or shattered. This looked too much like François' hotel room.

Garett handed her a clip. "Special ammunition, two legs or four, if it's coming at you, fire."

She popped her clip out and replaced it. Reece stepped away from the three of them and scanned the rooms, his face tilted upward.

"Three, maybe four. Minimal blood in here." His face was somber as he turned to Garett. "Not so that way." He stared at the door to the kitchen. She could smell it, too.

Garett waved his gun at the stairs. "Reece, Sean, check upstairs, stay together."

Micaela stilled herself and wiped the memories of François' murder from her mind. She couldn't find Ethan's aura. She reached out to Prudence and heard soft sobs. She ran toward the kitchen and the back door.

"Outside. He's outside."

Garett stepped in front of her. A shield. His job. He spoke into a small microphone clipped to his collar. "Meet us out back."

She and Garett raced down the hallway to the kitchen area. She could hear the pounding of feet overhead as Reece and Sean ran to catch up. With awful familiarity, she recognized the smell of blood and viscera. On the kitchen floor lay one of Ethan's guards, his right arm torn from his body. His detached head stared at them from the granite counter of the center island. She turned away, no time to look; they had to find Ethan, find Connie. She sprinted through the rear door and down the path.

At the edge of the cemetery, Garett shoved her to her knees. "You've a lot to learn, O'Brien."

She fought back the impulse to break his grip and forge ahead, but that would only get her or some of her people killed. She pressed her palm against the nearby tree; it pulsed under her hand. A name from her childhood, repeated by Aine, whispered through the leaves.

"Help me, Morrigan. My friends need a warrior, not a child."

The beat of the tree became the tattoo of the bodhran. The energy flowed through her as it had that day training with Nikki. The air around her crackled. Reece and Sean had come alongside her.

Sean's voice sounded miles away. "Her eyes, the fire dances in them."

She held her finger to her lips. *How many times had they fought the enemy, in how many forms? Picts, Romans, English. But they had survived. How she wished she had her sword instead of this modern device. So much more final to remove the head.*

Micaela moved forward in a crouch to the edge of the clearing. The three quarter moon lit the scene. Parts of two more of Ethan's guards were strewn across the grass. Prudence and a second female specter, Sarah, she assumed, shimmered near the crypt. Prudence wept. Sarah screamed in rage. Her anger had made her solid and she had hurled the angel from her own headstone at an

254

attacker, knocking him out. Connie squared off with three of the attackers, slashing at them with a broadsword.

A large catlike creature stood over Ethan, claw raised. It looked part human and part feline. She decided she would freak out about it later. For now, Micaela fired wide, afraid she would hit Ethan. The shot got the beast's attention. She drew her breath to steady her aim and fired again. The creature was propelled back; a dark stain blossomed on its chest. Garett leapt forward and stood over it. He put another round in its head. Sean and Reece flanked Connie. It was Brussels all over again.

Ethan was slumped against a tree. Claw marks gouged his cheek and extended under his jaw to his neck. The creature clearly was trying for his throat. She spun around, gun raised in search of threats. Sean was pinned by one of the attackers. The man raised himself up to strike the final blow. She fired. His wound apparently not fatal, the man stumbled into the woods, chased by Sean and a large wolf-like animal. The third man lay still on the ground; Connie had finished her work.

Micaela dropped to her knees beside Ethan and took his hand. It was so cold. His shirt was drenched in blood. She gently pulled the fabric away. The creature had tried to gouge a hole in his chest.

Connie bled from wounds to her neck and abdomen. She pried the gun from Micaela's hand. "To heal he has to feed. I'm hurt too badly and Garett and the others are in pursuit."

Micaela turned to Ethan; his eyes were dull. "Ethan, help me. How do I do this?"

He shook his head. "Never again."

"Oh no, you don't get to die and leave me feeling guilty."

His laugh came out like the croak of a bullfrog. She grabbed him under the arm and raised him to a full sitting position against the trunk of the oak. Her other hand sought the oak for support and power. Earth magic that would protect her.

Micaela turned to Connie. "You've done this. How do I start?"

"He's afraid to feed on you."

"Why?"

"Afraid he'll want you too much to let you go. He hasn't let himself want any woman since Sarah."

Micaela grabbed Ethan's chin and made him look at her. "That is a really dumb reason to die. Now tell me what to do."

Ethan squeezed his lips together and closed his eyes. She turned to Connie. "Help me. I don't want to lose him."

"Even if he could play games with your mind, he's too weak now. Give him your neck. It's less painful than your wrist."

Shit. She tore off her jacket, shrugged off the holster and yanked her turtleneck off. She tried to position herself next to Ethan but the angle felt wrong. All the while, color drained from him. Stubborn Yankee. She straddled him a little off-center with her left ear lined up to his right shoulder. He continued to shake his head and clamp his lips together. He was behaving like a two-year-old.

"Give me your sword, Connie."

Connie wiped the blade clean against her pant legs and handed it hilt first to Micaela. At over three feet, it was large for the job but it was all she had at the moment. She slid the blade across her right palm. *Shit, that hurt.* Crimson oozed from the cut. She pressed it to Ethan's lips.

He refused to open his mouth. She smeared her blood on her neck and across his lips. She moved her hand under his nose. Ethan's eyes opened, hunger burned in them. Survival instincts kicked in. She yanked her hand away. She offered him her neck.

"I'm sorry, Micaela," he whispered before he pulled his head back and bared his teeth.

When she was fifteen, she'd had a spinal tap to test for the meningitis raging through her boarding school. The stab of pain as Ethan bit down was the same… short, horrible. Unlike the spinal tap, the pain was overwhelmed by a very different sensation.

Her body responded, her left hand grabbed his hair to hold him in place while her right hand trailed down his side and pulled his blood soaked shirt out to caress him. Muscles in her uterus tightened and she could feel the moisture soak her panties. She dug her nails into his back as a moan escaped her lips. Ethan answered with a low animal sound that rumbled in his throat. His hand moved along her ribs to her left breast. His fingers brushed against the nipple that strained against her bra. He pushed the lace-trimmed fabric aside and fluttered his finger over the erect tip. She pushed down against his lap. The hardness she met told her the response was mutual.

He gasped as he released her. His head rested against the trunk, his eyes half closed.

"How do you say thank you and I'm sorry at the same time?" He pulled her to him and stroked her hair.

She ran her hand down his back. It was so warm and muscled that she considered the merits of stripping down in the family cemetery. She heard a not-so-subtle cough. Connie and Garett stood at Ethan's feet, their backs turned, guns at the ready.

Ethan chuckled, "I think our guards would feel more comfortable if we went inside the house."

Heat flooded Micaela's face. Ethan handed her the missing turtleneck. As they stood up, his hand hovered inches from her elbow. When she staggered, he took her arm.

"You must rest. I took…" his voice trailed away as did his eyes.

"I'll be fine, Ethan. We had no other options. I just need to clean up before the others arrive." She adjusted her bra and retrieved the shoulder holster and her H&K. The immediate need was for safety, not satisfaction.

Garett offered her his coat. "Don't put the turtleneck back on, you'll never get the bloodstains out."

Her torso was smeared with blood from where she'd leaned up against Ethan. "Won't I ruin your jacket?"

"My employer provides a generous clothing allowance."

She slipped on the leather coat. It was several sizes too large, but it was warmer than nothing. "Garett, what happened to the other attackers? Where are Reece and Sean?"

"Reece caught up with one more. The other and the leopardess got away. Sean went ahead to organize a cleanup of the house. I'll arrange for new security and a crew for out here. Our guests have landed at Logan and should be here within the hour."

Damn. First things first, she needed to change clothes, and somewhere in all this, she and Ethan needed to talk... privately. She wanted to know what those creatures were. She had to make him understand that she wanted to help.

"Thank you." Prudence's voice on the wind.

"Be careful." A second voice whispered. Sarah?

38

Micaela stood in front of the full-length mirror and studied the marks on her neck. They had already faded to red slits, easily masked by concealer.

"They heal fast, especially if you carry the right magic." Connie lounged on the rose colored Victorian sedan chair beside the fireplace.

"Is it as much of a rush for you? I mean, it was …"

"You don't have to describe it. It's good for me, but not in a sexual way. Remember, he's not my type. For me it's more like sky diving, bungee jumping and base jumping all rolled into one."

"And just like that, you could end up dead, or worse." Micaela said.

Connie passed Micaela her make-up kit. "But you'd do it again, wouldn't you?"

"No, tonight was an emergency." The press of her hardened nipples against her blouse betrayed her. "I need to call my grandmother."

"I understand." Connie closed the door behind her as she left.

Micaela tried to call her grandmother. She needed to hear her voice, to know that everything was okay, to belay the concern that lurked in the dark corner of her mind. No answer; she must be out for a late dinner. Micaela went in search of Ethan before the others arrived.

Too late. He and Byrne stood in the door to the study. Ethan looked up at her; his face displayed no hint of what had occurred. New guards were already positioned in the foyer. Garett's preference for ex-military or paramilitary showed. The new guards carried Uzi's along with long blades in sheaths strapped to each thigh. One of the guards held the front door as she approached. His other hand was on the grip of the submachine gun. Through the open door, Micaela saw Liam taking luggage from the back of a stretch Navigator. Nikki came up the walk, her duffel bag arsenal slung over one shoulder. Micaela was not ready to face Liam. She held the door for Nikki.

"Can I help?" Micaela reached for Nikki's regular suitcase.

"Sure. Are you okay?"

"It's been an interesting week. Thanks for the early birthday present."

"Garett said you tried it out."

"Some target practice." Micaela motioned to one of the guards. "Can someone see that everyone is settled into their rooms? I'll get some coffee."

Micaela detoured around the spot on the kitchen floor where she had found the body of the first guard. The clean-up crew had made short work of it. Connie scooped coffee beans into the grinder on the center island. For a two-hundred-year old house, occupied by a vampire even older, the kitchen was a modern wonder of stainless steel and endless cherry cabinets and shelves. Micaela tried her grandmother again; still no answer. She slipped the phone in her pocket.

"Where are the mugs?"

"To the right of the sink." Connie nodded her head toward the cabinet. "Pardon my asking, but why are you in here?"

"Because I'm a chicken."

"Since when?"

"I don't know what to say to Ethan, or any of them for that matter. So I'll help you and by the time we get back in there, small talk will be done and we can get down to business."

Micaela loaded mugs onto a tray. She found a white porcelain creamer and filled it with milk.

"You'll need to talk to him eventually."

"I know. Connie, does Ethan feed on men?" It just slipped out.

"When necessary, Garett has made himself available as long as there is no imminent threat to Ethan." She leaned against the granite counter, her left eyebrow raised in question.

Micaela busied herself filling the mugs as she worried at her bottom lip.

Connie continued. "It's not always about sex or I wouldn't volunteer. But, it's not my place to discuss Garett's preferences or Ethan's."

Micaela froze in mid-pour. "Tell me the truth, is Ethan the only vampire in this group?"

"It's not for me to say. I'm sorry." Connie reached into the double door refrigerator and started to pull out an assortment of cheeses.

I'll take that as a no, Micaela thought. Ethan was a vampire; Ivan was too. Could that be the reason she had never seen Byrne during the day? It was plausible that he was in meetings; everything she knew about Knowth's holdings could put heavy demands on his daytime hours. *But*.

Sean's head popped through the door. "Can I do anything, Micaela?"

"I've tried my grandmother a couple of times. Can you ask Reece to check with Chief Running Deer? Maybe call Mrs. Ryan. It's not like her to be out this late." She busied herself setting cookies and brownies on a tray. "Do you have any cheese or something to snack on? I'm starved and brownies won't do it."

"My apologies, protein is much better after you've donated. Help yourself. Do you want the cook to scramble up some eggs?" Connie arranged some Brie, Cotswold, and Leerdammer on a platter.

"This should work." She piled the cheeses onto water cracker and made short work of them.

Sean returned and picked up the tray. "Reece called his grandfather. The Chief hasn't spoken to Una today. I called Mrs. Ryan, she hasn't seen her either. I'll keep trying. They're waiting for you in the parlor."

Micaela stood in the archway between the foyer and the parlor. Ethan leaned against a wall; his face was a mask of indifference. If she didn't know, she would have thought he was his usual aloof, arrogant self. Byrne chatted amiably with Sean, who looked at Byrne like he was a rock star. Liam sat next to Nikki on the sofa, his hands clasped in an iron grip before him. This was a room that contained one, maybe two vampires. They were about to discuss the activities of what she assumed--- correction knew--- was another vampire. Time to lay all the cards on the table. Aine had been right: the Death card, transformation.

"Can I get anyone a drink? Coffee? Beer? A nice cabernet?" She looked at Ethan. A slight twitch of his upper lip, a smile or a snarl, was the only movement in his stone face.

Byrne had taken the wing chair by the fire. Dressed in a herringbone blazer over a gray turtleneck and black slacks, his elbows rested loosely on the sides of the chair. He looked as if he had never left Knowth. "Have you located Una, Micaela?" he asked.

"No. What happened in Arizona?"

Sean took out his cell phone and went to the stairs in the foyer and started dialing again.

"There was an incident. Rebecca was unharmed but others were. Her assistant, Sebastian, he attended the meeting in Brussels, will review security. There may have been a spy in their ranks. Unfortunately, they were unable to take any of the intruders into custody." Byrne laced his fingers together, his lips tight.

She took a mental deep breath. *Here goes.* "Was she attacked during daylight or was she... help me out here Ethan, what's the right term... awake, alive?"

262

Byrne launched from his chair. She watched the swirl of smoke in Byrne's eyes as they changed from gray to black. Connie was at Ethan's side. Liam, no longer on the sofa, was on Byrne's right.

Micaela found herself between the two men with her arms extended to ward off confrontation. She hadn't even realized she'd crossed the room. "Stand down, the two of you." She spoke to Byrne first. "He didn't betray anyone. I stumbled into an emergency."

A voice whispered through her mind, her mother's voice, "You carry Earth magic, they are creatures of the earth."

She reached inside and found it, a warm glow, brown and green that expanded until it filled her limbs and flowed down her arm to Byrne. She felt the hard ground of winter and dialed her own aura down. Her magic touched him and found his aura, blazing with his anger. Now she knew understood why she had never sensed Ethan's or Byrne's auras. But why had she been able to sense Ivan's? Perhaps evidence that he was trying mind games on her. So it wasn't that vampires had no auras. They did, but on a different frequency: a slower lower one. Like ice crystals that formed when water molecules slowed to the point of near immobility. A cold aura. She wrapped her energy around it in a psychic embrace.

The tension eased from Byrne and was replaced by intense curiosity. He nodded to her. "You would have found out eventually."

"I needed to know. How could I survive, if you kept me in the dark?" His eyes had faded to the familiar gray. Liam stepped back.

Ethan waved Connie off and moved closer to Micaela. He stopped two feet away but she felt him as if she was in his arms again. He wasn't trying to control her the way Ivan had. It was the tide responding to the pull of the moon.

"We," Ethan nodded at Byrne and Liam, "talked endlessly about how to broach the subject. We didn't want to frighten or shock you."

263

Micaela shook her head and laughed softly. "Before this week, I thought I was unique, odd. Everything seemed so chaotic. I felt like Alice on the other side of the Looking Glass. Once the shock of Ethan being a vampire had worn off, things started to fall into place. When I realized that Byrne and Ivan are vampires, too, I felt less crazy. Not completely sane, but better."

Sean rose from his perch on the staircase landing. He rushed to Byrne. "This is amazing. The Connor is a vampire? How old are you?"

Clearly, he was taking this more in stride than she had.

Byrne smiled at Sean's child-like enthusiasm. "I am older than many of my kind. I was brought to my current state by a Roman praetor, Lucinius Gordianus, during the reign of Augustus Caesar. He though that by turning a Druid he could control all of what is now Ireland."

A praetor, she thought, a representative of Augustus Caesar? That would make him two thousand years old. Two thousand years of history, two millennia of feeding on humans.

Connie collected the empty coffee mugs. "Sean, can you get some refills?"

Getting Sean out of the room was a good idea. Hell, Micaela thought, this is more than she could get her head around, but he was so calm about it? Then again, Sean had grown up in the Bridewell Druid community that Micaela had avoided.

Sean dropped to one knee in front of Byrne. "I'm not a child. I've pledged my life to the Grove. I now pledge it you. You are The Connor." He turned his gaze to her and Liam. "I would serve the High Priest and Priestess of the Grove. Please do not let anyone send me away. The Goddess has caused me to be here for a reason."

Why was Sean addressing his priestess remarks to her? According to stories her father had told her, the High Priestess had been trapped in the Otherworld with the Tuatha de Danaan nearly five hundred years ago. She could no longer deny the magic she held, but what she had done was barely more than parlor tricks.

264

Byrne rested his hand on Sean's head. "You will not be sent away. Everyone needs to know the truth if we are to succeed."

Sean's gaze moved from Liam to Micaela. She was used to being the focus of meetings and to others looking for direction from her, but the look in Sean's eyes was a crushing fervor. She was torn between running away and folding herself into the safety of Ethan's arms. Instead she stood alone.

She needed Sean to focus. "Were you able to reach my grandmother?"

"No. Do you want me to drive there?"

"Give me a minute, I'll try her again." She stepped into the foyer to call and to think. Nikki followed her out. "It's nearly midnight. Where would she be?"

"I have no idea." Micaela hit the speed dial again and listened until the voicemail picked up. She put the phone in her jacket pocket. "Listen, Nikki, I'm so sorry I dragged you into this. Vampires. You must think we're all lunatics."

"Did you know that the word lunatic comes from the belief that the full moon changes human behavior?" Nikki leaned against the gate-leg table that held Ethan's Revere tea set.

"What are you talking about?" Micaela raked her fingers through her hair.

Nikki placed her hand on Micaela's shoulder. "Stop trying to be real world. Think about some of the things you've seen. The figures you saw during the attack in Brussels, what happened to François, Reece's miraculous recovery from an animal attack, Liam at the stone circle."

She started to speak but Nikki held up her hand to silence her.

"Yes, Liam told me about that. Why do you think the rest of us have not run screaming from the room, or grabbed wooden stakes?"

Micaela squeezed her temples. "So you are saying, in addition to vampires, I'm dealing with…" *All the outlines she'd seen,*

265

not animal, not human. The word and the shadows took form. If *vampires were real then so were ...* "...werewolves."

"Shapeshifters, actually. Although, that's not an entirely accurate term for us, either."

"Us. You're ..." Goddess, what was next?

"Remember the accident in Brazil I mentioned, the one that caused me to move to Europe and work for the special Interpol Unit? I was attacked by a were-jaguar." She shrugged. "Here I am."

Micaela stared into Nikki's eyes. They had turned from their regular café au lait brown to chartreuse and the whites had vanished. Micaela shook her head and looked again. Definitely not human.

"Shit. I need to think, Nikki. I need some air."

Micaela walked past the guards and down the lime walk to the French garden. Water gurgled in the dolphin fountain. She sat at the edge of the rectangular basin and watched the Koi drift through the water, hiding under lily pads. The sky was full of stars and a crescent moon grinned down on her in silent amusement at the insanity she found herself in. A cool breeze stirred the leaves above her head. A red fox peered at her from under a bush.

She headed down the path toward the cemetery not expecting to be alone. Those days were over.

Two guards followed at a respectful distance. She sat on a stone bench, yards from where she had fed Ethan to heal him. The second ghost appeared beside her. She was beautiful, even in death, soft brown hair, hazel eyes, and full lips.

"You're Sarah."

The specter nodded softly. "Has he hurt you yet?"

"Hurt me? Ethan?"

"He will, you know. He killed me." Sarah glared at her.

"He told me. It almost cost him his life this time. He tried to refuse me."

"Why did you save him, if he didn't want you to?"

"I'm supposed to let him die?" Was die the right word for a vampire?

266

"To save yourself, yes. He loses control when he feels too much. You will be sorry one day." Sarah stared at the stone angel still on the ground where it had landed. A spectral tear trailed down Sarah's cheek.

"You still love him after all these centuries." How strange, Micaela envied a ghost for loving so deeply. "He still carries the guilt. He still cares."

Sarah's gloved hands smoothed the wrinkles from her ivory satin skirt. "For all the good it does either of us to live in the past." Sarah wore what must have been the wedding dress she had never worn down an aisle. Micaela reached out to take Sarah's hand. Vapor.

Micaela pressed her palms to her knees and pushed herself from the bench. "It's too much. Not just Ethan, everyone. I just tried to touch you. I went from a nice normal life to this."

Her guards stood like the stone effigies nearby. Either they could see Sarah or they expected guests to talk to themselves.

"Yet, you speak to me and to Prudence as if we are at high tea. Your life could not have been truly normal."

The white marble of the Lowell mausoleum glowed in the darkness. She thought about her parents' memorial marker, her survival of the explosion that killed them. Everything since François' murder.

"No, I guess I'm not a normal, maybe I never was." She let out a long sigh and with it a lie she had lived.

"So, what will you do now? Leave again?" Sarah asked.

"I'll do the only thing an O'Brien can do." Micaela headed toward the house. As she walked down the path, she called Una again.

Liam waited at the edge of the lawn. "Can we talk, please?"

Micaela moved to the deeper shadow of an elm and slid to the ground. She patted the earth next to her. Liam sat on the ground facing her. Neither spoke for a minute, until she started.

"You're a shapeshifter?"

"We, priests and priestesses, can use magic to be voluntary shapeshifters. But, like Reece, I was attacked several years ago. Now, I carry a strain of the less voluntary sort."

Despite the darkness, she could see his face and what this conversation cost him. She reached out and took his hand. She could feel the tremble. "That night at the Knowth stones?"

"The moon was close to full, then the vision at the circle. My emotions were running high. I could feel the shift begin and I refuse to hurt you." His free hand cupped her cheek.

She leaned her face into his hand. "I'm sorry I was angry with you. I misunderstood the whole situation, including, I think, your relationship with Byrne."

"Nikki told me what you thought you saw. Being a donor, is part of my relationship with The Connor, the relationship the Farrells have always had. Since I became an involuntary shapeshifter, my blood is more potent."

"So, I saw you feeding him?" She still wondered what kind a rush it was for him. Sexual like hers or Connie's base jumping?

"To be clear, I like women. But when you are different, it's not easy."

She stood and pulled him to his feet and wrapped her arms around his waist. "I know."

"Ethan told me how you saved him. You are part of each other now." Liam cradled her head to his chest. His heart pounded in her ear.

"If that means he has some sort of control over me, no. I don't feel like I did after Ivan bit me. Ivan was a constant whisper in my mind. He was quieter after Aine cleansed the wound. After you and I went to the stones, he was gone."

Liam lifted her face to his. "How do you feel about Ethan?"

Micaela frowned. When she'd first met him she had thought he was handsome but arrogant. "Feeding him changed the way I see him, but he isn't in my skull."

"That's good." Liam kissed her forehead and they walked to the house.

She had questions and the answers to most of them were inside, except for one. Where was Una?

39

The rose-tinted light flowed from under the mosaic glass shade of the Tiffany lamps. It warmed Ethan's study and its occupants, and cast soft shadows on the floor and walls. Nice trick, Micaela thought, there wasn't a pasty undead face in the room. Liam crossed to the leather sofa. He was near Byrne and had a clear line of sight to Ethan.

She planted her knuckles on her hips and pulled herself up to her full five foot seven height.   "So, if I'm to be banker to the undead, I need some information."

Byrne's eyes sparkled. "Where would you like us to begin?"

"For starters, is there anyone who should not be here?" Micaela eyed Sean.

Sean stood. His hands on hip posture was a mirror of hers. "I will not, cannot, be shut out. How am I to help if I'm in the dark?"

Caught in her own words, she nodded. "Fair point."

Sean returned to his guard post by one of the large windows that faced the side garden. He gave Reece a quick head nod and flashed a very satisfied grin.

Byrne offered her his seat. "Please sit. I… we will tell you anything you need to know. You are among friends and nothing to fear. I gave my pledge to protect you." He stared at Ethan, who bowed his head.

She couldn't go to Ethan, so she moved as close as possible to Byrne. "Don't blame him for what happened. Someone, and I think I know who, tried to kill him. Ethan refused my offer."

"Yet, he fed. He had no right, no permission." Byrne was angry and her temper rose right along with his.

"What right have you to interfere? You are not my father. I knew what I was getting into."

"I made him responsible for you." Byrne glared over her head right at Ethan.

"He had no choice. I opened a vein and stuck it under his nose." She crossed to Ethan and stared directly at him. "I couldn't let him die."

Liam put his hand on Byrne's arm. "She's fine. Garett checked her."

"Garett checked me? How?" Micaela asked.

Garett spoke up. "I can also read auras, with a special talent for detecting changes from a vampire's control."

She closed her eyes and filed away another revelation. Her brain was bruised from information assault. She opened them to meet Byrne's steady gray eyes. Now that she had found the vampire aura, she could feel his age and the weight of his power. She could also tell he was worried. Correction, men never *worried*, no matter how old they were. He was *concerned*. He had reason to be. Ivan was out there and attacking others of his kind and members of Byrne's group.

There could be no more running away. She had to push forward. *Don't look back. One step in front of the other.* Someone had told her that a long time ago.

Nikki sat at the end of deep brown leather sofa. Liam and Ethan watched Byrne from their positions against opposite walls. Their faces held the same knitted eyebrows and tight-lipped concern.

Micaela paced the room. "Several members of the deal have been attacked, including most of us. We need to stop the person behind this. But I want to know who I'm dealing with and what I'm

271

up against." She had a pretty good idea of who was responsible; she just didn't understand how the vampire world worked.

Byrne continued, "To answer your earlier question about who belongs, Sean is a normal, but…" he said throwing a smile at Sean, "he is a valued member of the team. Garett is gifted but otherwise normal. Ethan and I, as you know, are vampires. Liam, Nikki, and Reece are shapeshifters."

Reece stood near a large leaded glass window, his body half-turned to face a small open pane. He breathed in the night air. Micaela realized he was using his animal faculties to search for the scent of an intruder.

She'd *saved* Reece. Would she have made the same decision if she'd known the cost? Of course she would, these were her people and death was permanent. Maybe.

"It's my fault, isn't it?"

"No, I have you to thank." Reece came to her and grabbed her hands. "If not for you, I would miss out on being a Dad, Peg would be alone."

She searched for his aura. It was brown and green and smelled of the pine forest at home. "But you're a werewolf."

Reece lifted one shoulder in a shrug. "I've always liked to hunt. Now, I just do it differently and during the full moon."

"Does Peggy know?"

"She's my wife, I had to tell her and give her the choice."

Liam and Nikki nodded their silent assents.

She was afraid to ask the other question, but she needed the answer. "What do you hunt?"

"What I've always hunted. Deer, bear, and sometimes moose."

"Did they catch the beast that did this to you?"

Reece frowned. "Yes. It was Gloria Waters. We had been childhood playmates when we still lived outside Providence with the main tribe. Reece and Ria, we were inseparable."

"How was she changed?"

272

"We're still trying to find out. She was a rogue, not part of the local pack or any other. We'd thought she'd moved out west."

Byrne spoke. "With the exception of rogues, like the one who attacked Reece, it is understood by most of us that it no longer benefits any to take human life for survival or sport. We have worked long and hard to protect our privacy and to maintain our existence."

"Who is we?" Micaela wanted confirmation.

"You have met some of the ruling members of the vampire community during this deal. There are others of our kind in most human communities at various socio-economic levels. If a normal is changed, they are paired with an old one who teaches them how to control themselves and live undetected among their former peers."

"What if they can't adapt?" Nikki asked.

"We cannot allow one of our kind to threaten the existence of all." Ethan spoke. He moved closer to Byrne, his head bowed. "That is part of the reason Byrne was angry with me. I was given an order and he believed I had violated it."

When he raised it, she tried to catch his eye, but he avoided her and faced Byrne. Ethan's lips moved in a voiceless apology to Byrne. His palms turned out, Ethan took a step toward Byrne. Ethan rolled his sleeves up and unbuttoned his shirt almost to the waist. There was no evidence of the deep gashes the creature had inflicted in his smooth muscled chest. He stood before Byrne. Micaela's breath caught in her throat. Ethan was offering himself up for execution. She started toward him but Liam took her arm and shook his head.

Byrne remained motionless for a moment. Then, in a motion so fast it was a blur, he grabbed Ethan. A small scream escaped from Micaela, Liam's grasp tightened on her arm. Byrne buried his fangs into Ethan's neck. Ethan's eyes closed and his hands dropped to his sides. A long minute later, Byrne released Ethan. Ethan bowed to Byrne and returned to his position by the entrance to the study, his face peaceful and head high. A small drop of blood slipped from the corner of Byrne's mouth.

"Call it a promise or an order, Ethan violated it." Liam whispered. "He submitted himself to the judgment of The Connor and re-pledged his loyalty and obedience. It's how we survive. How battles are won."

Micaela found a blank spot on the wall to stare at until the urge to scream passed.

"Vampires require human blood to survive, right?" she asked.

"True," Byrne said, "but there is ample opportunity to meet our nutritional requirements without the loss of life. Thanks to the popularity of our fictional kind, there is no lack of volunteers."

"Aren't you afraid someone will out you?" Even as she asked, she knew the answer.

He shrugged. "If they remember, who would believe them? They are often extreme fans of the genre, so their friends and family assume that any marks are the result of a trip to one of the vampire theme clubs that have sprung up."

Micaela would wager a month's pay that she knew who owned these clubs. Her phone vibrated in her pocket. A text message appeared on her screen. She grabbed the back of a nearby armchair.

Liam had moved to her side. "What's wrong?"

"It's Ivan. He says he's tried to speak to me and that taking Una was the only way to get me alone."

Liam pulled the phone from her grip. "The text says you are to come to Joshua's Cave in Brown's Valley. Where is that?"

Reece's voice was a growl. "It's where Micaela found me. I want to know how he got past my people. Someone will pay."

Reece's brown eyes had turned yellow; fury burst like solar flares from his skin. Micaela could see the muscles in his face begin to flow over the bone.

Liam whirled on Reece. Liam's eyes had changed color and his already deep voice took on a new rumble, but all his facial features remained in place. "You help no one if you shift in anger.

You are new to this. Step away and control yourself. Garett, take Reece outside."

Garett reached into a cupboard and removed a large gun. Micaela ran over to take the weapon from Garett. "Don't. He's just upset. Liam," she said as she turned to him, "you said it yourself that strong emotions can trigger a shift."

Garett popped the clip and showed the contents to Micaela. "Powerful tranquilizer darts, just in case Reece needs help controlling the beast."

She stepped aside. Garett grabbed Reece by the elbow and hauled him from the room. Micaela took back her phone. "I have to reply; I have to tell him I'll be there."

"You are not going alone," Nikki said.

"But if I don't... he'll know all of you are there."

Byrne looked at Liam. "Not necessarily."

Liam asked, "Micaela, remember when we visited the stone circle at Knowth?"

"How could I forget."

"You felt the magic in the stones, heard them sing. They took you to a time before." He moved to take her hands.

She could hear the music again, the bodhran like a heartbeat. Her hand went to her right sleeve. The vine tattoo was under it, bright against her skin. Liam pulled his shirt over his head. There where she had seen it was the triple spiral tattoo, the triskele.

"You were there."

"I was, then and now. Together we will make the magic needed."

Micaela traced his tattoo with her finger. It felt alive, joined with Liam but apart from him.

Sean looked like a barn owl, wide eyed and head swiveling. "'Tis true, the high priestess has come back from the Otherworld. All will be well now."

Byrne put a hand on Sean's shoulder. "First we must deal with Ivan and release Una. Micaela, text Ivan. Tell him you cannot talk right now because you are not alone. You'll slip away as quickly as possible."

The message sent; Micaela turned to Liam. "What do we do? How do we know it works?"

"We'll use a variation of a masking spell. It will hide everyone while you remain visible."

Ethan spoke. "Garett will test to see if it works. I'll go outside and brief him."

Micaela felt the aching sadness in his voice. She squeezed Byrne's arm. "Give me a minute, please."

She followed Ethan. "Ethan?"

He stood on the back porch. "I owe you my life, or existence, however you prefer to see it. There have been many times when I wished to join my family."

"You can't do that."

"No, but your destiny takes you elsewhere." He turned so she couldn't see his face.

She placed her hand on his arm and drew him around. The loneliness that stared back squeezed her heart.

"I know things have changed and I don't know where it will take me." She rested her hand against his cheek. "But right now, I have to get my grandmother back."

"I have become a 270-year-old adolescent, pouting when we have so much to do." He moved into the darkness of the trees. When he returned moments later with Garett and a much calmer Reece, Ethan's face had resumed its mask of arrogant blankness.

Garett nodded to Micaela. "I'll wait here with Mr. Lowell. After the spell has been cast I'll test it."

40

Micaela faced Liam. The silk oriental carpet had been rolled back so that they sat on the bare oak floor. The boards had been hewn and laid centuries ago but there was still the faintest spark of earth magic in them. The electric lights had been replaced by natural flames in the fire and tall tallow candles. Instinct told her that this magic would be stronger if it were performed outside, but security realities kept them indoors. So much rode on her ability to do something she had no idea how to do.

"Will they be invisible?" she asked.

"Someday. It is there inside." His finger rested over her heart. "For now, I want you to tap into my aura and use it like an auxiliary battery. We will create the equivalent of white noise to cancel out the auras of the others."

They had gathered everyone together. Nikki, Byrne, Sean, Connie, and Reece sat around the room in predetermined positions. Five points on a star. Liam rehearsed the words with her twice. He reached down, took her hands in his and stared deeply into her eyes. His gaze was steady and confident. He recited the spell in Gaelic to her; she repeated it, stumbling over one or two words. She tried it two more times with better results.

"Do you want to go over it again?"

"I'm ready," she said. *I have to be.*

She closed her eyes, exhaled and went inside herself. She found the stillness that was nowhere and everywhere. Liam began the chant. She joined in, the words flowing smoothly. From deep within she heard Una's voice, her mother's voice, and countless others reciting the words with her. She felt the hum of Liam's aura, then Nikki's. Her senses crawled through the room in search of each unique frequency. Her power, joined with Liam's, turned the invisible shimmers of energy into a riot of colors, smells, tastes, and sounds.

Byrne stood before the fire. His aura was the blinding white of the Arctic nights and was the lowest; which, as the oldest, made sense. Each shifter had his or her own flavor that told her their animal form. Nikki, on the Victorian sofa, was the lush green of the rainforest and the plink of water as it dropped from vines and leaves. Reece, on guard by the window, rustled with the green pines and crunch of oak leaves. Sean, the only normal in the room, quivered orange with the energy of his frustration and need to belong. She pushed further and found Ethan. He was a swirl of energy. Deep tones like church bells, explosions of past violence and a warm golden piece she couldn't understand until Liam's voice whispered through her mind. "It's you." She watched the fluctuations in Ethan's aura as he looked toward the house. He'd felt her touch.

As Liam had instructed, Micaela combed through her own aura to extract individual strands, each a complement to someone else's aura. She wound one around Nikki, then Sean, as she worked her way through the group. She placed her final strand around Ethan. Each aura blinked out. She could see Garett's face. He started toward the house. She didn't need him to come in. She knew it had worked. To anyone with ability that might be looking, the group's auras had vanished into darkness.

She opened her eyes. She and Liam were on their knees. Her fingers were still entwined with his, but their arms were extended from their bodies. His eyes glowed the green phosphorescence of the surface of a warm Caribbean sea. She could drown in those eyes. Liam rubbed his cheek against her face. She felt the soft rumble in his throat.

The door to the study opened and Garett entered. He moved from person to person, his eyes focused on a place inches in front of each one. He paused, shook his head. He ended with Ethan who stood just inside the door, then turned to Micaela and Liam.

A wide grin stretched across Garett's generally stoic face. "We're ready to roll."

Micaela drove alone in the BMW. She couldn't see the other cars in the rearview mirror but she knew they were there. Garett may not have been able to see their auras, but she could still feel them, a cobwebbed tickle along her own edges. It was almost three when she pulled into the farm's driveway. Adam rose from the darkness of the front porch and met her on the walk.

"No wards on any entry of the house." She had discovered since last Samhain that Adam, as next Shaman for the tribe, had his own talents.

She shook head. "Not a surprise, she never locked doors or windows, either. The others are hanging back. Have you been inside?"

"A kitchen chair on its side, but otherwise nothing. I don't get a sense of any violence. Una was fine when she left here."

She couldn't stay long. Ivan would expect her to check the house like a normal before she headed up the mountain, so she went in. The house was just as Adam had described, the overturned chair looked as if someone had stood up too quickly. Adam waited in the parlor.

"Micaela, where is everyone? I can't sense them."

279

"It's a masking spell. Liam and I erased their auras, in the hope that Ivan or one of his people will not detect them."

"Can you teach me?"

"When this is over."

"Deal." He handed her the SUV keys. "The Land Rover will handle the access road better. You'd better get going."

She pulled out of the driveway. The others were about a half mile down the road. Brown's Valley and Joshua's Cave were less than two miles from her grandmother's house, as the crow --- or was it the raven --- flies, but it took ten minutes for her to reach the access road. A half mile up the road, the trees closed in and she could take the SUV no further.

The narrow beam of a penlight lit her way as she moved on foot down the same path that Reece had followed almost six months ago. She didn't need to push on the threads to see if everyone was in place. She could taste each of them like the hint of spice carried on a breeze. Liam and Nikki were feline but different from each other, Reece and Connie canine. Then, to her left, she felt a new aura, not masked, very human, an undeveloped sensitive. Shit, it was Hendricks.

She had to stop him, protect him from his own good intentions. She didn't think she was ready to do this alone, but to reach out to Liam risked betraying the location of the others. She had no choice. She had to act quickly and hope no one noticed. She found his frequency, wrapped an eddy current around it and watched his aura vanish. She made a beeline through the trees to where he stood. He wore a pale gray jacket that even in the darkness screamed target.

"If you wanted a late night walk in a forest, Hendricks, you should have stuck to Central Park." She stood so the wind blew between her and the detective and away from Joshua's cave.

"He's taken your grandmother, hasn't he?"

"I have no idea what you're talking about, but if you leave now, you should be able to get a few hours sleep before your next shift."

"It's Vasilievich you're meeting. I followed up like you suggested. The hotel cameras didn't catch anything, but the City Center and street cameras caught Ms. Vilkas coming and going. We had to slow the film to see her."

Of course she moved fast, Micaela thought, she's not human. "You once told me I was in way over my head. If anyone's in over their head tonight, it's you. For your sake and my sanity, you need to go and let me handle this."

"Not a chance. I don't leave loose ends. They killed Leveque and they have to answer for that." He pulled off his jacket and left it at the base of a tree. Under the gray he wore black pants, black sweater. Much better. She heard the soft click of him releasing the safety off his gun.

"They will answer for what they did. Just stay back, please. If he thinks I didn't come alone…" She couldn't even think the words, let alone say them.

"Ten years a SEAL and twenty years on the force. I've done this a time or two."

She had no time to argue with him. Hopefully, he'd get out in one piece, physically and mentally. Micaela closed her eyes and entreated the Morrigan to guide her into battle. With Hendricks close behind, Micaela slipped into the woods. She picked her way carefully, soundlessly, the huntress. She couldn't hear Hendricks. He was as good as his word. But still, just a normal. She reached back for the threads; everyone was in place. She nudged Liam's aura towards Hendricks. She counted on Liam to keep Hendricks safe.

41

Crouched at the edge of the tree line and downwind from the campsite, Micaela counted five, no six, figures around a fire. Kat and Ivan were not visible, so that made eight. Una must be in the cave. Micaela had found Reece there less than six months ago. She recalled the low clearance and damp walls. It had one entrance. Total darkness began after the first few feet. The cave went back about twenty yards with a side room at the halfway point. Una would probably be there.

Voices from inside the cave travelled on the wind, but too low to distinguish words. Her fists clenched and her muscles tightened, ready to launch. Hendricks put his hand on her forearm. He shook his head to warn her off before he retreated deeper into the shadows. He was right; she needed her wits about her. She would have to thank him later. Kat and Ivan came out of the cave and entered the glowing circle. Even in the great outdoors, she wore her standard high-priced hooker look, a barely-there black leather mini dress. Her one concession to the surroundings was that the four inch heels on her boots were stacked.

"The Irish witch will not come." She slapped a dozing guard in the back of the head, sending him sprawling toward the fire. Micaela smelled burning hair.

"There you are wrong." Ivan helped the man to his feet. "She understands the importance of family and loyalty. She will be here."

"Then, she will not come alone. She is weak."

Micaela stepped out of the shadows. "Sorry to disappoint, Kat."

Ivan moved toward her. His voice soft, almost apologetic. "I did not know how else to reach you, Mischa. You broke the bond between us."

She stepped to her right to be in line with the cave entrance. Kat mirrored her move, placing herself between Micaela and Una.

Kat called out. "Sergei, I want to know if she came alone. Pavel, see if she is armed."

A large dark haired man approached. Micaela recognized him as the man in the lobby on the morning of Francois' murder. He began at her ankles and worked his way up her legs, slowly, lingering too long at her crotch.

She returned his leer with dead eyes. "Nothing there for you, Pavelich. Move on."

She probably shouldn't have used the little boy suffix. When he reached her breasts he kneaded them as if hunting for an imbedded microchip. She clenched her teeth. The son of a bitch would not get the satisfaction of even the smallest flinch from her. He stepped away and shook his head. She watched Sergei travel the perimeter of the clearing. His movements were similar to Garett's in Ethan's study. Sergei was scanning for auras. Like his comrade, he too shook his head and returned to stand behind Kat.

Micaela watched him with feigned curiosity. "Shall we play hide and seek, Kat? Should I call 'olly olly oxen free' so everyone comes out?" She heard the low rumble of a growl from deep in Kat's throat.

Ivan turned to Kat. "It is just as I have told you. She is strong, and, like my Elena, a woman of great passion and caring." He moved closer to Micaela.

"I want to see my grandmother." Micaela said.

Even without the bond, he was still handsome. His white blond hair glowed in the firelight. His broad shoulders were encased in a black silk shirt over wool slacks and riding boots.

"Sergei will release her as soon as you and I leave. I would not harm your *máthair Chríona*." Ivan had used the Irish for grandmother, which literally translated to Mother of my Heart. She pictured Una inside the cave.

Screw handsome. How dare he try to manipulate her. She bit back her anger and softened her voice forcing a tremor of fear to trickle out. "Then you understand how I feel, Ivan. Release her and I will go anywhere with you. Your dacha on the Black Sea, perhaps?"

"You will love it there." Ivan reached for her.

Kat's face distorted with rage as she advanced on Micaela. "Do you think we are fools? You are nothing. Ivan, do not waste your time on her and that old woman. You are a great Tsar, greater than all who came before or after you. It is our… your destiny to rule, not hers. Let us be done with them."

For a heartbeat, Ivan seemed to waver. At the edge of her awareness, Micaela could feel Liam and the others move in. Sean and Hendricks remained at the rear. She needed to stall. Sergei and Pavel watched Kat and Ivan. They looked bored, as if they had seen this show before.

She took a step away from Kat. "Why did you kill François?"

Kat bowed toward Ivan. "In the service of my tsar. François was going to warn you of our plans."

"AGF?" Micaela moved a quarter of a turn around the fire. An air pocket in a log exploded, a gunshot of sound and sparks.

Kat flicked a nod toward Sergei as she answered. He moved around the circle. "Yes, François and his master, Montbelliard, knew Ivan would control the wealth of the other members. They did not see the wisdom of cooperating. An example needed to be set."

Ivan edged closer to Micaela. "I saw how the French wolf looked at you. He would have come between us, Mischa. François had to go."

284

Her people were nearby. "Why did you attack the other masters or their representatives?" She stood at the eastern end of the fire; Kat, Ivan and Sergei were at the other compass points.

"Some remained obstinate. Most were not seriously injured. We have to consolidate our power, Mischa, if we are to be the rulers we are destined to be." He stared across the flames. She could feel his energy reaching out as he tried to regain control of her. She pulled up the drawbridge of her psychic castle. His eyes narrowed.

"You tried to kill Ethan Lowell, too." She kept talking and moving, looking for a way to the cave.

"He was getting too close to you." Ivan growled. "You were not supposed to be there. Why did you surrender to him when you would not be mine?" Just below the surface of his face, she could see the monster she had seen on the balcony in Brussels.

"I saved him. I did not surrender, Ivan. He now has a debt of honor to me… to us."

Ivan studied her face. His next probe was a battering ram against her psychic walls. She entreated the Morrigan to keep him from detecting the web of auras tangled in hers.

"It's true. He did not make you his own. He does not control you. You are more powerful than I imagined." He stepped toward her, his hands reaching out. "Think, Mischa, what we could do together."

Kat moved around the circle toward her. "She will not serve you, Baron. Not as you deserve to be served. Perhaps she would even try to rule you, instead."

Micaela moved toward him. Her voice dropped to an intimate whisper. "You don't want a consort who will serve, do you? That is why you loved Elena. She was your partner, your soul mate. Let my grandmother go and we will leave together. She's all the family I have left. You of all people can understand that?" She reached her hand toward him.

She heard Kat's yowl before the white blur slammed into her, throwing her to the ground. Micaela slapped her hand on the dirt to absorb the shock, as Nikki had taught her, and rolled away into the darkness of the trees. She skirted the edge of the circle until she was upwind from Kat. Kat crouched on all fours, her pupils so dilated that her eyes appeared black. She sniffed the air. When Kat had come after Micaela, her own people had burst from the shelter of the trees. Garett, Connie, and Reece fanned out toward Ivan's men. Liam took aim at Sergei. Byrne and Ethan flanked Ivan, creating a wedge between him and Micaela. Ivan tried to call to her and she could hear him trying to negotiate with Byrne. Ethan's aura erupted with rage. There would be no negotiating.

Snarls replaced voices as bodies reshaped. Kat had partially shifted. She was still on two legs, her shredded remnants of clothes over the white and black stripes of a tiger. Her dark hair had become a halo of fur around a face that was caught between tiger and human. This was the silhouette Micaela had seen in the Sonian Forest. A roar bellowed from Kat's human mouth, as she lunged for her. Its meaning was still clear: Ivan was Kat's and she was furious. Micaela leapt out of her path. Nikki appeared beside her; she was in partial animal form. The sleek black coat of the jaguar shimmered in the firelight while chartreuse eyes tracked Kat's movements.

Micaela grabbed Nikki's arm... forepaw. "Get Grandma to safety, promise me."

Nikki answered with a snarl of grudging agreement and darted into the trees. Kat's eyes tried to follow her, but the black fur vanished in the darkness of the forest. Micaela assumed Nikki was making an end run to the cave entrance. Kat eyes darted from Nikki to Micaela. She seemed indecisive for once, caught between her fury at Micaela and the need to block Nikki's path. In that moment, Micaela scanned the clearing. Liam, in lion-like form, snapped at the throat of a large white wolf that must be Sergei. The wolf whipped his head away. He circled Liam before he leapt and landed on Liam's back, clamping his jaws between Liam's shoulder blades. They rolled over each other and through the fire. The wolf howled in pain as the flames seared its back. Liam's claws slashed the wolf's chest.

Micaela could only make out shadows that might be Garett, Reece, and Connie. Sean and Hendricks appeared from the tree line. Hendricks had his gun extended in a two handed grip. Sean had what looked like a shotgun raised shoulder height. A flash registered in Micaela's line of vision; one of the weretigers dropped to the ground.

Kat's attention had returned to Micaela. The tigress sprang from her low crouch. Micaela tried to move away, but she had been too distracted by the others.

She heard Garett yell. "Run." Then he was in front of her, Kat's claw coming down in a wide sweeping arc into him. Her second arm swung up into his rib cage. She tossed him aside like a rag doll and turned on Micaela. Sean and Hendricks ran to Garett.

Micaela sprinted into the forest, hoping to draw Kat away. There was no time for stealth. She crashed through the trees; the leaves exploded under her feet. Limbs reached out like arms to grab her, hold her for the beast that followed. Branches slashed at her face, the sting of them a small taste of the blood that would follow. She knew the terrain; it was part of the Grove. If she kept running she would pass through it and reach the Pokanoket enclave and the warriors. She paused to catch her breath. A warm muzzle prodded her hand. She looked down; it was Liam in animal form. Was Sergei dead or did he follow? Liam urged her on. The trees were too dense. On open ground, she and Liam could fight Kat and Sergei if they had to. It would be all right if she just kept moving.

She burst through the trees of the Grove, just as she had dreamt so many times. Unlike her nightmare, her grandmother and mother were not there. The fire pit was cold, nothing but black ash. She looked around for a weapon, something, anything. On the other side of the circle, a silver mist welled up from the ground. Had there been a fire she would have mistaken it for smoke. She could hear the beat of a bodhran. Liam stopped in front of the veil and sniffed. He quickly lowered his head to his front paws in a genuflection. In the center of the cloud, the vapors had taken human shape. The figure was a man, over six feet, broad shoulders, and long curly black hair.

287

She saw a smile on his lips and knew him. Her father. He stood at the border to the Otherworld.

Was he there to help or take her to the Otherworld? No, she would not go, she would not admit that all was lost.

"Da. Help us."

He held out a glittering long sword. She didn't stop to think. She reached through the veil and took it from him. The blade was silver, warm, and hummed in her hands. Ogham was carved into it, a spell of power. The hilt was gold with oak inlay.

"You have wielded this before, my daughter. Let Nuada guide you." Through the mists a raven flew and landed on Micaela's shoulder. She turned and planted her feet, grasped the hilt with both hands and raised the blade above her head. The raven spoke to Micaela, the names of François and Garett. It whispered of her grandmother, Rebecca Black Owl, Ethan and the others. She could smell Kat and Sergei under the trees, watching and waiting. A cold rage welled up inside Micaela.

"No more!" she shouted. "It ends here, Kat."

Kat stood at the edge of the circle; her eyes wary. Micaela's movements were slow and measured. She would control the attack, force Kat's hand.

"This is my home, my people. Here, it is you who are less than nothing."

Kat snarled and snapped; she dropped to all fours. Her features became less human and more tiger-like before Micaela's eyes. Sergei, in full wolf form, stood half a body length behind Kat.

"Why do you think Ivan never chose you, Kat?" Micaela taunted Kat. Liam crouched at Micaela's side, his teeth bared, his growl echoing her words. His eyes locked on Sergei. This was her fight, hers and Liam's. The sword glowed like a beacon in her hands.

Kat leapt across the cold fire pit. Micaela held her breath and swung. The blade sliced through the air, creating a scarlet crescent on Kat's abdomen. Micaela felt more than heard Liam's growl. He smelled blood. So did Sergei. Sergei raced toward Micaela. Liam crashed into Sergei, knocking him over. Liam's jaws closed on Sergei's throat. They were so close that blood sprayed from Sergei's throat into Micaela's face.

Kat shook her head. She appeared dazed, but began to circle again. The blood flow from her wound had already stopped. Liam crouched over the wolf. Kat turned to see the motionless Sergei, already returning to human form. She roared in rage and came at Micaela. She stepped to the right, the sword over her head. This time she swung in a horizontal arc. She felt the edge slice though Kat's flesh and bone. She watched as Kat's detached head arced out of the circle while her body sprawled across the pit. Micaela lifted the sword and plunged it through Kat's chest. The ground darkened with blood as Kat resumed her human shape.

Micaela stared down at the body. Kat was dead and she had killed her. She had killed several people this week. It would catch up with her, but not now; she still had things to do. Micaela knelt and wrapped her arms around Liam's neck, her face buried in his fur.

"Thank you."

He rubbed his face against hers. Against her cheek and under her arms she could feel his muscle and bone begin to flow just as it had at the stones. He was already returning to human form. She looked for the sword. It had vanished along with her father and the mist. She stood and began the dash back to the cave. Were the others safe, was Una safe?

Her cry of joy at seeing Una was cut short. Her grandmother and Byrne knelt on the ground. Micaela could see an arm covered by the familiar black leather jacket extended between Byrne and Una. Micaela rushed to their side and leaned over Garett. He opened his eyes when she touched his face. Half his face was torn away, blood flowed from a wound in his chest.

"Ms. O'Brien…"

"Don't talk, save your strength." He had jumped in front of Kat to protect her and she was still Ms. O'Brien to him.

"Saved you, that's what matters." He closed his eyes; a rattling breath escaped his lungs and he was silent.

Micaela grabbed Byrne by the collar. "Do something. Bring him over."

"I can't." Byrne looked up at Ethan. "Neither of us can."

Liam and Nikki knelt on Garett's other side. Connie and Reece, still in their wolf forms, curled at his feet. Micaela laid her face on Una's shoulder, who stroked her hair and hummed an ancient song of sorrow and comfort.

Byrne squeezed her shoulder. "We'll take care of Garett. Don't worry."

Micaela pulled herself up and stared at Reece; his amber wolf eyes blinked back human tears. She grabbed Garett's wrist, her first two fingers seeking a pulse. She searched the air around him and found his aura still rooted in his body. She smiled up at Liam. "Get Adam. Garett's still alive."

Liam nodded to Reece who raced back to the field where the cars were parked. Micaela leaned over Garett. She placed her hands on either side of his face, leaned over and whispered to him.

"You can't quit on me. You're Spec Ops, right? Made of tougher stuff. Well, show me how tough you are." She reached out to his aura. It floated six inches from his body. He was going; she wouldn't allow it. As she had earlier, she grabbed threads of her own aura, but this time she wrapped them around just one aura... Garett's. She tightened her hold on it, bound it to him. She wasn't sure it would work for long, maybe just long enough for Adam to get there. She had nothing to lose.

Adam arrived and tossed his backpack on the ground. He pressed herbs between Garett's lips while Nikki helped insert the IV. Adam's eyes were solemn as he looked at Micaela. "We do not have the right to make this decision for him, not you, not me."

Micaela turned to Reece. "But when Reece was hurt like this..."

Reece had returned to human form. He took Micaela's hand. "They reduced the sedative after we pulled away in the ambulance. I was awake but the pain was dulled enough so I could think. This was my decision. What if this isn't what Garett wants?"

"But he works for Ethan, he feeds Ethan, and he knows what all of you are." Micaela turned to Byrne.

Liam spoke. "This life should not be forced on anyone."

Micaela wiped her eyes and watched as Sean and Adam carried Garett away. Reece trotted along behind. She turned to Liam. "Where are they taking him?"

"They will do what they can and perhaps know his wishes."

Micaela wrapped her arms around Una. "I'm so sorry for everything."

"It will be all right, you'll see."

She had to tell Una the truth and the words tumbled out. "I killed at least one person at Ethan's house. Da appeared. He gave me a sword. I killed Kat with it."

"Nuada's sword, the treasure of the warrior. You did what was needed and you used it well."

"Just not soon enough." Micaela stared at the path Garett had disappeared down.

She turned her attention to the clearing outside the cave. Bodies were everywhere. Detective Hendricks wandered through the carnage, shaking his head and muttering. Someone would have to make him forget everything.

Micaela stood up and looked around the clearing; there was one body she needed to see. "Where is Ivan?"

"Over here." Ethan motioned for her to follow. What remained of Ivan lay under a pine. His head was gone and his body had a gaping hole in his chest where his heart used to be. She felt nothing.

"Liam is burning the head and heart as we speak. No normals will know what happened here tonight." Ethan's eyes followed Hendricks.

She didn't like the idea of messing with someone's memory, but in this case she could live with the exception. It was better than imagining Hendricks living with the nightmares. She would have enough of her own.

42

Garett had regained consciousness and was healing quickly. Adam told Micaela that Garett had a warrior's soul and sat at the Reservation fire with the others and listened to the Chief's stories. Garett had offered to teach members of the enclave a few things he had learned as a SEAL if they would reciprocate. Reece volunteered to teach him how to hunt.

In the weeks that followed, Micaela immersed herself in work. She had a request for a proposal to act as investment banker for a biotech firm out west. Before even beginning the proposal, she researched the two owners. They were thirty-something wunderkinds. One had been All-American track until a freak accident left him in a wheelchair. Otherwise, there was nothing unusual in their backgrounds. It looked like a refreshing change, far from Europe and New York. The proposal required long hours that kept her from her empty apartment.

But her days were not empty. She called Una daily, although sometimes Una was on her way out to a movie or dinner with Chief Deerfield. Micaela was amazed anything was accomplished with everyone checking in on her. Her assistant, Judy, was never more than a sneeze away. Nikki insisted on training or dinner every day. Liam called every morning, Ethan every evening. They were wonderful, kind and caring, which worried Micaela. People she cared about ended up dead or damaged.

The last week of April, she returned from a shareholders meeting for a national supermarket chain to find Liam waiting at her apartment. He had let himself in using the set of keys she given him. After everything that had happened, she felt safer knowing that Liam, Nikki, and Ethan had keys.

Liam sat in the wingback chair with Grady asleep in his lap. He gently put Grady on the cushion and came to Micaela. He wrapped his arms around her.

"How are you doing?"

"I can't sleep most nights." For only the fourth time today, she pushed back the tears; it was getting better. Yesterday had been five times.

"You had to kill Kat. Many others would have died. You know that, right?"

She pulled back. "I know that up here." She tapped her forehead. "But it still hurts here." She laid her hand over her heart.

They walked out to her terrace and sat side by side on lounge chairs in silence until darkness fell. Micaela finally spoke. "I've put the condo on the market."

"That was fast."

"I told the realtor to price aggressively. It's time to go home."

"Anything I can do to help?" He laid his hand on top of hers. It was so warm. She looked up at the night sky. The rising moon was near full again. He couldn't hunt in Central Park. Hendricks had "forgotten" almost everything, but they couldn't take chances.

"No, everything's arranged. I'm not going to wait for the apartment to sell. The movers will be here next week."

"Una will be glad to have you home." His voice was a purred whisper.

"Well, not exactly home. You know the old barn, the one you slept in? I hired Henry, Reece's cousin, to convert it into proper living space. It should be ready in a few weeks. I figure Una and Chief Deerfield might not want me underfoot for long."

Liam chuckled. "I'm sure they'll appreciate the privacy. What about Moran & Boru?"

"Brian says I can work the way my father did. I'll spend part of the week in the Boston office when I'm not travelling and come down to New York, as needed. Judy wants to move back to Boston to be with me. She worked for my Da in Boston. She says she can't imagine working for anyone but an O'Brien. Seamus says he's talking to Mary about coming north. That way he can drive me between Bridewell and Boston."

"Where will you stay when you do come to New York?"

"I have a friend, Parker, who's out of town. I can stay at his loft, or in a hotel," she said.

"I'll get you a set of keys for the Knowth loft in Tribeca. It has two bedrooms and a Jacuzzi on the rooftop patio." His smile was more sheep than lion.

Liam spent the night on the couch. She was glad he didn't push his advantage, although being held had its appeal. He flew back to Ireland the next day, but promised to return in time for Beltaine and her birthday. Ethan would be there, too. Nikki had taken a leave of absence from the NYPD and stayed in Boston to help Ethan with security while Garett recovered and adjusted.

The following Wednesday, the moving vans were loaded and on their way to Bridewell. She stopped for a late breakfast at a deli in Sleepy Hollow. Returning to her car with a large coffee in her hand, she heard a little girl speak.

"Look Mommy, there's a big black bird on that car. It's smiling at me."

She looked about seven, and had curly red hair arranged in the traditional long spiraled curls. She wore a green velvet brocade step dancing costume. Micaela rounded the bumper to the driver's door; the raven stayed put. She waved to the girl and her mother. "That's a good luck sign. It means you'll do very well today. Where's the feis?"

The mother answered. "At the Community Center in Bridewell, Massachusetts." She took her daughter's hand. "Come on dear, we still have quite a drive ahead of us."

"Perhaps I'll see you there."

The raven cawed softly.

Micaela whispered to her feathered companion, "I know, but Henry can let the movers in. We can watch the competition and still be on-time for the Beltaine gathering."

If you enjoyed this book, please go to the Dark Dealings page and post a review, like and tag it on as many of these sites as possible:

Amazon Kindle Books

But **most of all**----tell your friends

You can follow me and my publishing company

On Facebook at:

K.Victoria Smith

Three Worlds Productions

On Twitter at:

@kvictoriasmith

@3WorldsProductns

Visit our website at:

http://www.threeworldsproductionsllc.com/

or my blog at

Storyteller's Grove

CPSIA information can be obtained at www.ICGtesting.com
Printed in the USA
LVOW05s1602191113

361953LV00003B/831/P